Forces of Nature

CHERIS HODGES

Kensington Publishing Corp.
http://www.kensingtonbooks.com

DAFINA BOOKS are published by

Kensington Publishing Corp.
119 West 40th Street
New York, NY 10018

All Kensington Titles, Imprints, and Distributed Lines are available at special quantity discounts for bulk purchases for sales promotions, premiums, fund-raising, and educational or institutional use. Special book excerpts or customized printings can also be created to fit specific needs. For details, write or phone the office of the Kensington special sales manager: Kensington Publishing Corp119 West 40th Street, New York, NY 10018, attn: Special Sales Department, Phone: 1-800-221-2647.

ISBN-13: 978-0-7582-7660-5
ISBN-10: 0-7582-7660-5

First mass market printing: May 2013

10 9 8 7 6 5 4 3 2 1

Printed in the United States of America

Acknowledgments

There's something about the country. As a small-town girl myself, I always wanted to play in the grass and visit—not work—on a farm. Too bad I was allergic to everything. In *Forces of Nature* we do go to a farm, where Crystal and Douglas have an unconventional relationship that started with handcuffs. . . . I hope you enjoy their story.

I want to thank all of the readers who have supported my work over the years; from your e-mails, tweets, and Facebook messages, I feel so blessed. This is always the hardest part of writing a book, because I feel like I'm always forgetting someone, but charge it to my head and not my heart.

Thank you to some of the most supportive people I could ever have on my side: my agent Sha-Shana Crichton, my sister Adrienne Hodges Dease, Louise Brown, Michele Grant, Farrah Rochon, Phyllis Bourne, Yolanda Gore, Beverly McDuffie, Erica Singleton, Wendy Covington, Tiffany Strange, Tashmir Parks, Connie Banks Smith, Carlton Hargro, Mary C. Curtis, and as always, my mom and dad, Doris and Freddie Hodges.

I'd like to thank the book clubs who have hosted me and supported my work, including, the Sistahfriends book clubs—Columbia, Charleston, and Atlanta—the Building Relationships Around Books group, Real Readers Real Words group, the Black Romance and Women's Fiction book clubs.

Follow me on Twitter @cherishodges and be sure to friend me on Facebook/cherishodges.

Prelude
Reeseville, 1974

Douglas Wellington Jr. was filled with rage as he watched her with him. Joel Hughes thought he was so much better than everybody else because of that damned farm. Thought he was the town's golden boy because he went off to college and returned to Reeseville to work on the farm. People thought that farm was special because of the history and mythology that went along with it. First property in the county owned by African Americans—so what. The farm had been passed down through the Hughes family for over a century, each generation adding to the allure of it. So. What.

Douglas was making history himself. He had money and was no longer "Junior" from the wrong side of the tracks. Erin Hamilton needed to recognize that. He loved her more than he loved the woman he'd married, a practical clone of Erin. The same complexion and height. But Evelyn Wellington lacked the softness and tenderness that Douglas had always admired in Erin. In high school, they'd dated briefly, before *he* came along and stole her away. She'd been kind to Douglas when other girls turned their noses up at him. His good grades and love of reading impressed Erin, while others laughed at him and called him a nerd.

She'd never judged him or his shoes with the holes in the soles. But that boy was gone and here was a man with everything. How in the hell could she choose Joel Hughes—a glorified farmhand—over him? His eyes clouded with anger as they kissed and Joel's hand fell to her belly. Was his Erin pregnant? Pregnant with Joel's child? This should have been *his* future! She should've been having his child and allowing him to give her everything that her heart desired. Everything that his money could buy.

Douglas's manufacturing company, Welco Industries, had revolutionized the economy of Reeseville, North Carolina. He'd brought jobs that paid real money into town. Many of the properties that he couldn't even visit as a child now belonged to him. He purposely went after people who he felt had wronged him in the past, buying their houses that he had admired as a child only to tear them down.

Money changed things and changed the way people viewed him.

Douglas Wellington Jr. was even a member of the Duval County Country Club, a place that wouldn't even allow him to shine shoes there when he was a teenager. Still, he didn't have the one thing that he wanted more than anything. He didn't have Erin by his side.

"Why are you doing this to yourself?" Waylon Terrell asked his forlorn friend. "She's moved on and you're married!"

"Shut up," Douglas snapped. "There's always been something about Erin, and I wanted to marry her."

"Things didn't work out the way you wanted. What are you going to do about it? It's not as if you have room to complain," Waylon said. "You've done pretty damned well for yourself."

Douglas glared at him. "And so have you. Were it not for me, you'd still be working on that farm like a mule."

Waylon folded his arms across his broad chest. He enjoyed working in the business office at Hughes Farm. His friend had no idea what that farm meant to Duval County. They grew vegetables and sold some of them to the local market and gave away thirty percent of the produce to the local food bank and a few churches. During the last two years, the farm had been bleeding money, but Joel and Erin would not change their operation and they were looking for sponsors. When Waylon suggested that Erin talk to Douglas, he didn't know that his friend was still obsessed with her. After all, Douglas was about to be a father and they both were married. Waylon fell for Douglas's line about wanting to help the county, wanting to create jobs and help people in Waverly who felt hopeless.

Still, Douglas was hell-bent on revenge. Waylon wanted to warn Joel, especially since they'd grown so close while he was working on the farm. He knew Douglas had the means to make life hard for the Hughes family. Waylon even knew of the plan Douglas had been working on to purchase the land. But, Douglas paid well, much better than the Hughes family, and Waylon was trying to save enough money to start a life with his girlfriend, Dena Hopkins. She was in law school at North Carolina Central University in Durham and Waylon had plans to help her establish her law firm in Reeseville, because he knew his opinionated and spitfire woman would not be happy working for anyone else. Douglas had agreed to throw some work Dena's way, even though he didn't care for Erin's best friend. In his eyes, Dena had been the cause of their split in high school. Dena had invited Erin to the party where she and Joel had shared their first kiss. Still, for whatever reason, Waylon believed Douglas respected his relationship with Dena—but watching him quasi-stalk Erin and Joel, he had to wonder if he was wrong about that.

"D, man, don't you think you should let this thing go? You and Erin have both moved on, and it's best that you just focus on your business and your family," Waylon reasonably suggested.

"If Joel Hughes could take care of his farm and his woman, she wouldn't have approached me about being a sponsor for that farm and their community outreach. If they're having money problems, then I have the solution. I'm going to buy that land right out from under Joel."

"That's not going to happen. That place is historic, part of this county's folklore, and he'll never sell. Especially not to you. Everyone knows you're buying property just to level it."

"He may not, but I have a meeting with Ryan Hughes next week. If the old man is thinking about selling, I'm going to push him in that direction." Douglas had a sinister gleam in his slate gray eyes, and Waylon couldn't help but shiver. He knew Ryan Hughes was dealing with an illness, which was why he'd handed over most of the daily running of the farm to Joel and Erin. The last thing Waylon wanted was to allow Douglas to take advantage of the older man in this state. He had to tell his friend what was going on.

"D, that's underhanded and you can't do that."

"The hell I can't. See, that little boy from Waverly is dead and gone. I'm a grown man and

I'm going to get everything that I want. All these people who wrote me off are going to suffer."

"What about your growing family? Didn't you say Ev was pregnant?" Waylon questioned.

"Yes. Hopefully she will give me a son and then she can be on her way," Douglas said coldly. "I know that she doesn't love me and truthfully, I don't love her at all."

"She does love you."

"She loves what I represent, and my money. I'm not fooled," Douglas said. "I know what she's doing when she's spending weekends in New York. I can't even be sure that it's my child she's having." Sighing, he glanced at Joel and Erin again as they embraced tenderly. "That bastard took away the one thing that was most important to me and I'm not going to rest until I do the same to him."

Waylon wanted to jump out of the car and warn Joel about Douglas's scheme, but he sat there and watched his friend stare at Joel and Erin as they got into their car.

"She should be with me," Douglas bemoaned. "If it's the last thing I do, I'm going to have her again."

"Do you really think she's going to want you if you destroy her husband's life?" Waylon asked.

Douglas smirked. "If she doesn't, then she can suffer right along with him."

Waylon hopped out of the car, telling Douglas

that he had to meet Dena. He knew that he had to warn the Hughes family about what Douglas was planning. If he told Dena, she'd tell Erin and Joel what was going on.

"I hope you know who butters your bread," Douglas called after him. "Tell anyone about my plan and I'll make sure you don't spend one more day with Dena."

Chapter 1

Crystal Hughes was mad as hell and the person behind this madness would feel her wrath, she decided as she ripped the notice she'd received in the mail to shreds. "Welco!" she muttered. Crossing the vast living room, Crystal grabbed her purse and keys from the coffee table. That company and its mysterious—at least from Crystal's point of view—owner wanted to own everything in town. Well, Hughes Farm was not for sale.

What was it that Douglas Wellington III had been quoted saying in the paper last week? *If Main Street can't keep their lights on, why should I have to share my bulbs?* How heartless! Crystal knew this man didn't give a damn about Reeseville. If he did, he'd know that helping, not buying, was the way people made it through rough times in this small town. Crystal wasn't even sure if old man Wellington even lived in Reeseville. If he did, he wouldn't want to destroy Hughes Farm. *Bastard!*

Dashing out of her plantation-style house, Crystal nearly bowled over two teenagers planting rosebushes near her steps.

"Miss Crystal, is everything okay?" asked Renda Johnson as Crystal placed her hand on her shoulder.

"Yes, I'm just in a hurry. What are you and MJ doing?" Crystal forced a smile at Monique and Renda, two sisters who lived in the Starlight House, a group home that sat a stone's throw from Crystal's house. No one else in Reeseville wanted the home for wayward girls anywhere near them. People said that the girls would be a danger to their neighborhoods and would lower their property value. But Crystal, who owned more than one hundred acres of land in west Duval County, subscribed to the notion that one good turn deserved another. "To whom much is given, much is required," Grandmother Hughes would always say. Crystal told the board of county commissioners that Starlight could have as much space as they needed. She treated the girls in Starlight just like the sisters she never had, and in return, they treated her to surprises like planting rosebushes in her yard, raking her lawn, and working in her community garden without any complaints.

Placing her hands on her hips and smacking a wad of gum, Monique stood up and looked Crystal in the eyes. "Well, it was supposed to be a surprise. But we found those orange rose-bushes you were talking about. Why are you up so early?"

Nervously, Crystal twisted the green jade ring on her index finger. There was no way she could tell these girls about Welco's plans, plans that would level everything on her property. In their short lives, they'd seen so much disappointment and despair, and Crystal wasn't going to let evil Welco Industries add to it. She'd grown tired of watching this company buy up Reeseville as if they were playing Monopoly. In the last three years, Welco had purchased much of the land around Reeseville, building small factories that Crystal would bet her farm had been causing the increase in allergies around town. Did Wellington care? No. He simply said that people should take more vitamins.

But what she was most peeved with Welco about was the supercenter they'd built down-town, which caused the Fresh Food Market to close because they couldn't compete with the cheap prices of the supercenter. The Fresh Food Market had been the only grocery store in town where local farmers could sell their vegetables and fresh meats. When it closed, some of the smaller farms in Reeseville had suffered. Then Welco came along and bought them.

"Just some business in town, sweeties," Crystal replied. "Thank you so much for my surprise, though."

Mrs. Brooke Fey, the director and on-sight operator of the house, walked over to Crystal and the girls. "Ms. Hughes, I hope MJ and Renda aren't bothering you this morning," she said, surveying the scene in front of her.

"Oh no. These girls have given me something that I've wanted for a long time. Now, I really have to go." Crystal ran to her car, nearly tripping over her Birkenstock clogs and ankle-length rainbow-colored skirt. She started the car and peeled out of the driveway, leaving two black skid marks on the pavement. *This isn't going to happen. Welco isn't going to buy me!*

It wasn't nine a.m. yet and Douglas Wellington III, president and CEO of Welco Industries, was popping aspirin. His head throbbed like a heartbeat because the board was on his back, his assistant couldn't find the documents he needed for his ten-thirty presentation—and did she just say a woman was threatening to chain herself to the front door if he didn't meet with her immediately? This was not happening. Not today.

"Amy! Amy! I don't have time to meet with some kook. Call security or something. But what you need to do more than anything else is find my proposal!" he barked into the phone. From his desk, Douglas scrutinized Amy's small frame as she slumped over her desk. He knew he was too hard on her, but today wasn't a day for anyone to expect kindness from him. The board of directors was growing impatient about the time it was taking to get the business park project started. Douglas had no idea the owners of Hughes Farm would put up such a fight over that land. From what he understood, the farm wasn't a working farm with livestock and whatnot. Basically, they grew vegetables. In Douglas's opinion, there was enough dirt in Reeseville to plant a garden anywhere. It had been his great idea to hold off on any other projects until the business park was built. It wasn't as if Welco was losing money, but they weren't making money either. That was a problem Douglas had to fix—especially if he was going to keep Clive Oldsman off his back.

Twirling a silver ink pen between his fingers, Douglas picked up the phone and dialed Waylon Terrell's number. Waylon was his father's best friend and Douglas's godfather. In business, the only person Douglas trusted other than himself was Waylon. Were it not for his godfather, Douglas wouldn't be in the position he was in today. On days like this, that wasn't a good thing. He hadn't planned to follow in his father's footsteps. In fact, he'd spent a great deal of his life trying to be everything that Douglas Wellington Jr. was not, even if they were both coldhearted businessmen.

Luckily for him, he had Waylon in his life to control the board most of the time. Waylon had mentored him and guided him though some of his toughest business decisions.

"Hello, godson," the older man said when he answered.

"Waylon, the board is driving me crazy," Douglas admitted. "I know they want me gone and I'm beginning to think Amy is working against me too."

"Calm down, son. These guys want you out of Welco, but your father groomed you your whole life for this. Don't let these old bastards push you around. Take a deep breath and show them who Doug Trey is."

Hearing his nickname brought a smile to Douglas's face. "All right, doc," he replied. "Did you take a look at my business park plans?"

"Uh, I haven't really looked over them. I'm

retired, remember? I'll get back to you in a few days, but isn't this decision already made?"

Sighing, Douglas wished he'd gone to Waylon before presenting this business park idea to the board. What if he was going about building this place the wrong way?

I can't second-guess myself; that's what they expect.

"You're still there?" Waylon asked, breaking into Douglas's thoughts.

"Yeah, yeah. I'm going to go. We'll have to have dinner sometime this week," said Douglas. He said good-bye and hung up when he noticed Amy standing at his door. "What?"

"Sir," she said nervously. "That woman won't leave. She's handcuffed herself to my desk, sir. With her free hand, she keeps knocking papers off my desk."

Muttering a string of curses and profanities that would make a sailor blush, Douglas snatched his phone off the hook and dialed security. "There is a woman who needs to be removed from the building. You'll notice that she's wearing handcuffs," Douglas growled at the guard. Slamming the phone down, he walked over to the door and peered at the woman cuffed to Amy's desk as she dug in a huge brown sack. Thinking she might have a gun, Douglas immediately pulled Amy into his office and slammed the door. They ducked behind his desk, waiting for the woman to make her next move.

The artificial beauty of the Welco lobby grated on Crystal's nerves, from the potted silk plants to the shiny marble floors and the huge windows allowing bright sunlight to saturate the building. *But there's no life force here,* she thought as she looked around.

Crystal spotted a menacing security officer walking toward her, his massive hand at his side, gripping his flashlight. Dropping her bag to the floor, she sat down on the marble crossing her legs Indian style. This wasn't her first time standing up—rather sitting down—to corporate security. She and some of the girls from the Starlight House had protested at the local mall because security officers had harassed a number of young people for no reason. The Reeseville Mall ended up donating a hundred thousand dollars to the Starlight House to stop the weekly protests and the security guards were trained how to deal with diverse youth. Crystal's reputation as a community activist was born the day the settlement was announced. But she worried about living up to her family's legacy. Hughes Farm, which meant so much to the community, had been handed down each generation and she refused to be the one member of the family to mess things up and lose it.

She also didn't want to be viewed as some liberal nut either. Still, there was a right and a wrong way to do things. Many in the community already questioned if Crystal could handle running the farm and why she allowed the Starlight House to be built there. She'd heard the murmurs around town about her not doing as good a job with the farm as her parents. People questioned why she stopped raising livestock, accused her of being a hippie, and said she was going to ruin what took decades to build.

Maybe those whispers helped spur her anger toward Welco. People expected her to fail, and Welco buying out the farm wasn't going to prove her naysayers right. If she had to protest every day or sue to keep what was her family's, then she would. Douglas Wellington III was going to rue the day he tried to take over her farm. This was only the beginning.

The Welco security officer, who reminded her of an ogre from Greek mythology, snarled at her before saying, "Ma'am, unlock these handcuffs and leave."

Rolling her eyes, Crystal stood up to the towering guard. "If you want me to leave, get Wellington out here, otherwise, I'm camping out. What's right is right. I don't want to make a scene, but I will and the whole town will see it." Crystal threw her hand up, illustrating how close they were to the big bay window. Slowly, she returned to her seat on the floor.

The security officer ripped his radio from his hip holster as Crystal pulled a bottle of water from her bag. "All right," the officer said. "Show me that you don't have a gun in that sack and I'll see about getting Wellington out here."

Crystal looked at him quizzically as she opened up her bag to show him the contents: two more bottles of water and three apples. "Why the change of heart?"

Placing his hand on her shoulder, he smiled. "He ain't my favorite person, either. Hold tight." The officer waddled down the hall and disappeared behind glass double doors.

Crystal drank her water slowly, waiting for something to happen. *When is old Wellington going to appear?* she wondered, her frustration increasing, She'd already built an image of this monster in her mind—pencil thin, receding gray hair, a potbelly, and crooked teeth. Only a monster like that would want to displace people for the almighty dollar. Only a man with ice water in his veins rather than blood would view people as if they were a commodity to be bought and sold. Not Crystal—she wasn't for sale.

Moments later, a tall man, moving with the

grace of a panther and the body of a Greek god, crossed the lobby and planted himself in front of her. Crystal gazed up at him, momentarily speechless as he stared at her with slate gray eyes. His full lips seemingly beckoned her to kiss them and those hands—big and wide with long fingers—she wanted them on her body, caressing her breasts, thighs, and everything in between. Rapidly, she blinked and swallowed hard. She needed to get her hormones together; she wasn't here to lust after this man, whoever he was. She was here to meet with Wellington and she didn't give a damn if they sent Denzel Washington to the lobby to meet her—Crystal wasn't moving until she got what she wanted. Still, the man looking at her was fine as hell.

His face told a story of annoyance, with a scowl darkening his handsome features and his wide nostrils flaring with anger. "Are you going to just stare at me or do you have something to say?" His voice reminded her of a sensual sax, hypnotic and melodic. Her body was electrified at the thought of him whispering sweet words of passion in her ear.

"I'm not talking to anyone but Douglas Wellington." Crystal's voice wavered, but not from fear. Carnal desire described what she was feeling as she stared into his eyes.

"I *am* Douglas Wellington," he announced dryly.

Now on her feet, Crystal was dumbfounded. There was no way a man this beautiful could be as cold and callous as the man she'd dreamed up in her head. Where were his fangs, protruding belly, and horns? The scent of burning sulfur and brimstone? "What? You're Douglas Wellington?"

He folded his arms across his chest and shot her a look of irritation. "This is fascinating and all, listening to you repeat my name. But what the hell do you want, lady? Most people make a phone call and set an appointment to get a meeting. This is a distraction that's interrupting my workday."

Narrowing her dark eyes into slits, Crystal exclaimed, "My land is not for sale, you pompous ass. If you think for one second that I will allow you to come on to my property and just take over because you want to, you can forget it."

Douglas laughed and turned to walk away. "If you read the letter that was mailed to you about my company's plans, there was a number for my attorney that you can call. I suggest you do that," he said. "And uncuff yourself," he added, "otherwise, I'm calling the police."

"And I'm calling the press, jerk! Do you realize what you're planning to destroy all in the name of corporate greed? People need this land and I will fight you tooth and nail to make sure it stays in my possession. So, get ready to lose."

Douglas waved her off as if she were a gnat buzzing around his ear. "If you don't unshackle yourself by the time I get in my office, and then get out of this building, I will press charges when the police arrive."

Chapter 2

Douglas closed his eyes once he reached his desk. The first time he exhaled, he realized that he'd been holding his breath the entire time he was talking to that woman. Her beauty bewitched him, sending his heart rate into overdrive, until she opened her mouth. Her long legs, caramel skin, and ink black hair were burned onto his brain cells, and his loins ached for her. Douglas had never felt such a raw sexual yearning for a woman before. Standing up, he looked out into the lobby to make sure she'd left. To his surprise, she was still there, causing his desire to turn into anger. The last thing he needed was that woman sitting in his lobby distracting him. He picked up the phone to call the police, but he couldn't bring himself to complete the call.

Slamming the receiver down, Douglas stormed

out of the office just to come face to face with the woman again. Forcing himself to look past her angelic features, he glowered at her. "Didn't I tell you to leave?"

"And you think I'm a woman who does what she's told? I'll leave when you back off my land. You're not going to force me to sell it to you because you think you know what this community needs. Do you even live here? I bet you spend your weekends running around looking for other things to take over. You don't give a damn about Reeseville and the people who live here. You just want to add another feather in your cap."

Damn, she's fine when she's angry, he thought as she pointed her finger in his face and shook her head from side to side, causing her silky hair to whip across her face. Douglas wanted to reach out and touch her skin, it looked so smooth. But she was saying all the wrong things with those sexy lips of hers.

And did she realize that construction of the business park she wanted to block would employ more than fifteen hundred people in Duval County, especially the western portion of the county? That raggedy farm operation was worth more torn down than whatever she had going on there. Besides, this project was something he had to complete, something to honor his father. Douglas Wellington Jr. wasn't an easy man to love and Douglas hadn't wanted to be like his father at all. But since his father's death, he'd wanted to do something to honor his legacy, at least his public image—a man from the wrong side of the tracks who'd done well. This business project had been important to him, at least according to the old file that Douglas had found. No matter how pretty she was, this woman wasn't going to stand in his way.

"And another thing," she said, poking him in the chest. "People aren't for sale. You think because you have money that you can just get your way."

Douglas shook his head, wanting to kiss her supple lips and press her body against his; but at the same time he wanted to have her thrown in jail for trespassing. It was bad enough that he had to justify his decisions to the board. Now this woman was standing in the lobby of his company berating him. She was probably a plant by the board to disrupt his day so that he would be off kilter for his meeting.

"Miss, I'm asking for the last time. Please leave."

"The name is Crystal Hughes. And the Hughes Farm isn't going to be sold." She reached into her purse and retrieved a small silver key to unlock her handcuffs. "Back off or you will be in for the fight of your sorry life."

Laughing, Douglas reached out and touched

Crystal's arm. "Everyone has a price. Why don't I just add a few more zeros to the company's first offer and you can take your righteous indignation someplace else?"

Crystal grabbed her bottle of water and tossed its contents in Douglas's face. "Buy that, you jackass! This isn't over."

Douglas watched as Crystal stomped out the door, at the same time that Clive Oldsman, chairman of the Welco board of directors, walked in. She nearly pushed the old man out of the way as she stormed out.

Wiping the cool water from his face, Douglas tossed his hands up as Clive questioned him with a cold stare.

"What was that all about?" the old man asked.

"You know how people are in this town," Douglas replied. Amy rushed over to him with a white hand towel. Nodding thanks to his assistant and wiping his face, Douglas turned to Clive, who scowled at him. "Why are you here, Clive?" Douglas asked.

"Maybe we should go into your office and talk. We need to have this conversation in private."

Thinking that the last thing he wanted to do was be in a confined space with Clive, Douglas reluctantly led the man into his office. *What else can go wrong today?* he wondered.

Clive perched himself on the edge of Douglas's

desk. "The Welco Business Park project is moving a little too slowly, don't you think? The plans are right there. You should make it happen."

"What do you want me to do, Clive? Beat the residents out there until they sign over their land?"

Pulling a Cuban cigar from his jacket pocket, Clive chomped down on the brown stogie. Douglas sized up the older man, knowing the rest of the board sent Clive to spy on him. They didn't like him and thought he was too aggressive in some of the business decisions that he made. But one thing they didn't complain about was the amount of money they made.

"Don't light that in here," Douglas said forcefully. "This project will get done on time. I know what my job is and I would appreciate it if you all would let me do it."

Moving the cigar from one side of his mouth to the other, Clive leaned in and looked Douglas in the eye. "You're not doing your job, and quite frankly, we're tired of your incompetence. These nickel and dime projects aren't going to increase our revenues. We need this business park, so make it happen." Clive stood up and headed for the door, and then he abruptly turned around. "The only reason you're here is because the board has enormous respect for your father. Wellington men built this company, but before we allow old loyalties to destroy it, we will remove you as CEO and get someone more capable to take charge."

Leaping to his feet, Douglas rushed toward Clive. "You will not take this company from me. You're still making money, Clive. You're still a millionaire off these nickel and dime projects. So you can tell the board and anyone else that this project will proceed and I'm not going anywhere."

Clive slammed out of the office, leaving Douglas alone to wonder why he stuck around to take this abuse. Slumping in his chair, Douglas thought back to the days when his father ran the company and he did everything he could to run away from it.

He'd never had any intention of becoming CEO of Welco Industries, the company that robbed his father of his family, his health, and his life. Douglas wanted to strike out and do something different. His plan was to get into the music industry like Jermaine Dupri. Then Waylon called him and told him about his father's cancer. It was his senior year of college and he'd already gotten an internship with the record company, So So Def. He'd been on his way to meet with a singing group that he'd planned to introduce to Jermaine. Then the phone rang and his life changed forever.

"Your father needs you," Waylon had said.

"Not this again, Waylon. I don't want to join the family business."

"Stop being selfish. Do you know your father has colon cancer?"

That revelation had stopped Douglas dead in his tracks. Douglas Wellington Jr. was the closest thing to Superman that he'd ever known. His father couldn't have cancer. Pushing his dreams aside, Douglas returned to Reeseville to learn everything he could about Welco. When his father died, he took over and became the youngest CEO in company history. He would've considered that a great accomplishment had he wanted the job. But he felt as if he was wearing leather loafers that didn't belong to him.

Still, he tried to do what he thought his father would've done. He bought things, tore things down, put the name Welco everywhere.

I would have done better just painting a target on my back, he thought as he leaned back in his chair.

By the time Crystal arrived home, her blood boiled with anger. Douglas Wellington III was the most arrogant man who had ever crossed her path. How was she going to tell Mrs. Fey that they might have to move the Starlight House? Especially when no one else in the county wanted the home for girls anywhere near their property.

Sitting in the driveway, she banged her hands against the steering wheel. How was she going to fix this?

Do these companies do any research before they make these grabs for land? she thought as tears welled up in her eyes. Hughes Farm was much more than a piece of land. The farm had been in Crystal's family since the turn of the last century. Casio Hughes had been a sharecropper on the farm when it belonged to Simon Winchell. During the influenza outbreak of 1918, Simon's wife and two sons died, leaving him alone with more land to work than he could handle. The Hughes family fared much better. Casio's wife and four sons were spared and they took care of Simon, tending the land, burying his family, and comforting him. When Simon was stricken with the flu, he made a last-minute change to his will, leaving his land to Casio Hughes and his family.

Generation after generation of Hughes grew up in west Duval County. Up until 1985, the farm was fully functioning, producing tobacco, cotton, corn, and soybeans. But a declining agricultural economy forced the Hughes family to find another way to make a living. When Crystal's grandfather, Ryan, invested in the family's land, building single family homes and renting them to Section Eight recipients, the family and the land flourished. Following Ryan Hughes's death in 1990, Crystal's parents, Joel and Erin, took over and started the community farm after homelessness became a problem in Reeseville. Joel and Erin retired the year Crystal graduated from North Carolina A & T State University and turned the reins of Hughes Farm over to her. With a degree in agricultural science, Crystal had always planned on returning to Reeseville to make some differences on the farm. So far, though, she hadn't done anything with her degree. Crystal continued renting to low income families, growing vegetables in the community garden, and helping others the way someone helped her ancestors.

Emerging from the car, Crystal wiped her eyes and walked over to the Starlight House. Looking at the two-story wood-framed house decorated with gold stars, she knew that no one would take those girls in if Welco Industries had their way and bulldozed the house and everything else on the property. Knocking on the door, she took a step back, trying to figure out how to stop Welco's plans. One of the staff members answered the door. "Hi, Crystal."

"Lorraine, is Mrs. Fey here?" Crystal asked.

"She went in to town. Is something wrong? You look a little flustered." Lorraine beckoned for Crystal to come in.

Shaking her head and touching Lorraine's shoulder, Crystal couldn't find the words to say what was really wrong. "Just have her stop by my house when she returns, please."

Nodding, Lorraine agreed to do so.

On the walk back to her house, Crystal decided that the only way to fight fire was with fire. Glancing over her shoulder and looking at the girls working in the garden, she realized the media would love this story; it had the trappings of being a lead story. Displacing a group of girls for corporate greed would make the front page of every paper within fifteen miles of Reeseville. TV would pick up on the story too. Crystal could see the faces of the Starlight girls on the six o'clock news. "Douglas Wellington, you've messed with the wrong person this time," she muttered. Crystal ran into the house and began making calls to the media.

After the day Douglas had, he needed the drink that he held in his hand. The cold martini burned when it hit his throat. This was good. A hand touched his shoulder and Douglas turned his head slightly. "Deloris Tucker, what do you want?" His blood pressure had shot up at least a hundred points. The last thing he needed was to deal with this reporter. Douglas was sure that Deloris wanted to get a job with a big time newspaper, so she went out of her way to cover every story involving Welco as if it was some big scandal. He couldn't wait until she got her dream job so that she would stop being his ultimate nightmare.

"Not happy to see me?" she asked, smiling coldly. "I got a call from a Crystal Hughes at the office today. You're displacing kids now?" Pulling a digital recorder from her purse, she shoved it under Douglas's nose. "So, Mr. Wellington, is it true that Welco is making a play for Hughes Farm in order to build an office park?"

Glaring at the reporter, Douglas set his glass on the bar. "No comment."

Deloris threw up her hands. "If that's how you want it. But according to Ms. Hughes, this land is historic and the location of a group home that no one else wants to accommodate. If your plans go through, then those girls have no home. Do you really want to come off looking colder and more heartless than normal?"

"And if this business park doesn't go up, fifteen hundred people don't have jobs. Twenty delinquents having a home or thousands of families putting food on their table; which is best for Reeseville?" Douglas rose to his feet, pulled his wallet from his pocket, and dropped the cash for the martini on the bar. "Good evening, Ms. Tucker."

Douglas stormed out of the bar, hopped into his silver Jaguar, and sped out of the parking lot.

Lowering the convertible top, he headed for the highway. The wind against his face made him feel free. He needed freedom, needed to get away from all of the prying eyes that watched his every move. Douglas questioned why he took over Welco Industries after his father's death. Maybe the board was right and he was too young to handle the responsibilities of running the company. He couldn't be the P. Diddy of industry, but he tried to be pioneering with running Welco. Most of the time, the board balked at his more innovative projects. When he wanted to look toward investing in wind energy and natural gas energy, the board wasn't interested. Solar energy farms? Not at all.

When he'd said that he wanted to make Welco more of a part of the community, sponsor some events and things like that, Clive was the first one to scream that those social events would do nothing for the company's bottom line. Maybe if the company had done more in the community, people like Crystal Hughes wouldn't think of it as an evil empire. And maybe she wouldn't look at him as the devil.

The board had warned him about making himself the "face" of Welco. But while Douglas's plan was to make the huge company seem more personable, what he ended up doing was giving the press and people like Crystal Hughes a target.

Her name sent shivers down his spine. That woman was so sexy, so alluring, and such a pain in his rear end. Why couldn't they have met in a bar, Crystal wearing something low cut and tight, clinging to her luscious curves? He'd buy her a drink, take her for a fast ride in his Jag, and watch the wind blow through her silky hair.

Pressing the gas, Douglas opened the engine up, sending the speedometer over one hundred miles per hour. The excitement of speeding down the road made him tingle, much like good sex would. But who had time for a sex life? Douglas couldn't find a woman who was actually interested in him and not his bank account—another problem in making himself Welco's face.

But Crystal didn't seem like the gold-digging type. Quickly Douglas put the brakes on his thoughts. She might not be a gold digger, but she was the enemy. Sexy as hell, but his enemy nonetheless.

The next day, Douglas found out just how much trouble Crystal could be. He picked up the morning newspaper from his front doorstep and the headline jumped out at him. "Woman challenges Welco growth."

Sitting down on the top step, Douglas read the story intently. He wasn't surprised to see Deloris's name on the byline.

If community activist Crystal Hughes has her way, Welco Industries will not expand its development into west Duval County. Hughes, who owns Hughes Farm, said she received a letter from the company offering her $1.5 million for the hundred acres of land outside Reeseville.

"Hughes Farm is more than just a farm," she said. "When no one else in town wanted to let Starlight House build, I let them in. The crops that I grow out here feed hundreds of homeless people and allow the girls to help other people, which speeds their healing."

Hughes Farm is a historic part of west Duval County. According to records from the county clerk's office, the Hughes Farm has been in operation since 1918. While it is not a working farm, more than thirty low income families live in houses on the property.

"A farm is a nurturing place. That is what Hughes Farm is all about. We're helping families grow, we're helping the girls at the Starlight House flourish," said Hughes.

Douglas Wellington III, president

> and CEO of Welco Industries, said, "And if this business park doesn't go up, fifteen hundred people don't have jobs. Twenty delinquents having a home or thousands of families putting food on their table; which is best for Reeseville?"

Crumpling the paper, Douglas tossed it into the recycling bin on the edge of his porch. Standing, he cursed himself for speaking to Deloris because he knew she'd twist his words, like she always did. As he walked into his house, the phone rang. He didn't need to look at the caller ID display to know it was the office. Of course the board saw the paper and if Douglas knew anything about those old men, he knew they were not amused. Grabbing the phone, he barked hello.

"Mr. Wellington, this is Amy. The board has called an emergency meeting and they're here waiting for you."

He rolled his eyes to the ceiling and sighed. "Tell them I'll be there in fifteen minutes." Douglas hung up the phone and plopped down on the sofa. His temples throbbed relentlessly and he hadn't even had his first cup of coffee. Realizing that the longer he kept the board waiting the harder things were going to be, Douglas pulled himself up, showered, dressed quickly, and headed to the office, ready to take his lumps. Somehow, he was going to have to convince Crystal Hughes to sell him that farm—especially if he planned to keep his job as CEO.

Chapter 3

Crystal placed her newspaper on the table as she reached for her cup of organic, fair trade coffee. Satisfied that she had made some waves, she knew her work had just gotten started. Sipping the strong coffee, she closed her eyes and saw Douglas Wellington's face. His slate gray eyes haunted her. Why did he have to be so damned fine? He should've looked like the monster in her head instead of the man of her dreams. And what a dream she'd had about him last night, his hands all over her body, touching her in places she didn't know existed. Those lusciously thick lips kissing hers, sucking her bottom lip, his tongue darting in and out of her mouth. Heat rushed to her cheeks and moisture pooled between her legs as she recalled her dream.

Standing, Crystal walked to the back window overlooking the acres of crops growing in her backyard. The man starring in her erotic dreams wanted to take this away. The man of her dreams was cruel and callous, putting the almighty dollar above the needs of people. She picked up the newspaper and reread Douglas's comments. How could he make judgments on people he didn't even know? The Starlight girls weren't delinquents; they'd just had a bad turn in life. Some of the girls came to Starlight after years of abuse or for committing a petty crime, but after a few months, the difference in the girls was clear to anyone who bothered to look.

Crystal found herself proud of each girl who emerged from Starlight House and became a productive member of society. The girls who completed the program successfully went on to college, many heading for her alma mater, NCA&T. Two former Starlight girls had written a book about the program. *Maybe I should give Douglas a copy so that he would know who these kids are that he maligned,* she mused.

She looked back out over the land and took another sip of her coffee. What if Douglas Wellington saw what this land meant to people? What if he walked the fertile soil and understood the history of Hughes Farm and why selling it would be a loss for the entire community and not just her family?

Turning toward the garden, she watched several girls from the Starlight House picking ears of corn and peppers. Those vegetables would be washed and donated to the homeless shelter in downtown Reeseville. People needed to know how much of a difference the farm made in the lives of these girls. Crossing the room, Crystal grabbed her phone and called a friend at the local TV station.

"Moses Johnson," he said when he answered.

"Good morning, Moses. It's Crystal."

"I was just about to call you. I just read the paper."

"Then why don't you get a camera crew down here. Some of the girls are in the garden and I have a lot to say about Wellington's comments this morning. How dare he talk about those girls that way! That slimy son of a . . ."

"Whoa, Crystal, calm down. Better yet, save it for the cameras. We'll roll a crew that way and have you on the noon news," he said.

Smiling, she told him thanks and hung up the phone. Round two was about to begin. Douglas Wellington III didn't have any idea who he was messing with.

About an hour later, a news crew from Channel 12 pulled into Hughes Farm. Crystal and some of the girls stood in front of the camera as the reporter set up her shot. Seconds later, Crystal was taking the reporter and the cameraman on a tour of the farm, showing them the crops, the group home, the greenhouses where she grew rare roses and orchids, and finally the steps of her home.

"This house," she said, "is over four hundred years old. But if Welco has its way, it will be reduced to rubble. History will be erased, and why? So the company can increase its profits?"

The reporter nodded to the cameraman to cut. "Thank you, Ms. Hughes," she said. "This is very compelling."

Crystal smiled and shook hands with the petite blond. "Thank you for coming out here."

The woman returned Crystal's smile before hopping into the news truck. Crystal wondered if they were heading to Welco Industries. A lightbulb went off in her head and she turned to MJ and Renda. "Grab some markers and meet me on my front steps in thirty minutes."

The girls looked befuddled, but they followed Crystal's directive while she ran in her house, grabbed her keys, and then hopped into her car heading for the local office supply store. If there were going to be news cameras at Welco, she was going to be there with picket signs and the very delinquents Douglas wanted to make judgments about. Can you say "round three"?

"Totally unacceptable," said Clive Oldsman. "Why would you say something like this to a reporter? What in the hell were you thinking about? This makes you and Welco look just like the assholes Crystal Hughes says you are."

Douglas leapt to his feet as Clive tossed the newspaper in his face. "Look, this is going to blow over. Every time we develop land around here, someone complains. Do you want to scrap our plans and scout another site because of one newspaper article? I'm sure Ms. Hughes has made her point and we shouldn't hear anything more from her. Now, you all have taken up enough of my time today. Good day, gentlemen." Opening the door, Douglas waited for the six members of the board to leave. Everyone exited except Clive, who closed the door behind them.

"You'd better make this go away. Our stock is already taking a beating and this can only make it worse," he hissed.

"I know that," Douglas said. "But even with the so-called beating that you say our stock is taking, we're still raking in profits. So, what's your damned problem?"

Narrowing his eyes at Douglas, Clive sighed. "You're nothing like your father. He must be turning in his grave as he watches you run this corporation into the ground."

"Why don't you get out of here before I say or do something I might not regret," Douglas replied.

"What I *regret* is the board appointing you president when you obviously can't handle it."

Unable to control his anger, Douglas grabbed Clive by the collar. "You pompous son of a bitch! My family built this company and you're not taking it away from me. The business park will get built, the stock will rebound, and you will resign from this board."

Jerking away from Douglas, Clive straightened his shirt and shook his head. "You'll be out of this company before I will. You can bet the bottom line on that." He stormed out of the conference room.

Douglas closed his eyes, counted to ten, and prayed for a quiet rest of the day. But as he walked into the lobby, he knew his prayers wouldn't be answered. A camera crew rushed toward him. "Mr. Wellington, Mr. Wellington," the reporter called out. "Do you really plan to level Hughes Farm? Do you stand by your comments in the *Reeseville Gazette*?"

Throwing his hands up, he said, "I have no comment. Now get off my property."

A few board members who were lingering by the door turned around and followed Douglas into his office. Fred Jones, Dorian Harper and Willis Reed stood in the doorway of Douglas's office. Fred spoke first. "This is ugly."

"Very," said Dorian.

Douglas, who'd taken a seat behind his desk, folded his arms across his chest. "We've dealt with worse. Do you remember what happened when we brought Welco-Mart to north Duval County? People said our store would kill all of the mom and pop local businesses. But when those same people saw we used local businesses to build the shopping center and the salaries that Welco-Mart paid, things died down." Reaching in his desk drawer, Douglas retrieved a bottle of aspirin. Flipping the cap off, he dumped two pills down his throat and swallowed hard.

Willis nodded. "When we built Welco-Mart, we controlled the press. Seems as if Ms. Hughes has the media eating out of her hand. Douglas, I believe you will take care of this, but this Crystal Hughes woman is going to be a problem."

A sexy problem. Why does she have to be so fine and so difficult? Why does she have to haunt my thoughts? Douglas stood and ushered the three men out of his office. When they walked into the lobby, they saw Crystal, an older woman and seven girls marching on the sidewalk holding picket signs. "Welco hates children," the signs read.

Douglas's attention fell on Crystal, who was dressed in a pair of skin-tight jeans that accentuated her luscious curves and taut ass and a white tank top that clung to her supple breasts and exposed a sliver of her flat stomach. Her flowing hair was parted down the center and hung on her shoulders in two thick braids, framing her beautiful face. For the first time, Douglas noticed her doe-shaped black eyes, perfectly shaped nose, and those lips. He'd dreamed of those lips since she chained herself to Amy's desk. Crystal was a classic beauty, the kind of woman he'd shower with diamonds and gold. He wanted to peel those clothes from her body and make slow love to her in a room filled with roses and candles.

One of the girls pointed to the entrance where Douglas and the board members stood. The group started to chant loudly, "Hey, hey, ho, ho, Hughes Farm will not go!"

Douglas felt Crystal's angry stare focusing on him, but even with a scowl on her face, she was beautiful. Opening the door, he walked outside and sneered at the protesters.

Willis grabbed his shoulder and shook his head. "Don't make a scene," he warned.

"I won't. Maybe I can reason with them." Douglas just wanted a chance to talk to Crystal. Slowly he crossed over to her, standing inches from her. She lowered her sign and glared at Douglas.

"Ms. Hughes, this is cute, but you can picket here all night and nothing is going to change. The city council and county commission have given us the go ahead on this project, the land will be rezoned, and everyone around you has sold their land to Welco. Why don't you do the same?"

Crystal's grip tightened around the wooden handle of her sign. Douglas had no clue if she was going to strike him or not. Instead, she hoisted her sign high above her head and began chanting, "People aren't for sale, people aren't for sale. Hey, hey, ho, ho, Hughes Farm will not go."

Gently taking her by the arm, Douglas pulled Crystal aside. "Ms. Hughes, we can't have this out here. This is a business; I'm going to ask you to move across the street."

Snatching away from him, she hit him on the shoulder with the sign. "You know what? I'm sick and tired of you thinking that you own this town and all the people in it. Were you picked on as a child? Do you need to buy things to make up for other shortcomings in your life?" She looked pointedly at his crotch.

Douglas laughed. "You're funny. Just stop standing in the way of progress and maybe we can be friends. And if you'd like to find out about what you're looking at, then I'd be happy to show you just how wrong you are."

Narrowing her eyes at him, she swung the sign, which he caught this time. "Not even if you were the last man in the galaxy! And the only way you'll get my farm is over my dead body." She tore away from him, rejoining the other protesters, and chanted even louder.

Even though he didn't want to, Douglas went inside and called the police. He'd tried to warn her, he reasoned.

As the officers leapt out of their cars, Douglas regretted his decision. He watched from his office window as the police begin to cuff the protesters. When he saw Crystal in the clutches of an oversized officer, he wanted to rush outside, pry her from the man's grip, and usher her inside the office. Then he would check her for injuries, kissing her tender wrists if they showed signs of hurt.

Shaking his head, Douglas tried to make himself believe that Crystal needed to go to jail, even though he knew it wasn't true.

Crystal caught Douglas's stare as she was stuffed into the back of a police car. If her hands hadn't been in cuffs, she would have flipped him off. How dare he! The protest was peaceful. Now he stood in the window gloating because she was being carted off like a criminal. The cop took off down the street toward the Duval County Detention Center. Sighing, Crystal realized that she may have caused trouble for the Starlight girls. If Douglas pressed charges, some of the girls at the protest might end up in a juvenile detention center because of previous criminal charges.

"All right, miss, out of the car," the officer said as he opened the door.

"Enjoying yourself?" Crystal snapped. "You

arrested us for no reason. What are you going to charge us with?"

"Nothing," said a voice behind them.

There was no mistaking that voice, rich and smooth like an expensive leather coat. Crystal whirled around, staring into slate gray eyes. Douglas walked over to her as the police officer unlocked her handcuffs.

"You shouldn't have called the police in the first place." She rubbed her tender skin and glanced up at Douglas. "Why aren't you pressing charges?"

"I don't need the bad press. Ms. Hughes, what is it going to take for you to end this and let Welco handle its business?"

Placing her hands on her hips, Crystal shook her head from side to side. "This isn't business to me, it's my legacy. My family has owned this land for nearly one hundred years and worked on it many years before that. So, if you think I'm going to step aside and let you bulldoze it, you'd better think again."

The sly smile that spread across Douglas's face enraged and excited her all at once. Turning away from him, Crystal shivered inwardly. How could she desire this man, this sexy, arrogant, pompous, alluring man with the haunting eyes? *He's evil,* she forced herself to think. Facing

Douglas with a fresh anger, she pushed him out of her way.

In a surprising move, Douglas grabbed her arm. "Ms. Hughes, why don't we calmly discuss Welco's plans over dinner? We can behave like civilized adults."

Crystal snatched away from him and stared at him incredulously. "Did you just ask me out to dinner? Have you lost what's left of your mind? I wouldn't eat with you if my life depended on it." Shivering with anger and disgust, Crystal raised her hand to slap Douglas, but he gently took her small hand in his bigger one and brought it to his lips, softly kissing it.

Electricity surged through her body as his lips touched her skin. Crystal wanted to pull away . . . she knew that she should pull away . . . but she didn't.

"Good day, Ms. Hughes. By the way, how do you plan to make it back to Hughes Farm? I'd be happy to give you a ride home," he said after dropping her hand.

Stepping back and nearly stumbling over a pine tree root, she shook her head. "I don't think so. I'd rather walk than ride with you."

Douglas raised his eyebrow as the other protesters were released. "But what about them? Let me help you all get back home. I even brought my limo so that I can take all of you back safely."

Crystal rolled her eyes and was about to call him a pretentious bastard trying to woo people with his wealth, but she didn't want the girls to have to walk three miles back to the van at Welco. "Is this supposed to impress me?" she snapped.

"No, it's supposed to get you and those young ladies back to your van."

She sighed and gritted her teeth. He did have a point. Crystal reluctantly agreed to allow Douglas to give them a ride. He led Crystal and the seven girls to his limousine. Excitement rippled through the girls. MJ looked at Crystal as if to ask her if it was all right to get in. She nodded and MJ slid inside. Douglas stood behind Crystal as she got into the limo. His scent of patchouli and natural masculinity frazzled her senses, causing the hairs on her neck to stand on end. But when he placed his hand on the small of her back in an effort to help her in the car, she lost it on the inside at least. The simple touch made heat radiate throughout her body, transporting her to a dark bedroom with candles burning and smooth jazz playing in the distance. His body was entwined with hers and . . .

"Ms. Hughes, is there a problem?" Douglas asked.

Quickly, Crystal climbed into the car. "You're my problem," she muttered.

Smiling knowingly, Douglas sat across from

her. "Ladies, I'm sorry about all of this, so why don't I treat you all to lunch?"

The girls smiled and giggled, but Crystal folded her arms across her chest. "Are you sure you want to feed a bunch of delinquents?" she stated as a not so subtle reminder to him and the girls of why they were protesting in the first place.

Douglas ran his hand across his smooth head. "That was an unfortunate statement and I'm sorry."

"Are you sorry enough to not tear our home down?" MJ asked.

Douglas looked out the window and sighed. Crystal enjoyed watching him twist uncomfortably in his seat.

"Aren't you going to answer her?" Crystal asked acidly. Bonnie, a Starlight House employee, watched the banter between Crystal and Douglas as if she were watching the Williams sisters play tennis.

"This isn't an appropriate conversation to have here. Let's just go have lunch and save this conversation for another time and place."

"Oh, we *will* have this conversation," Crystal said.

Douglas knocked on the window separating the driver and the passengers. "Raul, take us to B & D's Diner." He turned to Crystal. "Thanks to Welco, that diner has become a staple in this community."

Rolling her eyes, Crystal crossed her legs. "Do you think that one diner is going to change the fact that your company is buying land in this town like you're playing Monopoly? Why don't we just call this place Welcoville?"

Laughing, Douglas pulled a piece of lint from his pin-striped trousers. "You're funny, Ms. Hughes. But what you fail to realize is that Welco Industries is Duval County's largest employer. And even if you don't want to admit it, you benefit from my company."

Is there no end to his arrogance? she wondered as she stared into his eyes, his beautiful eyes. Glancing down at his hands, she remembered the jolt she got when he touched her earlier. Inwardly, she quaked with desire, and if they were alone in the limo, surely she'd be in his arms, kissing him, tasting him, making love to him, this monster who wanted her property.

"Stop this car," she said. "Let me out."

Bonnie and the seven girls looked at Crystal. "What's wrong?" MJ asked.

Crystal looked at Douglas. "I can't stand to breathe the same air as this jerk. But you guys have a good lunch and I'll see you back at the farm."

Douglas shook his head. "Ms. Hughes, it would be irresponsible of me to put you out in the middle of nowhere. When we get to the diner, I'll be happy to call you a cab."

Crossing her arms across her breasts, she sighed and sank back in the plush leather seat, forcing herself to look out the dark window and not at Douglas Wellington.

Chapter 4

As Douglas ushered Bonnie and the girls into the restaurant, he turned and looked at Crystal, who was standing near the pay phone. Her quiet beauty struck him—doe-like eyes, pouty lips, and a button nose he wanted to kiss desperately. And that hair—if he could only run his fingers through it and feel the silkiness of it against his skin. His body responded to the fantasy of having Crystal wrapped around him. Shifting his weight from one foot to the other, hoping to hide his erection, he turned away from her.

"Ms. Crystal," MJ called out. "Are you coming in?"

"No," she replied. "I don't have an appetite. You go ahead with Bonnie."

MJ nodded and followed the others inside. Douglas, however, lingered outside, stealing glances at Crystal. She was the closest thing to a goddess walking the planet. He mustered up the courage to approach her.

"Ms. Hughes, this doesn't have to be ugly," he said, fighting the urge to touch her.

"Not as long as you get what you want, right? This may impress teenagers, but I'm a grown woman and it will take more than lunch to buy me off."

"Can you be reasonable? Think of the jobs this business park will create. The unemployment rate here is twenty-two percent; I'm trying to do something about that. Just the construction of the business park will cut that in half."

"And what do you think will happen to those girls? No one wanted them before and nothing has changed. As long as Starlight House needs a place to stand, I'm going to make sure it happens and I will fight you with everything I've got."

Smirking, Douglas said, "You'll lose. I have endless resources and all you have is righteous indignation."

"You son of a . . ." Exhaling loudly, Crystal covered her face with her hands. "I hope you're prepared to fight, Mr. Wellington."

"Call me Douglas."

"There are several things that I would like to call you."

He flashed a camera-ready smile. "Really?"

Crystal narrowed her eyes at him. "You jerk. I

hate you and what you're doing to me and those girls."

"Look, Ms. Hughes, you will have enough money to start over. Reeseville is full of empty land. You can build another farm; we've made a generous offer to you."

She lunged at him, grabbing the lapels of his jacket. "Why can't you find another place? Why does it have to be your way or no way?"

Wrapping his arms around her slender waist, he pulled her closer to him. "How long have you wanted to touch me like this?"

Crystal let him go and pushed away from him. "Roguish behavior doesn't become you."

Cocking his head to one side, Douglas smiled again. "You grabbed me, Crystal. And to answer your question, Hughes Farm is the perfect location for this business park. It's accessible to public transportation, and many of the people who need work live right in that area. Why don't you stop being selfish?"

Crystal rolled her eyes. "Me, selfish? I'm not the one trying to take over the world. You're greedy and selfish and a jackass."

"So eloquent," he ribbed. "The offer stands, and it's a very generous offer. Take it now and end this madness in the press."

Stomping her foot on the cement, Crystal glared at him with anger flickering in her eyes. "This is about you playing the hero. I guess the story is going to get leaked that you liberated the protesters who picketed your business. So transparent."

Unable to fight the feeling any longer, Douglas wrapped his hand around the nape of her neck, pulled her close to him, and kissed her deeply. To his surprise, she didn't fight him as his tongue explored the sweetness of her mouth. She didn't push him away as his hands roamed her back, cupped her heart-shaped behind to pull her even closer.

Douglas's body felt as if a volcano had erupted inside him as Crystal clutched his back. Her touch excited him, made him want more than just this kiss. The engorged flesh between his legs nearly burst from his trousers. Abruptly, Crystal stepped back from him and dashed down the street as if she was fleeing a ghost. Just as Douglas decided to take off after her, his cell phone rang.

"What?"

"Is that anyway to greet your godfather?" Waylon asked.

"Sorry, it's been one of those days."

"I know, I've been watching the news and reading the paper. Doug, are you sure that you're doing the right thing?"

"The board isn't backing down on this project, so it has to be the right thing."

"I didn't realize that you were trying to buy out Hughes Farm. That land is damn near sacred."

"Why?" Douglas asked. "It's just an old farm."

Waylon sighed. "Son, do some research. Hughes Farm was the first piece of property that was owned by African Americans in this county."

"Why are you people so stuck in the past? Welco is African-American owned, so what is the big deal?"

"If you do some research, you will understand, and when you do, make the board understand that this is not the place to build this office park."

"I don't need this right now. I got to go." Douglas hung up the phone and walked inside the restaurant to dine with the girls, although his mind was on the feel of Crystal's petal soft lips.

I'm such a fool, Crystal thought as she stopped to massage her aching feet. She'd walked two miles to the farm, her body covered in sweat, but not from the humid air—from the heat she and Douglas created when they kissed. Kissing Douglas was impulsive and reckless. This man was the same person who wanted to take her land. And her heart? She wanted to write the kiss off as a ploy to get what he wanted. But why did she kiss him back? Why did her legs quiver as he traced her mouth with his succulent tongue and why did she enjoy it so much?

"Crystal," Brooke called out as she rushed toward her. "What happened today? I was watching the news and I saw you and the girls getting arrested."

"Everything is fine. Wellington actually took the girls to lunch. Bonnie is with them and . . ."

Brooke's blue eyes stretched to the size of quarters. "He did what?"

Waving her hands in the air, Crystal said, "It's all to counteract what he did. I hate him! He thinks his money and his charm are going to make me cave, but I won't."

Looking confused, Brooke shrugged her shoulders. "But he didn't press charges, right?"

"No, he didn't. And thank goodness, because a few of the girls would have been in big trouble."

"If I'm overstepping, let me know, but I think you acted recklessly today," she stated, crossing her arms over her breasts. "Sometimes, your causes threaten us more than Welco Industries can. I can't believe Bonnie went along with this nonsense."

Crystal exhaled loudly. "Brooke, I don't see how teaching these girls, who have been stepped on their entire lives, to stand up for themselves is a threat."

"It is when they get arrested and end up on the evening news. These girls aren't at Starlight because they're model citizens. They have minor records, but one infraction could make them major. Now, I appreciate you granting us this space, but you have to stop putting my girls in the middle of your battles."

"I'm fighting for all of us. What do you think is going to happen if Welco gets its hands on this property? Do you think anyone in Duval County is going to welcome a new Starlight House?"

Anger flickered in Brooke's eyes before she replied, "I'd take these girls into my home before I let you risk their freedom for your issue of the moment."

Sighing, Crystal rolled her eyes and started to walk away. Brooke reached out and grabbed her arm. "I'm not finished. This buyout from Welco affects all of us, so why don't you have a meeting with the company instead of picketing them? Come at them in a professional manner and maybe you can stop them from forcing us to move."

Snatching away from Brooke and trying to keep her temper in check, Crystal said, "I appreciate your concern and I will contact a lawyer and try to get a meeting with Mr. Wellington."

"I appreciate that. Any idea when the girls will be back?"

Crystal's breath caught in her chest—that man was going to come on her property. "Uh, why don't I just go get them?"

But before she could leave, a black limo turned up the winding dirt road leading to the Starlight House. Brooke rushed over to the limo and helped the girls out of the car, while Crystal watched, hoping for a glimpse of Douglas.

Through the tinted windows of the limo, he watched her standing at the edge of the road. Closing his eyes, Douglas relived their kiss. Crystal tasted like sweet manna and felt like a soft cloud. He must have her in his life and in his bed. But how could that happen when she hated him for trying to take her land? *If she really hated me, she wouldn't have kissed me,* he thought.

"Mr. Wellington, thank you for lunch," MJ said as she climbed out of the car. "Does this mean you aren't going to take our home away now?"

Inwardly, he shuddered, but he flashed a plastic smile. "You have a good day, young lady."

MJ stomped away and Douglas returned to watching Crystal as the driver turned back to the road.

Before they made it back to town, Douglas's cell phone rang again. "Yeah?"

"Douglas, it's Fred. What's going on with you and those protesters? It was all over the news."

"I've taken care of it. Don't worry, this will be over soon," Douglas said confidently.

"It better be. I don't know how much longer I

can protect you from Clive. He wants your head on a platter, and some of the other board members are starting to agree with him."

Dropping his head, Douglas squeezed his nose. "Can I help it that Hughes Farm means so much to people in the community? Let me handle this so that we can begin construction this winter."

"But how do we know this Hughes woman isn't just holding out for more money?"

"She's not like that," he said defensively.

Fred groaned knowingly. "Is there something going on with you and this woman that we need to know about?"

"I have another call coming in, I have to go." Douglas clicked his phone off and tossed it in the empty seat in front of him.

"Back to the office, sir?" the driver asked.

"No, take me downtown to the Arctic," he said, referring to a popular bar.

When the limo arrived at the speakeasy, Douglas hopped out before his driver opened the door. Quickly, he shot inside, took a seat at the end of the bar, and ordered a vodka martini with extra olives. The bartender handed him the drink and Douglas downed it in a few gulps, hoping the alcohol would take his yearning for Crystal's kiss away. It didn't. The warm burning sensation heightened his senses and he wanted more of her lips. Tapping the bar, he ordered another drink. This time, he sipped it slowly with his eyes closed.

"Doug?" Waylon asked. "What are you doing here?"

Opening his eyes, Douglas faced his godfather. "Needed to get away."

"The board?"

Douglas wanted to say yes, but the truth was he could handle the board; it was his feelings for Crystal that were causing his problems.

"Doug?"

"It's that woman, Crystal Hughes."

Lifting his eyebrows, Waylon smiled. "I saw her picture on the news. She is a fox."

"And she has the softest lips." Douglas stopped speaking, fearing that the alcohol had loosened his lips a little too much.

"Don't tell me that you have gotten personally involved with this woman. That is the last thing you need to do. Trust me."

Douglas stared blankly at Waylon. What could he say? Of course he wasn't personally involved with her, but every time he closed his eyes, he saw her face. When he tried to sleep last night, she invaded his dreams, pressing her body against his.

"You are, aren't you?" Waylon questioned.

"No, though I'd like to be. She's an amazing woman and so damned sexy."

Waylon slapped him on the shoulder. "Are you

insane? I know your father and I told you not to mix business with pleasure. And need I remind you how unethical this relationship will be?" What Waylon didn't tell his godson was a relationship with Crystal Hughes would be like turning back the hands of time and he was sure the result would be the same as it had been years ago. More bitterness, more pain. He couldn't stop his friend all those years ago, but he'd do everything to keep Douglas from making the same mistake.

"Don't worry, we're nowhere near starting a relationship. She thinks I'm evil for wanting her land."

Waylon sighed, waved for the bartender, and ordered a double bourbon. "I think she's right. Did you do what I asked? Have you looked into the history of Hughes Farm?"

Douglas gripped his glass like a vice. Waylon was supposed to be on his side, his ally. "No, I haven't, and it doesn't matter what the history is. At this late stage, finding another location would set back construction and push us over budget. Besides, this was important to my father. I'd think you'd be behind me on this. This was the last project he'd been working on before his death. And if finding a new place for those girls to live is the only holdup, then I'd be happy to help, but . . ."

"This has nothing to do with what's on that

farm now. Hughes Farm is the first piece of land owned by an African American in Reeseville. When the textile industry went belly up in the county, Hughes Farm still made millions because that family had the insight to cash in on the 'organic' craze. Hughes Farm is a source of pride and it should be a historic landmark. You really need to leave this alone."

Standing, Douglas grabbed his drink and finished it. "I don't need to hear this right now. Maybe someone should have told me this earlier. And why does it matter so much to you? Besides, if it was so historic and important, why did Dad want it years ago?"

Waylon cleared his throat, then placed his hand on Douglas's shoulder. "You're the one in charge; you should have done your homework. Put the martinis down and find another site. I know I asked you to come back here and run the company after your father died, but you don't have to follow in his footsteps with every project. He made some bad decisions and you don't have to take up where he left off."

"Isn't that what the board expects? Me to be his clone? This business park plan was written in such detail that I thought it was going to be a cake walk."

"Fix this," Waylon said as he moved Douglas's

glass out of reach. "Read the entire file and stop half-assing your job."

Douglas rose to his feet, feeling like a five-year-old who'd just been scolded, and walked out of the bar. He climbed into the limo and grabbed a bottle of water from the minibar.

"To Welco, sir?" the driver asked.

Douglas nodded as he leaned back in the soft leather seat.

Arriving at the office, Douglas breezed up the back steps hoping to avoid reporters or any straggling board members. He made it to his office without running into anyone.

"Any messages, Amy?"

Like a robot, his assistant handed him a stack of pink slips. "And Clive Oldsman was looking for you. He said he'll be back."

Muttering words too profane for a lady to hear, Douglas slammed into his office. When he sat down behind his desk, he flipped through the stack of messages. He stopped after seeing Crystal's name. Grabbing his phone, he dialed the number on the slip of paper.

"Carlyle, Hopkins and Robinson, how may I direct your call?"

"I must have the wrong number. I'm looking for Crystal Hughes," Douglas said.

"Hold on, sir," the woman said.

Seconds later, another woman picked up the phone and introduced herself as Dena Hopkins.

"I thought this was Crystal Hughes's number," he said.

"I'm her attorney. We want a meeting, Mr. Wellington."

"For what?" Douglas asked, putting up his guard. He hated that he had gotten so distracted by Crystal's beauty when he had business to take care of.

"My client doesn't want to lose her land and we would like to talk about other ways this could be handled."

"I'll meet with you, but the result will be the same. What time would you all like to come in?"

Dena sighed. "Mr. Wellington, if you're not willing to negotiate, then we should just meet in court."

"Court?"

"Yes, court. My client has made it clear that she isn't giving up without a fight and we are prepared to take this all the way," she said. "We'll see you tomorrow at nine a.m." Dena hung up before Douglas could respond.

Deciding that he had to play hardball with Crystal, he called his team of corporate lawyers.

Chapter 5

The shrill ringing of the phone jolted Crystal from her nap, and it couldn't have come at a worse time, because she'd been dreaming of making love to Douglas. She snatched the cordless phone from the base and growled hello into it.

"Crystal, it's Dena. I just had a conversation with Mr. Wellington and he has agreed to a meeting with us."

Swinging her legs over the side of the sofa, she felt a warm rush through her body at the sound of Douglas's name. "When?"

"Tomorrow morning at nine. He wants us to meet him at his office. Now, you know how much I adore your fighting spirit, but I need you to let me do the talking."

"Fine, I'll be there. Thank you for getting to work on this for me," Crystal said.

"You know how close I've always been with your parents, and there is no way I'm going to let Welco come in with this land grab. I see the apple didn't fall far from the tree," she said cryptically. Crystal was puzzled by Dena's tone, but moreover, she wondered if she should've called her parents before involving their lawyer.

The last thing she wanted was for her parents to leave their sunny retirement home in Miami to come back to Reeseville and get into this dogfight. *They trusted me to run this farm and I'm not going to go crying to them like a baby,* she thought as she walked into her bedroom to find a suitable outfit for the meeting. As she flipped through the clothes in her closet, Crystal decided to wear a charcoal gray pencil skirt and pink tunic. She couldn't wait to see Douglas's face when she showed up looking the part of a professional and not a protester. Then again, she couldn't wait to see Douglas's face again, period.

What if there was another way? she wondered as she pressed her finger against her lips. She had to get Douglas to stay on the farm for more than a few minutes. What if he stayed there for a week and saw the inner workings of the farm? Felt the peace and tranquility of the land and saw what a difference being there made in the lives of the Starlight girls. Unless he actually was the heartless bastard who called those girls delinquents, there was no way he'd continue with the plans to demolish Hughes Farm. She wondered, though, would this plan make matters better or worse?

The next morning, Crystal woke up early feeling nervous about the meeting. She'd promised to take a backseat and allow Dena to do all the talking, but would it be possible to hide her attraction to Douglas Wellington? Would being that close to him, engulfed in his manliness, turn her brain into mush, or worse yet, cause her to revisit the dreams she'd been having about him? Rising from the bed, she headed to the bathroom, showered quickly, then dressed. Pulling her hair back in a bun, Crystal decided to grab breakfast once she got into town, although her stomach was in knots and she didn't think she'd be able to keep any food down at all. If she and Dena could get through to Douglas and he backed off her land, then she'd be convinced he wasn't evil and would take him up on that dinner offer.

Crystal didn't date much as her main focus was always working on the farm. Plus, there weren't a lot of men who met her lofty standards, a man with a sensitive soul, love of land, animals, and art. *That ain't Douglas Wellington, so stop thinking about him,* she told herself as she walked to her car.

Nervousness flowed through her body like

blood through her veins as she drove up to the Welco Industries building. She inhaled deeply, hoping that the burst of oxygen would calm her nerves. Strengthening her resolve, Crystal emerged from the car, smoothed her skirt, and walked into the building. She recognized the security guard from her last visit to Welco.

"Back again," he said when he looked up at her. "Where are the handcuffs?"

"I have an appointment this time," she said, shooting him a sly smile.

"Let me check." He picked up the house phone just as Dena walked over to them.

"He's not giving you problems, is he?" Dena asked.

Crystal shook her head and stifled a laugh. "We're old friends."

Dena leaned against the desk, waiting for the security guard to get off the phone. "Well, is Mr. Wellington ready for us?"

"Yes, ma'am. He's on his way out to see you all."

Crystal's breathing became shallow as she spotted Douglas and another man walking in her direction. She assumed the wiry white man walking with him was one of his many lawyers. As usual, Douglas looked incredibly sexy in his custom-tailored navy blue suit and crisp white shirt and the overhead lights dancing on his gold cuff links. His intoxicating cologne filled the air and frazzled her senses. Crystal looked away and focused her attention on Dena, the woman her mother always called a five-foot-five force of nature.

"Ladies, my office is this way," Douglas said, his voice sounding like a sweet symphony to Crystal.

The foursome walked into Douglas's office where three more suits were waiting. Crystal turned to Dena after they'd taken their seats. "Looks like they have the entire legal staff here."

"It's just a ploy to intimidate us," Dena replied confidently, then faced the four lawyers. "Gentlemen, my client and I only have one thing to say—we're not moving."

Dena stood and touched Crystal's arm so that she would follow suit.

"Then what was the purpose of this meeting?" one of the attorneys asked.

Dena reached into her leather briefcase and withdrew a blue document. "This is a summons to appear in court. We're seeking an injunction to stop any construction near the farm. Obviously, you all thought this was about money and to get what you wanted all you had to do was add more zeros to the check. Well, it doesn't work like that. And, if this was about a negotiation and not intimidation, all of you wouldn't be here." She waved her hand at the cavalcade of lawyers. "Let me be clear, this isn't my first time at the rodeo and we won't be intimidated by these high-handed actions." She passed the document to Douglas.

"What?" Douglas snapped, leaping from his seat when he looked at it.

Crystal folded her arms across her chest and cocked her head to the side. "I told you I wasn't going to roll over and play dead for Welco Industries." Dena shot a look to Crystal telling her to save it.

One of the lawyers cleared his throat and rose to his feet. "Let me see that." He took the document from Douglas's hand.

Dena nodded toward the door and she and Crystal took their leave.

Douglas ran after them, catching Crystal by the arm. "Do you really want to throw down the gauntlet like this?" he asked. "This will get ugly, and if you and your attorney think that was intimidating, wait until we get inside the courtroom."

"Please take your hands off me," she replied breathlessly. The touch of his hand against her skin rippled through her nervous system, causing her to quake inside.

"Crystal, you can relocate, you can buy more land. . . ."

Focusing her stare on him, she pushed his hand away. "This isn't about the land, this is about a legacy. This is about my family's blood, sweat, and tears. So, take your money and shove it."

"I'm shoving it under your nose. I would advise you to take it. You won't win in court."

Dena stepped in between Douglas and Crystal, placing her hand on his chest. "Mr. Wellington, you have more to lose than my client—tread lightly. Crystal, let's go."

"You don't want to do this," Douglas called out after her.

Crystal waved her hand in the air, dismissing him as she and Dena walked out the door.

Douglas stood against the wall, watching Crystal's hips sway as she left. He didn't want to fight with her and he didn't want to get nasty to get that land, but if he had to, he would. This was business and if she wanted to run with the big dogs, she was going to need more than some small-town lawyer to win. At the end of the day, though, he hoped Crystal would forgive him when it was all over. In an ideal world, she'd be standing by his side when the business park was built, sharing in his success. Douglas walked back to his office and dismissed his legal staff. In the quiet of his office, he began to look into the mythology of Hughes Farm. The vast number of articles that popped up on the screen shocked him. Leaning back, Douglas read the history of the farm, starting with Casio Hughes, a sharecropper who first took ownership of the farm in 1921, following a lengthy court battle with the Winchell family after the reading of Simon Winchell's will.

So, fighting runs in the family, Douglas thought as he rubbed his aching eyes. The next article detailed the success of Hughes Farm over the next fifty years, from cotton to tobacco to soybeans, and finally to a low-income housing community. He began to see why Crystal was so protective of the place. But if the land was this historic, what had his father been trying to accomplish by purchasing it? The file about the farm was old and thoroughly researched. Even at the time of his death, Douglas Wellington Jr. had been trying to bring the farm under the company's umbrella. *Why is this happening? The woman of my dreams hates me and I have to take her land.*

Douglas stood up and walked to the window overlooking sleepy Reeseville. The skyline of the town wasn't impressive like Charlotte or Atlanta, but Welco could make it that way. With the right development, Reeseville could be a progressive city with booming employment and growth. But what was it going to take to make Crystal understand that? Hopefully the court case would be over soon and he and Crystal could reach some kind of middle ground and get to know one another better. He needed her in his life; her aura was so positive and vibrant. No woman had ever touched him the way Crystal had. And no woman had ever told him no either.

Crystal's no different, he thought, adjusting his tie. *I just have to get her to see things my way.*

Sitting at an outside table at the Main Street Café, Crystal quietly sipped a cup of green tea. The scene in Douglas's office replayed in her mind. He wasn't going to give up until he got what he wanted and Crystal wasn't about to let that happen. *How can I appeal to his human side? He knows what it's like to have a family tradition. Hell, if someone wanted to take Welco he wouldn't roll over and let it happen.*

Draining her teacup, Crystal grabbed her cell phone and called Welco Industries.

A drone voice answered the phone. "Welco Industries, how may I direct your call?"

"Douglas Wellington, please."

Classical music played in Crystal's ear as she tried to think of something to say.

"Mr. Wellington's office," his assistant said.

"Is Mr. Wellington available?"

"May I tell him who's calling?"

"Crystal Hughes."

Moments later, Douglas breathed her name, sending shivers down her spine. "This is a nice surprise."

"I don't want to fight dirty, but I will," she said. "Why don't you come out to the farm and see what it means to the community?"

"There's no doubt that Hughes Farm is important to Reeseville, but I don't see how spending any time out there will change anything," Douglas said. "However, if this is your cute way of accepting my dinner invitation . . ."

"You've only briefly seen the land. There's nothing like waking up and smelling the dew-covered roses and honeysuckle. I'm pleading with you, please consider it," she said.

"Fine, I'll consider it. But what about this injunction?"

"Spend a week at Hughes Farm and I'm sure you will change your mind about wanting to destroy this land to build a business park."

Douglas laughed. "I doubt that, but I will take you up on your offer, Ms. Hughes. When do you want to make this happen?"

"This weekend, I'll fix up one of the guest cottages and you can move in," Crystal said as the wheels spun in her head. Sure, her plan was hokey and Douglas might not change his mind. But Crystal believed that nature, and especially the beauty of Hughes Farm, would have some kind of impact on him. Maybe seeing how much people depended on the food she raised there and how much the Starlight girls needed a home would give him pause. Dena wasn't going to like it one bit, though.

"Ms. Hughes, I look forward to it. I'll have someone bring my things over Saturday morning."

Crystal smiled, knowing that once Douglas got on her turf she would be able to change his mind by any means necessary. But would she be able to keep things strictly professional? *Of course I can,* she thought as she pulled cash from her purse to pay for her tea.

A half an hour, one muffin, and two more cups of tea later, Crystal called Dena. There was no way she could keep her plan under wraps. Besides, she needed Dena to get their court appearance pushed back.

"Absolutely not," Dena balked when Crystal made her suggestion. "What do you think having that man on your property will do? He'll probably draw up new plans for the business park. Where did you come up with this hair-brained idea? A Lifetime movie?"

"Dena, this is my decision. Let's be real about this. Douglas has a legal staff that can tie us up in so much red tape."

"Is there something I should know about?" Dena asked suspiciously.

"What's that supposed to mean?" Crystal toyed with the half-eaten muffin she'd been nibbling on.

"You just speak of him with such familiarity. Have you forgotten that he is trying take your property? Your family legacy? City council is in Welco's pocket, and we have a fight on our hands," Dena said gruffly. "Just what in the hell do you think inviting him to stay at the farm will accomplish? If anything, he'll get more ammo to use against us. Let me tell you something about men like Wellington: they are not sentimental. Roses, fresh fruit, and crying little girls don't mean a damned thing to them."

"Dena, calm down. This will work, trust me. I have some tricks up my sleeve that might not hold up in court."

"Do I want to hear more?"

"Dena, if Douglas Wellington has a human side, once he sees how dependent people are on this farm and its history, there will be no business park at this location."

"One week—and do your parents know what you're doing?"

Crystal inhaled sharply, attempting to cool the hot anger boiling in her stomach. Did Dena think that she was a child and couldn't make a decision without getting the approval of her parents?

"Dena, I can handle this, all right? I don't want to involve my parents. They left this farm to me and I think I've done a damned good job running it."

"And I agree, but this is a big deal, Crystal, and Joel and Erin should know their farm is under attack."

"It's my farm now and I am protecting it. One week, Dena, and things will change."

"We'll see," Dena said, then hung up.

Without paying attention to the pedestrian traffic on the sidewalk, Crystal collided with a man, which sent her car keys flying out of her hand. As she knelt down to retrieve her keys, his big hand covers hers.

"I didn't see you there," Douglas said, still holding on to Crystal's hand.

"Guess I'm still standing in the way of progress, huh?" she said sarcastically. Slowly rising to her feet, still holding hands with Douglas, she stared into his eyes and smiled. "I'll take my keys now."

Douglas twirled the key ring around his finger. "Why don't I buy you a cup of coffee?"

"I don't want any coffee," she said as she reached for her keys.

Douglas held the keys above his head. "Then you can have tea."

Rolling her eyes, Crystal agreed and she walked into the café with Douglas. She stood behind him at the counter as he ordered a large espresso for himself and an apple cinnamon tea for her, which was actually one of her favorite drinks from the café.

"How presumptuous of you," she said as she took the steaming cup from him. Douglas placed his hand on the small of her back and led her to a corner table. Crystal sat down and crossed her legs. Her face grew hot under Douglas's piercing stare. She grabbed her cup as he silently sipped his coffee, but he never took his eyes off her.

"What kind of game are you playing, Mr. Wellington?" she asked after taking a sip of her tea.

"I could ask you the same thing, Ms. Hughes. What do you expect to happen at your farm next week?"

"I expect the Grinch's heart to grow to the size of a normal one," she replied as she set her cup on the table between them. "Douglas, this county and this town need Hughes Farm. Why can't you understand that?"

"Why can't you understand that this business park is going to happen and a lot of out of work people will have jobs?"

"My keys," she snapped.

Douglas handed them to her, but closed his hand around hers. "Has anyone ever told you that you're sexy when you're angry?"

The feel of his skin against hers caused her heart to palpitate. As much as she wanted to fight her attraction to him, she couldn't help being turned on by his touch. He had a body that looked as if it was built for unspeakable pleasures, and those eyes. She wanted to get lost in them as he undressed her and ran his hands across her skin.

"You're such a sleaze," she snapped, rising to walk away, but her heel caught in a tear on the rug. Before she hit the floor, Douglas scooped her up in his arms.

While he held her, Douglas looked deep into Crystal's eyes as a fire burned between his legs. He'd never desired a woman this way before and if he didn't have her, he felt as if he would explode. Maybe it was because she was forbidden fruit, or the fact that she was the first woman to actually tell him no and mean it, but he wanted her more than he wanted his next breath. Carnal desire took over and he captured her full lips with his. Douglas felt the bite of Crystal's fingernails on his shoulder as she responded to his scorching kiss. And just for one heated moment, they were oblivious to the stares and whispers of the other café customers; all either of them cared or could think about was the sweet inferno building between them.

Then reality slapped Crystal, making her push away from him and tear out of the café. Douglas followed her, determined to find out if she shared his yearning for her. Taking long strides, he caught up to her, grabbed her elbow, and forced her to face him.

"This is the second time you've kissed me," he said.

"Funny, but I think this is the second time that you've violated me, Mr. Wellington."

Stroking her cheek, Douglas smiled. "Crystal, I can't fight being attracted to you anymore, which is why this proposal of yours isn't going to work."

Snatching away from him, Crystal narrowed her eyes and hissed, "You can't expect that I'm going to let you share my bed after what you're trying to do? Go to hell."

"Only if you lead the way," he called out as she stomped off. "I'd follow those hips anywhere."

Chapter 6

The week leading up to Douglas's visit to Hughes Farm, Crystal wanted to call everything off, because for the last six days her mind had been clouded with fantasies of kissing him, touching him, and making love to him. Stalking across the room and peering out the window, Crystal watched an unfamiliar pickup truck pulling into the driveway. As the vehicle stopped, she was mesmerized by the man, clad in fresh blue jeans, a crisp white T-shirt, and a New York Yankees baseball cap, as he hoisted a duffel bag over his broad shoulder. She'd never seen Douglas dressed like a regular person and she was sure the outfit was new. *That man has probably never owned a pair of jeans in his life.*

As Douglas raised his hand to knock, Crystal opened the front door, not caring that it was obvious she'd been staring at him from the window. "You're early," she said.

"Isn't that better than being late?" he asked as he gave her a slow once-over, admiring her T-shirt and the way it clung to her breasts.

"No, it isn't. Either way, it's rude. I don't even have your room ready in the guest cottage," she said as she stepped aside, allowing Douglas to enter the house.

He stood in the middle of her living room, which was decorated with a southwestern flair. Nodding, he said, "Nice touch. Classic."

"If you have your way it will be rubble," she said as she closed the front door. "Where are my manners? May I take your bag, get you something to eat or drink?"

Douglas smiled and shook his head, and then he headed for the caramel-colored leather sofa. Sitting, he dropped his bag on the floor.

Anger cruised through Crystal's body as she watched Douglas pick up the remote and turn the television on. Just seeing him sitting there as if the house belonged to him rattled her to the core, especially when she wouldn't mind joining him on the sofa and losing herself in his sweet, hot kiss.

"What do you think you're doing?" she snapped as she picked up the bag and threw it in his lap. "This isn't stately Wellington manor and I'm not one of your servants."

Douglas furrowed his brows as he looked up at her. "I thought you said my room wasn't ready? What did I do?"

"Oh, I . . . I . . ." Crystal's face grew hot from embarrassment as she turned away from Douglas. "I'm going to go check on the room."

Dashing out of the living room, Crystal headed out back to the small cottage where Douglas would be staying. As she opened the door, she felt a masculine presence behind her.

"You expect me to live here for a week?" Douglas said. His lips were so close to her ear that she shivered as he spoke. "This is a cute dollhouse, but I'm a big man, darling."

She looked around the space and had to admit that "dollhouse" was an accurate description of the cottage, with its lacy slipcovers over the sofa and love seat and the matching curtains. Crystal always thought the cottage was a comfortable place, but she wasn't a man of large proportion. However, there was no way she and Douglas could sleep under the same roof. Not with the way she was feeling and thinking about him. Folding her arms across her chest, Crystal glared at him. "What am I supposed to do, give up my house for you?"

"No, we can share a bed," Douglas said with a grin.

Crystal turned toward the door. "I'll bring you some clean towels."

He blocked her exit by pulling her into his arms; he brushed his lips against her neck. "I hope you don't plan on sneaking in here tonight and violating me as I sleep."

Pushing away from him, she pulled the door open and dashed out. *I can do this,* she thought as she walked up the back steps to her house. *Douglas Wellington isn't going to take my land or my heart.*

Douglas wondered what to expect for the week as he stood up and walked to the front windows. Interestingly enough, the cottage faced Crystal's bedroom. He watched as she walked into the room and flicked on the light. He dropped the curtain quickly so that she wouldn't see him. Staying in the small cottage was starting to look better and better, he thought as he headed for the bedroom. Turning the light on, Douglas shook his head at the sight of the twin bed and old English dresser. *This is definitely a dollhouse.*

Dropping his bag on the small bed, which had a yellow and white comforter on it, Douglas began to unpack his clothes and wondered how he could stop thinking about Crystal. After getting settled in, he decided that he might as well explore the property, even if he'd rather be exploring every tantalizing inch of Crystal Hughes. He looked up at the house, hoping to catch a glance of her as he started his walk. When he didn't see her, he decided to head for the garden. The beauty of the scene before him instantly took his breath away.

Crystal was dressed in a pair of dusty overalls with her hair pulled back in a loose ponytail, kneeling down with a basket of corn, peppers, and tomatoes trying to help a young girl with another basket. Douglas rushed over to her, grabbing her basket before she lost her grip on it.

"Thanks," she said, lifting the smaller basket into her arms. "Mercer, are you all right?"

"Yes, ma'am, I just can't do anything right. I can't even pick vegetables to make the soup with." With her shoulders slumping, Mercer started to walk away, but Crystal stopped her.

"Mercer, don't let what other people say about you cloud your self-esteem. You can do anything you put your mind to and when you and the other girls make this soup, there are going to be several people who appreciate it." Wrapping her arms around the girl, Crystal hugged her tightly.

Douglas couldn't help but be touched by Crystal's gentle way with the girl. He could see the girl beginning to smile as they embraced.

"You go on inside," Crystal told Mercer before ushering her toward the greenhouse.

"You're pretty good with these girls," he said as she took her basket from his hands.

"It's not hard to be nice to people. You should try it sometimes."

Douglas smirked, sarcastically thinking how nice he would like to treat her if he could get one night alone with her. "I am nice to people," he said. "Why do you think I'm such a monster? I'm just a businessman."

"Who wants to monopolize this town and county," she shot back. "And why? How can you look at this place and think it would be better served as a business park? What about the beauty of the land and what it means to these girls?"

Turning his back to her and running his finger across a cornstalk, Douglas said, "Why are you making this personal? It's a standard business deal. Something that my company and I do all the time."

"Can you hand me those cabbages over there?" she asked, ignoring his last comment.

"Changing the subject?" Douglas closed the space between them and pulled her into his arms. "This doesn't have to be painful."

"But it is. This isn't just about me and my family's legacy, it's about the community in general. This place is one step away from being Welcoville and you know it."

Shrugging his shoulders, he passed her the vegetables. "Who else is trying to turn this rural place into a viable city? Crystal, people are suffering here. They need jobs and money and Welco is just stepping up to the plate and giving the people what they need."

"People need more than money and jobs; they need to know someone cares about them." She pressed her hand against his chest, attempting to push away from him. But Douglas grabbed her hand and kissed it.

Unable to pull away, she fell against his body and their lips brushed against one another's. Douglas capitalized on the rare opportunity to kiss her as he captured her lips, savoring the sweet taste of her mouth. He expected her to fight him, but to his surprise she melted against him. Their bodies fit together as if they were destined to be one. He roamed his hands up and down her back, feeling every luscious curve as he glided down her hips. A soft moan escaped his throat as the kiss became deeper, wetter, and hotter—until Crystal pulled away.

"This is so wrong," she said, freeing herself from his embrace.

Douglas reached out and grabbed her arm, "Crystal, you want me just as much as I want you."

Wiping her hand across her face, Crystal snatched away from Douglas and returned to the house. As he watched her walk away, he fingered his lips, reliving the searing kiss he shared with her. He made up his mind to have her, no matter what.

* * *

Crystal wished she could explain away her attraction to Douglas Wellington. She knew this man wanted to take her land away and would probably sleep with her to do it. *This is crazy! Why am I letting this man get to me?* she thought as she poured herself a glass of water, hoping that it would cool the fire burning inside her body. Slowly she sipped the liquid, but her mind couldn't get past the sensation of Douglas's lips against hers, his hands all over her body. The back door opened and as Douglas appeared in front of her, she dropped her glass.

Bending down to scoop up the broken glass, she asked, "What are you doing in here?"

Douglas knelt down and took the sharp glass from her hand. "I need towels and an extra blanket. I guess I should have knocked."

"You think?" she snapped.

Douglas seemed to ignore her attitude as he walked over to the trash can and dumped the shards of glass in it. "So, what do you have planned for dinner?"

Crystal folded her arms across her chest and eyed him incredulously. "Whatever my plans are, they don't include you."

"How am I going to see the majesty of this farm if you keep me tucked away in that little dollhouse? I want to taste the fresh veggies and whatever else you grow here." A smile spread across his face as if he wanted to say something else, but restrained himself.

Crystal returned his smile with a wry one. "Fine. If you want majesty, then we can have dinner at the Starlight House—that is if you don't mind dining with delinquents."

Folding his arms across his chest, he said, "You're not going to let that go, are you?"

"You said it. Have you changed your mind about the girls?"

"I didn't mean what I said. I was angry and that reporter twisted my words. You know, Welco would happily relocate the girls. I'd even be willing to let some of the girls do an internship with the company."

"Is that supposed to give you absolution for destroying my property?"

Looking away from her, Douglas reached for a dish towel and wiped the water from the floor. "Let's get something straight," he said. "My business park is going to go up, whether you like it or not. But there is something bigger here than business. You feel it every time I touch you, every time I kiss you."

He stood and focused his full stare on her. Crystal felt hot underneath his penetrating gaze, and she wanted to tell him that if they were in another time and space she would have no problem sharing herself and her life with him.

But he was her sworn enemy. He was big business and everything that she'd lobbied against. Falling for him was out of the question. Steeling herself, she faced him with her arms folded across her chest. "I'm a woman and I have hormones," she said. "But there is nothing between us and there never will be."

"Didn't your mother tell you to never say never?"

"If you want to have dinner with me, meet me in an hour at the Starlight House. I'll make sure you get towels and a blanket. You can leave now."

Douglas closed the space between them. "If you say so. I'll see you at dinner." As he walked out the door, their bodies touched slightly, causing Crystal's breath to catch in her chest. He winked at her as he closed the door behind him, and as much as she wanted to hate his arrogance, she couldn't help but want him even more.

About an hour later, Crystal and Douglas headed over to the Starlight House to join the girls for dinner. She glanced at him as they walked across the yard, noting his change of clothes. He was wearing another fresh pair of jeans and a multicolored button-down shirt. His fresh scent of patchouli and Irish Spring soap was almost too much for her to bear.

Brooke greeted them at the door with a quizzical look on her face. "Crystal, I didn't realize you were bringing a guest for dinner."

She reached out and placed her hand on Brooke's shoulder. "I thought if Mr. Wellington saw the good that goes on here, he would change his mind about building a business park on this land."

Smiling at Douglas, Brooke stepped aside to let them in. "Mr. Wellington," she said, "I hope you like meat loaf and potatoes."

"I'm sure I will," he said. "It's been a long time since I've had a home-cooked meal."

"Well," Brooke said as she led the couple into the dining area, "every meal here is prepared by the girls. Most of the time it's really good. By letting the girls cook and clean, we are teaching them responsibility and adding a little discipline to their lives."

Crystal pointed to where MJ and Renda sat. "This is my usual table," she said. "But you are under no obligation to sit with me."

Douglas smiled at her and before he could say anything, Brooke interjected.

"Mr. Wellington, I would love to discuss the history of Starlight House with you over dinner." She pointed to a table in the front of the dining area. "This is where the staff sits and I would be honored if you join us."

"All right," he said, though his eyes were on Crystal.

She refused to return his gaze, afraid that her attraction would betray her.

MJ walked up to Crystal and wrapped her arms around her waist. "Miss Crystal, I knew you were going to save this place. Has that man changed his mind?"

"I'm working on it," Crystal said as she sat down with MJ and Renda. She smiled at the girls and looked down at their plates. "So, what's good?"

"That guy is good looking. Is he your boyfriend?" Renda asked.

"Not at all. He's here because I want to show him how important this place is to all of us. Then maybe he won't tear it down."

MJ wrung her hands and focused an intense glare on Crystal. "What if it doesn't work? If he tears this place down, where are we going to go?"

She wrapped her arms around MJ's shoulders and squeezed her tightly. "I'm not going to let that happen; I'll do whatever it takes to protect us and this farm. That includes Starlight House. You guys are extremely important to me."

"We know," Renda replied.

"Then you know I'm a fighter. But sometimes you catch more flies with honey than you do with vinegar," Crystal said as she stole a glance at Douglas. He was seated at the table with the Starlight staff, looking back at her.

She quickly looked away from him before their eyes could lock. Crystal wished her hormones would stop racing.

After dinner, Crystal hurried back to her house, trying to avoid Douglas. She knew if she saw him again that she wouldn't be able to resist.

Closing his eyes, Douglas was about to explode. He couldn't listen to Brooke Fey talking about Starlight House anymore. He got it. The house was a last chance ranch for girls who weren't bad but had been in bad situations. He understood that people in Reeseville didn't want to give the girls a fair chance and despite this lack of trust, they proved themselves at the Starlight House. Sure, what she'd said made sense, and Starlight House seemed like a great place, but it didn't offer as many jobs as the business park would. He would be more than happy to build a new house for the girls. *Why don't these women get it?*

"Ladies, thank you for dinner and for telling me all about Starlight House, but I really have to go back to my quarters and freshen up."

Douglas rose to his feet, shook hands with Brooke and the rest of the staff, then bolted out of the dining hall in search of Crystal. When he arrived at her front step, he stopped and glanced at the door. Should he just walk in and take her into his arms again? Or should he return to the little house and fantasize about her?

"Do you need something?" Crystal called out from behind him.

Douglas turned around and smiled. "I was wondering why you ran out on me over there."

"Because I had to put towels and blankets in the guesthouse, per your request," she said before pushing past him.

Douglas grabbed her arm. "Where's the fire, Miss Hughes? I'm still waiting on my tour."

She pulled away from him, smiled dryly, and walked up the steps of her house. "Why don't you meet me here in about an hour? There is something I want to show you."

He returned her smile. "What do you want to show me?"

"The magic hour."

Skeptical, Douglas agreed to meet her. "Should I wear anything special?"

"Comfortable shoes, Mr. Wellington," she said before disappearing inside.

Douglas couldn't deny his attraction to her any longer, and he wasn't going to. He was going to have her and his business park. Scampering off to the guesthouse, Douglas prepared for his evening with Crystal.

Before long the moon lit the sky and Douglas was ready for his excursion with Crystal. As he stepped outside and glanced up at the diamond-like glow of the stars in the sky, he was taken by the quiet beauty of the farm. It had the look of a postcard with water from the irrigation system glistening on the manicured blades of grass, and off in the distance the vegetables cast warm shadows over the land. The farm looked like something ripped off *Little House on the Prairie.*

A hand touched him on the shoulder. "Ready?" Crystal asked, looking down at his shoes. "Nice sneakers."

"Are these comfortable enough?"

"Depends on you. Can you keep up?" She smiled, then took off running down a small dusty path.

Douglas followed, struggling to keep up with her because he was watching her behind bounce up and down.

She looked over her shoulder. "You're kind of slow there, Mr. Executive," she said.

"I'm not used to this. I usually do my running on a treadmill." Douglas stopped and leaned against a tree.

"Luckily for you, we're here," she said, pointing to a small mirrored pond. "Look up."

Douglas followed her directive and turned his eyes upward. The ink black sky resembled velvet sprinkled with jewels. "Wow," he remarked as the light reflected from the pool. He glanced over at Crystal, who was awash in the glow of the moon and looking like an angel. "This is beautiful."

"My parents said sunset is the magic hour. That is when God shows us His beauty and we should take time and reflect on it. That's why they built this pond. We used to come out here and have dinner sometimes." Crystal closed her eyes as she talked. "But for me the reflection of the moon and the stars were surreal and beautiful. Like an expensive painting that should be hanging on the wall of a museum."

Douglas stepped closer to her, wrapping his arms around her slim waist. "It really is gorgeous." His lips were dangerously close to her ear. He wanted to gently kiss her lobe, take it between his teeth and send chills down her spine.

She opened her eyes, facing him and shaking her head. "How can you possibly want to destroy this?"

"Do we have to talk business now?"

Before she could respond, Douglas captured her lips in a smoldering kiss. He felt her body tremble as if she was trying to resist him but couldn't. Taking advantage of her lust, Douglas deepened his kiss, pulling Crystal so close to his body that she could feel every inch of him. Their clothing provided little barrier between their hot bodies, and he felt her feminine heat against his burgeoning groin. Placing his hands on her ample behind, Douglas tried to bury himself inside her.

She pressed her hand against his chest, breaking off their kiss. "You can't keep doing that," she exclaimed.

He gently stroked her arm. "Why? We both enjoy it. Crystal. I want you with everything in me. You are the most alluring and beautiful woman that I've ever met and—"

"Is this your new ploy, trying to get me to change my mind about selling this place in between kisses and caresses?"

Holding her face between his hands, Douglas stared into her eyes. "I have real feelings for you and I'm sorry that it has to be this way."

She pushed his hands away and frowned. "Am I supposed to believe you, knowing that you want this land to become the latest acquisition of Welco Industries? If you are really genuine, you will drop this proposal or at least find a new place to build your park."

"And then what? You have your farm and thousands of people still don't have a job. I'm in a tough spot here," he said, walking away from her. "You're the first woman that I've met who doesn't care about what Douglas Wellington represents. You actually hate it."

She nodded and laughed. "You're right. I actually think you're rather sleazy," she said.

Douglas encircled her waist and brushed his lips against the nape of her neck. "But you really love it."

She turned around and smiled at him. "I wish you weren't Douglas Wellington the third. Why couldn't you just be Joe Regular?"

"Why couldn't you live two miles up the road?"

Surprisingly, Crystal leaned in and kissed him, hard and savagely. His body erupted at her touch. And just as quickly as she kissed him, she pulled away. "This is so wrong. You're my enemy and I should treat you as such."

Crystal dashed away from him, leaving him standing there staring at his confused reflection in the pond.

Chapter 7

Crystal paced back and forth in the kitchen wishing she didn't crave Douglas's kiss, his touch, his taste, and his smell. She wanted to make love to him more than she needed to breathe, but how could she be sure he wasn't trying to use her attraction to get what he wanted?

Is he that cruel? she wondered as she walked over to the sink and got a glass of water. Glancing out the window, she spotted Douglas as he emerged from the woods. He reached into his pocket and retrieved his cell phone. Crystal smiled, knowing that the phone wasn't going to have any reception on the farm property. She laughed loudly as he twisted his body hoping for the faintest signal. She was tempted to open the door and hand him her cordless phone. But who was he calling? Maybe he was telling the board that he was wearing her down. Well, if he talked on her line she could listen. *That would be wrong,* she reasoned as she turned away from the window. *But this is a war and I plan to win.*

Crystal opened the door and stood on the back steps. "That's not going to work out here."

Douglas snapped his head up as if he was startled. "What?"

"Your cell—the trees block the signal. That's another reason why it's so peaceful out here. There are some places where cell phones shouldn't be allowed and this is one of them."

"If you say so," he stated as he walked up the steps. "But I do need to make an important phone call. I didn't notice if there is one in the dollhouse."

"There isn't a phone out there, but you can use the phone I have in the kitchen."

Douglas smiled at her. "Is this your way of keeping me close to you?"

Crinkling her nose, Crystal scoffed at him. "I'm trying to be a gracious hostess, but if you want to contort your body hoping for one bar of signal strength, then knock yourself out."

Closing the space between them, Douglas gently grabbed her chin. "Loosen up, Ms. Hughes, I was just making a joke. Do you mind if I use your phone? I need to check in with the office."

Pushing his hand away, she stepped aside and allowed Douglas to walk into the kitchen. Though tempted to eavesdrop, Crystal walked into her living room, took a seat on the sofa, and flipped through her copy of *Ebony* magazine. Ironically, Douglas and his company were profiled in the issue.

I just can't get away from this man, she thought as she looked at the handsome picture of Douglas staring back at her.

Peeping around the corner, making sure Crystal was out of earshot, he dialed up his godfather.

"This is Waylon."

"Hey, it's me."

"Where are you? I didn't recognize the number."

"I'm at Hughes Farm and I think I've made a huge mistake." Making this admission wasn't easy for Douglas, since this was the biggest project he had ever posed to the board. "This place is more than just a piece of land."

"I hate to say I told you so, but I did. What are you going to do?"

Rubbing his hand over his face, Douglas replied, "I don't know. It's too late to scout another spot."

"It's never too late, and if Ms. Hughes doesn't want to sell, what can you do? The board will have to understand that," Waylon sagely replied.

"And you know that isn't going to happen." Douglas imagined what the board would say if he went to them asking for another chance to find a spot—yes wouldn't be an option. "I should've taken your advice. If I had checked this place out I would have never suggested this as a site."

"The place or Ms. Hughes? I think you're smitten with her."

Placing his hand over his face to cover his smile, Douglas knew that he couldn't deny the fact that he had fallen fast and hard for the lovely Crystal Hughes. But after talking to Brooke Fey and the staff at Starlight House and watching the girls who lived there, how could he think about putting up a business park when these people were saving lives? Then again, if he bought a bigger house for the girls, Starlight House would be able to help more girls.

"This has nothing to do with Crystal," Douglas lied. "Sure, she's a beautiful woman and all of that, but this is business and I have a hard decision to make."

"Hope you learned a lesson in all of this," Waylon said.

Douglas imagined his godfather leaning back in his easy chair, twirling a cigar around in his hand because he knew he shouldn't smoke it, with a big smile on his wide face. "And what would that be?"

"Always listen to me. I told you not to go after Hughes Farm. That place is magical, historic even. So, I'll do this. I'm going to put my feelers out there and see if the board is open to moving the location of the business park and you will be free to woo that woman."

"This has nothing to do with a woman," Douglas said.

Waylon laughed heartily. "This is certainly more than just business. Have a good week."

When Waylon hung up, Douglas pondered what he said. It was true that this was more than just about business. He wanted to get inside Crystal's mind and her heart. He wanted to know all of her hopes, dreams, and fantasies, then he wanted to be the one to make them come true.

"Are you done?" Crystal asked as she walked into the kitchen.

"Yes," he replied, removing his hand from the receiver. He closed the space between them, focusing his gaze on her face. "Thank you so much."

"You're welcome. Would you like to join me for a cup of tea?" she asked, walking over to the refrigerator and pulling out a pitcher of sun-brewed ice tea.

"That sounds great," he said. "Where are the glasses?"

Crystal smiled at him and pointed toward the table. "You sit down and let me take care of this."

Following Crystal's directive, Douglas sat at the round wooden table and watched her as she removed a block of ice from the freezer, dropped it on the counter, then picked at it with an ice pick. In one fluid movement, she chipped off enough ice for two glasses of tea.

"I guess having an ice maker would be bad for the environment," he said as she walked over to the table with the tea.

"That's right, just like tearing down this place, bringing in a bunch of bulldozers and gasoline-powered machines with all of those exhaust fumes."

Groaning and leaning his head on the table, Douglas said, "I thought we were having a drink and not a lecture."

"You know the most important thing to me is Hughes Farm. In the short time you've been here, you have to see the impact that it has on so many lives."

"And, Crystal, more people would be served by jobs in this community if we followed through with what I've proposed. That's all I'm trying to do," he said as he took the glass from Crystal's outstretched hand.

"We're never going to see eye to eye on this. Having you here is a bad idea," she said. Crystal looked into his eyes and wished that she could tell him the real reason why she couldn't sit still, the real reason why she was breathless every time he walked into the room. Every time he looked at her, her heart skipped a beat and her temperature rose. Even the way he held that glass, slowly bringing it to his lips, made her wonder what those lips would feel like against her hard nipples, buried in the valley of her womanhood. Her glass slipped from her hand, crashed to the floor and shattered to bits. "Damn," she muttered as she and Douglas began to mop up the tea and pick up the glass. "I'm not usually this clumsy."

"Where did you go? Should we start using plastic cups? Or are those bad for the environment too?" he asked.

"Oh, hush. I'm fine," she said as she turned away from him. She was more than a little embarrassed about her lapse.

Smiling, Douglas placed his hand on top of hers. "I'm aware of how you look."

"Don't do that," she snapped as she snatched her hand away from him. "Let's be clear on what's going on here. I want you to change your mind about building on my land."

"And I want you to kiss me again," he said, stepping closer to her and filling her space with his scent. Crystal fought to keep from shivering as he wrapped his arms around her waist. The warmth of his breath tingled against her ear and her knees turned to jelly, making it hard not to collapse against his chest.

Fight it! her inner voice cried out. Crystal stiffened her back and pushed away from him. "I want to do no such thing and I think you should leave. I have things to do."

"Anything I can help you with?" he asked as he leaned back on the counter.

Crystal swallowed a laugh. "You want to help me mop, sweep, dust, and fold laundry? Ha!"

"I understand, you don't want to be alone with me because you can't keep your hands to yourself," he said with a sexy smirk that was nearly Crystal's undoing. "But don't say I didn't try to pull my weight."

"All right," she said, deciding to call his bluff. "You can clean the kitchen." She tossed a dish towel at his chest, which he caught effortlessly. Sighing, she wondered if there was anything that man couldn't do.

"I have to clean the kitchen alone?" he asked more seductively than should've been allowed by law. Crystal inhaled as if she was about to launch into a yoga pose and nodded yes before making a hasty exit from the kitchen. Her best bet, at least in her mind, was to go to the laundry room and let her lustful thoughts of Douglas be drowned out by the spin cycle. On second thought, all of that spinning and vibrating would only intensify her longing, lustful need and throbbing between her thighs. She'd dust the living room. That was safe enough, wasn't it?

Making a turn for the supply closet, she grabbed the furniture polish and dust rags. As she passed the kitchen, she glanced at Douglas and his cleaning efforts. Surprisingly, he was up to his elbows in soap and water scrubbing the teapot. A beat passed before he moved the pot to the other side of the sink and thoroughly rinsed it. He caught Crystal's gaze and winked at her. She quickly turned away and dashed into the living room. Her heart was beating like a steel drum and all she could think about was Douglas hoisting her up on the kitchen counter and stroking her like she needed cleaning. As she started waxing the table, she knew it was her mind that needed a good scrubbing.

Douglas dried the dishes and placed them on the counter, not sure as to where they should go. He chuckled as he recalled the look on Crystal's face when he caught her gazing at him. Sweet and sexy. Was every part of her like that? How was he going to convince her to give him a taste of that sweetness? Drying his hands, Douglas decided that he'd mop the floor before going to find Crystal. Sure, household chores weren't his normal weekend activities—that's what he paid his housekeeper for—but something about being in Crystal's kitchen made him feel at ease.

I'd better not tell her that or she will swear that it's the majestic nature of this land and we'll be fighting again, he thought as he opened the cabinet underneath the sink in search of Pine-Sol. Of course, all he found were organic cleaning products with confusing labels on them. Smiling, he decided this was a great excuse to go and find

Crystal. Heading for the living room, Douglas was stopped dead in his tracks as he watched her bent over, polishing the solid oak table in the middle of the room. With each stroke, her booty wiggled a little and Douglas wanted her more than ever. Who knew housework was sexy, he pondered, then cleared his throat, causing Crystal to stand up and end his erotic show.

"Yes?"

"I was getting ready to mop and I didn't see any Pine-Sol and I don't quite understand the products you have underneath the sink," he said in a low tone that reminded Crystal he was more male than she'd had in her kitchen in years. Hell, ever. But this man was not the one she should be having those kinds of thoughts about. He wanted to tear down the very house where she wanted to make love to him. Shaking her head, she tried to focus on the question at hand. Cleaning products. "Right," she said. "I don't clean with harsh chemicals, 'cause it's bad for the environment."

"Okay, but which one of these products cleans the floor?" he asked as they walked into the kitchen. Crystal bent over again, giving him another full view of her perfectly shaped behind. Again, he just wanted to reach out and grab it.

"Here you go," she said, turning around with a white bottle in her hand. "Cleans better than Pine-Sol and it's made right here on this farm."

"Is there anything you don't do here?"

Crystal placed her hand underneath her chin as if she was thinking, then said, "Nope. Well, we don't sell out."

"Ouch. Do we have to go there with every conversation?" he asked, taking two steps closer to her. "You know what I want right now?"

Quivering as his warm breath tickled her upper lip, Crystal was about to ask him when the phone rang, giving her a needed escape. "I have to get that," she said, then moved to the cordless extension on the edge of the counter. Douglas watched her every move as she picked up the phone and said hello. While she talked, he watched her full lips move and nearly lost it when she ran her tongue across her bottom lip. Was she actually talking or was he in the middle of the best dream he'd had in months?

"Dena, that isn't necessary," he finally heard her say. "I have the situation under control."

Douglas didn't like the panicked look on Crystal's face and it took everything in him not to grab the phone and tell her lawyer where to go and how quickly she could get there. Why was he so protective of this woman, at least in his mind? According to Crystal, he was the one causing her harm because of the business park. Just like she wanted to keep her family legacy alive, he wanted to honor his father's last wishes. This business park was a major part of it. Instead of grabbing the phone, he observed, stewing silently.

"Okay," she said with a sigh. "I'll see you in the morning." Then Crystal hung up the phone and turned to Douglas.

"What was that all about?" he asked.

"Just some legal stuff," she said with a shrug. "Anyway, back to the mopping. This is concentrated, so you don't have to use a lot of it to get the floor clean."

Douglas offered a mock salute. "Yes, ma'am," he said. Crystal looked around the kitchen and nodded in approval.

"You did a good job for a spoiled rich boy."

"There's more to me than just good looks and money," he said with a wink.

Crystal turned away from him, thinking about his other stand-out attributes: soft lips, sweet tongue, and hot hands. "I'm going to finish polishing the furniture. The mop is behind the refrigerator," she said, then dashed out of the kitchen.

Once she was alone in the living room, Crystal thought about her conversation with Dena.

"Your parents aren't happy about this scheme of yours," the attorney said.

"You called my parents?" Crystal said incredulously as she locked eyes with Douglas. Why was he looking at her like that while Dena was painting him as the spawn of the devil?

"I hope you know he isn't against using your weak-

ness to get what he wants," Dena said. "Something I'm pretty sure he learned from his godfather, a man with no qualms about using any and everything at his disposal to get what he wants. You're playing with fire."

"I don't understand what you're talking about and how his godfather has anything to do with this."

"Trust me, Crystal, men like Douglas Wellington and Waylon Terrell are as ruthless as they are handsome. We need to work toward a real legal solution to stopping Welco and spending the week with Douglas isn't going to change anything. You are setting yourself up for a heartbreak and loss of what your family has worked so hard for. Do you really want to be the Hughes who loses Hughes Farm?"

"Dena, that isn't necessary. I have the situation under control."

"Listen," Dena interrupted. "I'm bringing over some legal papers that you need to look at tomorrow and I want to have some words with Douglas Wellington."

"Okay, I'll see you in the morning," she said. Then she hung up the phone and locked eyes with Douglas again, wondering if she had made a mistake, as Dena said.

Crystal returned to polishing, though the table had a shine on it that was close to that of a mirror. As she rose to her feet, she grabbed her cleaning supplies and headed for the supply closet. When she walked out the door, she ran chest first into Douglas.

"Where's the fire, Crystal?" he asked as he wrapped his arms around her waist.

"Will you get your hands off me?" she said, her voice shaky.

"Sorry," he said without releasing her. "I finished mopping. What's next?"

"I have to do laundry and you can mop the bathroom."

"How about a break?" he asked. "Because I find it hard to believe that you spend your Friday nights cleaning."

"And just what do you think I do on the weekends?" she asked, looking down at his arms around her.

Douglas relented and let her go. "Well, I think you sip ice tea under the stars. You said this place is magical . . . so show me some more magic."

"How about I show you to the bathroom so that you can finish helping me. You volunteered, remember?"

"You're a hard woman," he said.

"Douglas," she said, "maybe we can take that walk after we're done. Then you can see more of what this farm has to offer and understand just what tearing it down would destroy."

"And I need you to understand that you're the most beautiful woman that I've seen in a long time and I can't get the thought of your kiss out of my mind."

Crystal gasped, but Dena's words blared in her head, bringing her back to reality.

"Down the hall on the left," she said.

"What?"

"The bathroom. I'm going to do laundry."

"Why don't I help you with the laundry instead?"

Crystal inhaled and thought about the lacy underthings waiting in the basket and Douglas touching them as he loaded the washing machine. "No, thank you."

His smile made her heart skip a beat and her blood boil. "If you need a break or this is too much work for Douglas Wellington the third, then feel free to go back to your quarters. I really don't need your help."

"What are you afraid of?" he asked. "After all, you invited me here."

"You have a really big ego," she snapped. "I invited you here because you need to see . . ."

Douglas grasped her chin, tilting her mouth upward, and then he captured it in a hot, sultry, and knee-shivering kiss that threw Crystal's mind off balance. What warning had Dena given her? Aww, hell, it didn't matter, she thought as his tongue probed her mouth, meandering around as if there was nothing wrong with them kissing again. As if he wanted nothing more from her than to make love to her until their bodies melted together.

As if he didn't want to destroy her family's

legacy. That thought sobered her. Crystal pulled back, swallowing the lust inside her and trying to push up anger. It didn't work. "Douglas, you can leave now."

"Leave as in go back to the dollhouse?"

She nodded, then took off down the hall. Douglas followed her, grasping her shoulder and making her look into his eyes. "What's going on here?" he asked.

"You're keeping me from my laundry," she snapped.

"You don't give a damn about that laundry. Every time I kiss you, you want to run out of here as if your pants are on fire. If they are, I'd be more than happy to put it out."

"Douglas," she said, her voice low and seductive to his ears, "there's nothing for you to put out and if you think for one second that I'm going to sleep with you tonight, you can forget it."

"I have no intentions of sleeping with you—tonight. But soon enough, you will be ready and I'm going to be right here. The first, the last, and the only time I will turn you down is tonight."

"Turn me down?" she asked incredulously. "You're out of your mind."

"I know you're not ready," Douglas said with a smile. "Soon enough you will be."

Crystal rolled her eyes and wiggled his hand from her shoulder. "You should really get out of here before I simply lose control and ravish you. Since you've turned me down and all," she sarcastically said.

"One more kiss?" he asked, then leaned into her. While Crystal fully expected a soul-shattering kiss on the lips, Douglas surprised her with a tender peck on the cheek. She fought to keep her face neutral, since he didn't need to know what she was expecting.

"Good night," he said, then turned down the hall to leave. Crystal started to stop him, but she just stood still and waited to hear the door close. When she heard the slam, she realized that she'd been holding her breath. Expelling a sigh, she turned back to the living room and to her surprise, Douglas was sitting on the sofa.

"I thought you left," she said.

"And I thought you were so hot to go do your laundry," he replied with a blinding smile. Despite every logical thought in her head, telling her to kick him out, Crystal sat down on the sofa beside him. "Besides, you owe me a walk."

"What's your game?" she asked.

Douglas inched closer to her and slipped his arm around her shoulders. "I could ask you the same thing," he replied. "Let's take that walk."

Sighing, Crystal agreed. Maybe getting out of such close quarters with Douglas would allow her to think, give her a chance to show him more of the farm and its majestic acres. Who was she fooling? Being outside with him was going to leave her just as tense and frazzled as she felt right now—with his strong arm around her.

They stepped out on the porch and Crystal stole a glance at Douglas, who was looking up at the sky as if he was transfixed by the clearness of it all. She smiled.

"Looks like you're beginning to see the magic and I haven't even started the tour."

"Funny," he replied. "I'll admit the stars look brighter out here."

"Yet you want to cloud the sky with smoke stacks and plumes of smoke from your business park."

Douglas shook his head. "And give thousands of people jobs to go to every day so that they can put food in their family's mouths. You think this is all about growing my company when it's much deeper than that."

They stepped off the porch, heading toward a path that Crystal pointed to. "But what about the people who already depend on this farm? The Starlight girls, in particular? Don't you understand some things can't be measured in dollars and cents?"

"Money makes the world go round, Crystal."

"And since you have a lot of it, you just expect the world to dance because you dropped some dollars?" She fingered her hair and shook her head. "Douglas's personal strip club?"

"You just can't admit the good that Welco has done for Reeseville, can you?"

She stopped walking and faced him with her head cocked to the side. "Good? I guess closing the Fresh Food Market doesn't count. How many farms went under because that grocery store couldn't compete with that supercenter of yours?"

"And how many families can count on a store where they can meet all of their needs without having to drive all over town? If the Fresh Food Market was meeting the needs of the community, then what would a little competition hurt?"

"You just think throwing money at people solves everything, don't you?" She dropped his hand and shook her head. "Money is nothing more than paper."

"You act as if you don't like money, but you're not hurting. Do you even know what most of the people in this town are going through while you sit here on you precious land handing out fruits and vegetables. I'm creating jobs, not salads."

"Maybe that's why I can stand up to you when everyone else in this town just gives you what you want. I will not let you take this farm from me and the people who need it."

"And what about the people who need jobs? Look past this farm and look at Reeseville. People need this business park. I'm not trying to do a land grab here, but I want to make this town a better place."

"You don't give a damn about this town!"

"You're not the only one with roots here,"

Douglas retorted. "My family is from here as well. And though we don't have mythology like Hughes Farm, my father wanted to do something here. Provide jobs and opportunities that no one else in Duval County wanted to give to poor people."

Tilting her head to the side, Crystal was taken aback to hear Douglas speak with such passion about his family's business. Still, Welco was a heartless corporation, no matter what story Douglas wanted to spin.

"Why here? Why this farm?" she asked. "If you really care that much . . ."

"Crystal," he whispered, "this is just business."

She glared at him and shook her head. "And until you realize that it's more than that, I don't want to have another conversation with you. Dena was right. This was a horrible idea." Crystal spun away from him and stalked back to her house.

Chapter 8

Inside and alone, Crystal wanted to scream. Douglas wasn't going to change, he was all about money and there was nothing she could do to get through to him. Why hadn't she listened to Dena? This wasn't some romantic movie, this was a businessman, a sexy man whose lips seemed to be drawn to her like magnets. And boy did those kisses leave her feeling weak.

Not weak enough to give in to his buyout however, and if he thought kisses and hot caresses were going to sway her, he needed to think again. Or maybe she was being swayed. Swayed toward letting him inside her bedroom, between her thighs and inside her hot and waiting valley. *Stop it,* she thought. *That man is bad news and losing your heart to him is about as smart as losing your farm to his company.* Sinking back on the sofa, she tried not to think about the warmth of Douglas's touch. As she closed her eyes, the phone rang, interrupting her naughty fantasy before she even got started on it.

"Hello?" she said breathlessly into the phone.

"Crystal, what in the hell are you doing?" her mother asked in a calm tone that obviously belied how she really felt.

"I guess this is about Dena's call," Crystal replied. "Mom, I have things under control and I'm not going to lose our farm."

"Should your father and I come home and help you? Dena told me that you're up against Welco and her arch rival, Waylon." Crystal could've sworn that she heard her mother chuckle.

"This is the second time I've heard his name tonight. What is this all about?"

Erin expelled a breath and said, "That's Dena's story to tell, and I think your father and I may need to pay a visit because both of you have more than business on your mind. Douglas Wellington Jr. was a hard man and I can only imagine the business lessons he taught his son. That being said, daughter, what made you think it was a good idea to invite him to move in for a week?"

"He hasn't moved in. He's staying in the guest cottage and . . . what do you mean by 'Douglas Wellington Jr. was a hard man'?"

"This isn't the first time they've come after this farm, Crystal," Erin said. "Your father was so bitter after that battle. Why do you think we moved?"

"Why didn't you all tell me any of this before?" Crystal asked, now on her feet pacing back and forth.

"Because it wasn't information that we wanted to saddle you down with," she said. "And we thought the land grab was over. I guess we were wrong. I haven't told your father that you have that man's son staying on our property."

"Is there something else that you're not telling me?" Crystal asked.

Erin sighed again and told her daughter that she would check in with her on Monday.

"Mom, don't . . ." The dial tone sounded in her ear before she could say "hang up."

Now, this is just getting weirder. My mother doesn't keep secrets from me! Crystal glanced at the phone and started to call her mother back. Instead she dialed Dena's number. Dena wasn't just the Hughes family's lawyer, she was an old friend of the family. She and Erin were best friends. Crystal was sure that Dena could shed some light on what her mother was trying to hide.

"Hello?" Dena said.

"Dena," Crystal said. "We need to talk."

"Have you gotten that man off your property?" she asked.

"No, and that's not why I'm calling you."

"Then what is it, Crystal? I hoped your mother

would've talked some sense into you and told you what a silly game you're playing."

"No, but she did tell me about Douglas Wellington's father."

Dena fell silent and Crystal knew she'd hit a nerve. "Your mother told you what, exactly?" Dena asked.

"That he was a hard man. What did she mean by that?"

"That's your mother's story to tell and obviously, she didn't tell you."

"Funny," Crystal said. "That's the same thing she said about you and Waylon Terrell. Now, someone is going to give me some answers!"

"Crystal, we all have a past and your mother and I don't want you to repeat the mistakes we made."

"What mistakes?" she asked, annoyed that both her mother and her lawyer were trying to pull the wool over her eyes.

"You don't want to be involved with the Wellington clan," she said. "You're going to have to trust that your mother and I know what we're talking about. Crystal, those who don't learn from history are doomed to repeat it. All you need to know is Welco has always wanted this farm."

"Why, though?" Crystal asked as her mind filled with the thought of Douglas's kiss. "I have no clue what you and my mother are talking about."

"If you're lucky, you never will, Crystal. Trust me when I tell you that Douglas will do anything to get what he wants and if that means pretending to love you, he'll do it."

She sighed and sank into the sofa. "So, this happened to you or my mom?"

Dena groaned. "Douglas has to go if you really want to save your farm. You're going to win this through the courts, not through whatever fantasy you thought would play out this week."

After hanging up with Dena, Crystal was even more confused than she was when she'd called her.

Douglas walked past his quarters and headed back to the reflective pond Crystal had showed him earlier. Underneath the moonbeams, the pond looked like a silver mirror. He wished that Crystal was by his side. He wished that he could stop the purchase of her property, but his hands were tied. Dipping his finger in the water, he watched as the ripples wrinkled his reflection. This land was unique and part of him regretted putting the wheels in motion to tear it down. But going back to the board now would mean that he'd be removed from his position, and he couldn't disappoint his father's memory. He'd taken the CEO position because it was what his father had wanted. And when Douglas had discovered documents that had been marked "Hughes Farm," he thought that getting this land would be a way to honor his father. The Douglas Wellington Jr. Business Park would capture what meant most to him, Douglas surmised. Growing up, Douglas was acutely aware that Welco had been his father's top priority. He couldn't recall playing catch or watching football with his dad. Everything had been about business. There had been days when Douglas waited at his father's feet while he wrote reports and ignored his son. Had it not been for Waylon, Douglas's childhood would've been relentlessly sad.

Still, he wanted to build this tribute to his father.

Thinking about the file, Douglas wished that his dad was around to answer why Hughes Farm was so important to him. The notes on the farm had been vague, but since they'd been his father's, Douglas assumed that he didn't need to do any more research, despite Waylon's urging for him to do so. This was his father's baby and more than anything else it would be a gain for the county.

But why was this farm so important to everyone? *I need to see that file again. Maybe I missed something about why he needed this place.* Since he wasn't going to have the pleasure of Crystal's company, he decided to go to his office and take a look at his father's notes about Hughes Farm.

Walking back toward his truck, Douglas saw the lights were still on inside Crystal's place. Was she thinking of him as he'd been thinking of her? He started to forget the file, stroll up to her door and give her a good-night kiss that would stay on her mind all night. As he was about to do just that, the lights went out inside the house. He hopped in his truck instead. He had a week to get Crystal to realize that she wanted him inside her bedroom as much as he wanted to be there.

Starting the truck, he drove slowly up the driveway, feeling as if he was leaving some utopia and heading back to a reality that he wasn't sure he wanted anymore. It was getting a little too easy for him to understand why Crystal was fighting so hard to save her family's farm. And he'd only been there for a half a day.

Who was he kidding? It was Crystal that he was enchanted with—as he had been since the day she handcuffed herself in his office. Maybe it was because she hated his money and forced him to work to earn her trust. Maybe it was how sweet she tasted every time he kissed her. Or maybe it was the burning heat of desire that smoldered inside him every time their eyes locked.

I have got to get this woman out of my head. She's standing in the way of progress and no matter how sexy she is, she is still a distraction, he thought. And as much as he tried to remember that this was simply business, Douglas knew business had nothing to do with what he was feeling and what was going on. That's why he needed to know what his father had been trying to do with that land. Why was it so important to him?

"Does it really matter?" he mumbled as he picked up his cell phone to see if he had service now that he was a few miles away from the farm. He saw the blinking icon for his voice mail and a couple of text messages. When he clicked on the first text message, he smiled at his godfather's warning.

Don't forget your true purpose for being there.

"That's been long forgotten," he muttered. "And that's why I've got to see this file." Before he could drop the phone onto the passenger seat, it rang.

"Yeah?" he said.

"Douglas, it's Deloris, and I've heard the craziest rumor," the reporter said.

"I don't have anything to say to you," he retorted.

"Is it my fault that you're so quotable? Are the rumors true? Are you staying with Crystal Hughes at the Hughes Farm?"

"No comment," Douglas said, then clicked the end button. *How does this woman know my every move?* he thought as he turned into the parking lot of Welco Industries. Looking at the dark office building, he wondered if he should give the board what they wanted—his resignation. Then he could leave the company and do something he wanted to do. *Like Crystal.* Douglas looked around as if he expected to see someone else standing near his truck.

Giving up his position in the company would seem like a slap in his father's face, though. After he figured out what his father's plans were for Hughes Farm, he would make a decision about his position with Welco Industries.

Climbing out of the truck, he headed inside to his office. On nights when Douglas wasn't out of town, looking for something discreet and meaningless, he'd find himself in his office working, trying to make up what he thought had been failure to his father.

So when Waylon told him to research Hughes Farm, it hadn't mattered because Douglas knew his father wanted that land.

Now, he wished he'd been more businessman and less son seeking his dead father's approval. Walking into his office, he turned the lights on and saw that his file cabinet drawers were slightly ajar. He never left his cabinets open. "Who's in here?" he bellowed. After getting no reply, Douglas opened the drawer where he kept his father's file on Hughes Farm and his diary.

"Shit," he groaned as he pulled all of the contents out of the drawer. The diary and the file were gone and he was pissed. Douglas had found the diary last year and hadn't brought himself to read it. Part of him knew there was something dark in those pages that he wasn't ready to read. But one day, he planned to read it. Now it was gone. Grabbing his desk phone, he called Amy.

"Hello?"

"What happened after I left the office?" he growled into the phone.

"Mr. Wellington?" she asked.

"Get here, now!"

"Y-yes, sir," she stammered.

Douglas slammed down the phone and continued his search. Why did someone want that file? There wasn't anything in that file that could help . . . Crystal! Did she have someone on the inside? Had she used this plan to get him away from his office, cut off from communications, and now she had the file that . . . No. He wasn't going to believe that she would be that underhanded. But why wouldn't she play dirty? Crystal made it clear that she would do anything to save her farm. He wasn't going to put stealing past her. But he couldn't come out and accuse her.

So, how was he going to broach this subject to her? Douglas picked up the phone and dialed

Crystal's number, but he hung up after the first ring. What was he going to say to her? He couldn't just hold the phone and listen to her saying hello. That's what stalkers do. Pacing back and forth in his office, his mind danced from anger to desire as he thought about the missing file and the touch of Crystal's hand on his shoulder. The sensations that ran through his body as he recalled her soft moans as they kissed inside her house almost negated the negative thoughts he'd been having about what had been taken from his office. Until Amy walked in. His mind shifted back to the business at hand.

"Who was in my office?" Douglas boomed.

"I—I don't know. When you left, I got a call from—"

"Amy, when I'm not here you know that you're not supposed to leave your desk without locking my office. We've had this discussion before."

"I didn't, sir. I didn't leave your office open. Mr. Terrell came by looking for you and you weren't here."

"You're saying my godfather went into my office?" Douglas was about to fire her for telling what he thought was a lie.

"No," she said. "Mr. Terrell left and I walked him to the elevator. When I returned your office door was open and I thought you were back. I looked in the office and no one was there. I closed the door and then I left."

Sighing, Douglas thought about what she said and who would've gone into his office. It had to be one of the board members. Other than himself, Waylon, and Amy, they were the only people who had carte blanche in the building. That was going to change. Douglas sent Amy to her desk to wait for him while he called security.

"Mr. Wellington," the security chief, Rex Harris, said. "How can I help you, sir?"

"I don't want anyone to be allowed up on my floor unless it's myself, Amy, or Waylon Terrell. Change the security code on the elevator to eight-three-nine-seven," he ordered.

"Yes, sir," he said. "Is there a problem I should be aware of?"

"Not yet, but we're trying to avert that. If anyone gives you shit about the new rule, make sure you inform me."

"Yes, sir, but are you—"

"Are you questioning my orders?"

"No, sir," Harris said nervously. "I just want to be—"

"Do as I say and there won't be any problems." Douglas hung up the phone and wondered if Harris was part of the problem. He called Amy into his office and motioned for her to sit in the leather chair across from his desk.

"Yes, sir," she said.

"There's a file missing from my office that could have impact on the business park."

"I did—"

Douglas held up his hand. "I'm not accusing you of anything, right now. But we have to find that file and I need to know how that file got out of this office. You need to get me the video surveillance and have it sent to this address by an outside messenger company," he said as he wrote down the address to Hughes Farm. As he slid the paper over to Amy, he watched her face for a reaction. She should've known the address and she should've asked him a question about why he was staying there. But she said nothing. Douglas felt as if he had found the leak.

"You can go now," he said to the frazzled assistant. As soon as Amy left, Douglas called his head of security back.

"Yes, sir?" Harris asked.

"I need the security video from midnight Thursday through ten p.m. today," he said. "And when my assistant calls Monday morning to ask for a copy of this same video, give it to her and don't tell her that I already have a copy of it."

"All right. I can have this downloaded and sent to you in the next half an hour," Harris said. "Sir, are you sure there isn't more that I need to know about what's going on?"

"If you needed to know more, I'd tell you. This week I need you to keep an eye out on my office."

"No problem. Do you want me to add another camera to your office?" he asked.

"Yes, and I want it to be undetectable," Douglas said. "If you can install it tonight before my assistant gets in on Monday that would be great."

"All right. I'll be up there after the download is complete," Harris said.

"Thanks," Douglas said. After hanging up the phone, he started to call Crystal, but decided against it. She probably didn't even know he'd left.

Chapter 9

Crystal wanted to slap herself. Was she really waiting on her front porch to see when and if Douglas would return to Hughes Farm? Really? First of all, it wasn't as if he was her man, and secondly, he wasn't obligated to stay at the farm simply because she'd invited him.

Still, where in the hell did he go? And why did she care so much? Who cared if he had a hot date with some airhead, stick-thin girl with breast implants and long fake hair? *Good for him*, she thought evilly. "Douglas needs a brainless woman who thinks everything he does is right and that is not me," she muttered. Taking a sip of her iced tea, Crystal decided that she would sit outside for another five minutes and then she would go inside and fold her laundry. She told herself that she wasn't going to worry about where Douglas was or who he was with. It wasn't her business and she had no need to rack her brain over it. As she rose to her feet, she saw the headlights of Douglas's truck pull into the long driveway. She sat down and tried to pretend that she hadn't been waiting for him. When the truck stopped, Crystal fully expected to see Douglas get out of it with another woman. But the sight of him walking toward her porch alone allowed her to breathe a sigh of relief.

"Good evening," he said when he noticed her sitting in the dark.

"Evening. Back from a hot date?" she asked, then immediately grimaced. "Never mind. That isn't my business and I don't want you to think that you being here . . ."

Douglas held his hand up, silencing her as he stepped up on the porch and stood in front of her. He smiled at the white tank top and spandex shorts she wore. "I had some work to do at the office and since you made it clear that we weren't going to be together tonight, I had to find something to do with my time."

"'Be together'?"

"You know what I mean," he said with a slick smile. "But, here we are."

"Yes, here we are. Would you like some tea?" she asked.

"Sure," he said as he took a seat in one of the two rocking chairs on the porch.

"I'll be right back," she said, then dashed into the house. Once she was alone in the kitchen,

Crystal told herself that all she and Douglas were going to do on that dark porch was sip tea and talk. *I can ask him more about his father and see if I can find some clues that will help me form questions to ask my mom when I talk to her on Monday.*

She fixed the tea, grabbed a few freshly baked oatmeal-apple cookies, and headed outside. Stepping out on the porch, she noticed that Douglas was napping in the rocking chair. He looked so handsome when he was sleeping, she thought as she watched the rise and fall of his chest. As he ran his tongue across his bottom lip, she longed to taste him. Why did he have to be her rival, the man who wanted to take her land, instead of her lover? The man she could walk over to and wake with a hot, wet kiss?

"Douglas," she said quietly as she crossed over to him.

"Mmm," he said, stirring from his catnap.

"Your tea," Crystal said as she held the glass out to him.

Taking the glass from her hand, he smiled his thanks. "It's so peaceful out here," he said, setting the tea on the wrought-iron table beside his chair. "And private." In one quick swoop, he pulled Crystal on his lap.

"Hey," she exclaimed, but made no effort to move.

"Comfortable?" he asked, his lips against her ear. Crystal shivered and kept silent, even wrapping her arms around his neck and leaning her head on his shoulder. Why did being in his arms feel so comfortable?

Five seconds and then I'm letting him go. This isn't why I sat outside waiting for him. Wait, I really wasn't waiting for him. I was just sitting outside, she thought. Douglas stroked her thigh as they sat and Crystal felt her desire pooling in her panties every time his hand danced across her flesh.

Get up and go back to your corner! Crystal's voice of reason screamed as she fell deeper into Douglas's embrace.

"Your tea is getting hot," she said.

"So am I," he whispered, then captured her mouth. Douglas was an amazing kisser and as he sucked her bottom lip while licking the inside of her mouth, Crystal was brought close to an orgasm. Her legs quivered, her folds of flesh between her thighs grew wet like a river, and she moaned—loud, deep, and unabashedly.

Douglas deepened his kiss, moved his hands around her waist and pulled her closer. Oh, how he wished she was straddling his throbbing erection with the fullness of her bosom pressed against his chest. He wanted nothing more than to be buried deep inside her as she rode him while the chair rocked back and forth in the stillness of the night.

"Stop," she moaned as their lips parted and he flicked his tongue across her bottom lip.

"If you really wanted that, then you would unhand me," he said in a low voice that made her inner thigh throb.

Crystal dropped her arms from Douglas's neck and rose to her feet. "You're right," she said. "Enjoy your tea." She started for the front door and Douglas leapt from his chair and blocked her path.

"Okay," he said, placing his hands on her shoulders. "I'll behave."

She raised her right eyebrow at him and sucked her teeth. "I had some cookies, but you made me drop them. And they were freshly baked too."

"My apologies, but somehow I think the taste of your tongue was all the treat I needed tonight."

"Date didn't go as planned?"

Douglas tilted his head to the side and smirked. "I guess it would help your irrational dislike of me if you thought I'd gone on a date instead of to my office—like I said. Then all of those nasty thoughts you have about me in the back of your mind would be validated, huh?"

"Actually, the fact that you want to take all of this from me pretty much validates any nasty thoughts I have about you."

"Give me a sample of just how nasty those thoughts are."

Crystal slapped her hand against her hip. "I thought you said you were going to behave?"

He shrugged. "What did I do? You said you have nasty thoughts."

Crystal stared into his eyes so deeply that he shuddered. "Tell me something," she said in a low voice. "And don't give me the politically correct answer, but why this land? Why do you want my farm so bad?"

He wished he had an answer, something he could say that would make her understand this was about his father's dream. "Well," he began, "this isn't about turning Reeseville into Welcoville as you said before. Let me tell you something about me and my family. We wanted to help this county and this town become economically independent. My dad was born here and loved this place. He always felt that outsiders didn't understand what this place could be. We're between Charlotte and Greensboro, we have a rarely used rail system that can help in exporting goods throughout the country. That's why we're trying to build this business park. It was the last thing that my father was working on before he died."

"And you still haven't answered my question," she said. "Why this farm?"

"Because," he sighed, "it was important to my father."

His honesty was both refreshing and frightening. Had the Wellington family had a longstanding grudge against the Hugheses? Was this the Hatfields and McCoys?

"Why was it so important to your father?"

Fearing he'd already said too much, Douglas simply shook his head. "You know what," he said. "I'm still researching it, and when I find out, I'll let you know."

"That's bull," Crystal spat. "I'll get my own answers because you're not telling me everything and I will not let a few kisses and sweet words make me forget the truth—next month you want to level everything on this property. Goodnight." She slammed into the house leaving him standing on the dark porch with a puzzled look on his face.

Construction on the business park was scheduled to start in thirty days. He'd even talked to a few county commissioners and city council members to see if they could force eminent domain on the farm, since that had been part of his father's plan. Now, Crystal had him questioning why his father wanted this land so badly. It had to be more than business. He wondered if his godfather would come clean about it. He reached for his cell phone, then remembered he had no signal. *Shit.*

That little dollhouse Crystal had stuck him in didn't have a phone, either. He could try a smoke signal, or he could knock on the door and ask her if he could use the phone. Like she would allow that. Still, he didn't feel like driving into the town limits for a signal. Knocking on the door, he waited for what seemed like an eternity for Crystal to open the door.

"What do you want?" she asked.

"To use your phone if you don't mind," he replied, offering her a half smile.

"Sure," she replied, stepping aside so that he could enter the house. "When you're done, you know your way out." Crystal tore off down the hall and Douglas watched the tempting sway of hips, then headed into the kitchen when he heard what he assumed was her bedroom door slam.

Grabbing the phone, he dialed Waylon's number.

"Hello?" the older man said when he answered.

"Godfather," Douglas said.

"Something's wrong, huh, Trey?"

Douglas nodded as if Waylon could see him, and said, "Someone broke into my office and took the Hughes Farm file."

"What Hughes Farm file?"

Peeking around the corner, Douglas made sure Crystal wasn't creeping up on him before he said, "The one you and my father kept for years."

"Douglas, please tell me that wasn't the sole basis for your decision to go after Hughes Farm."

"So what if it was?" Douglas said in a near whisper. "Was the information in the file wrong?"

"It wasn't a sound business plan," Waylon said. "I think you should leave that place and you need to forget that file and go to the board with an alternative."

"And you already know that they don't want alternatives," Douglas said. "But why should I forget the file?"

"It was . . . Douglas, you have to clean this up."

"Did you take the file?"

"Now you're accusing me of being a thief? What's wrong with you, boy? You're the one who called me and got me involved in this without doing more than reading over an old file from your father. Don't call me this late with your accusations!"

Douglas removed the phone from his ear and looked at it. "Boy"? Who in the hell did Waylon think he was talking to? "Listen," he said, "I'm going to find that file and I'm going to find out what you're trying to hide from me." *And find out what's in my father's diary,* he added silently. Douglas wanted to kick himself for being so sentimental about this business deal and for not reading his father's diary. Who would want it? What was hidden on those pages?

Before his godfather could respond, Douglas forcefully hung up the phone and cursed as quietly as he could. When he started for the front door, he saw Crystal standing in the hallway.

"Is my phone okay?" she asked.

"Yes. Sorry about that."

She raised her eyebrow at him, but didn't say a word. Seconds ticked away as they stood there staring at each other.

Finally, Crystal asked, "Want a drink?"

"Do you have something stronger than tea?"

"Of course," she said. "Whiskey strong enough?"

Douglas chuckled. "You drink whiskey?"

She smirked as she moved toward the kitchen. "It's the drink of choice when a huge corporation tries to take your land."

"Ouch."

"Sorry, kind of," she said as they entered the kitchen and she turned the light on. Crystal reached under the counter and pulled out a bottle of Jack Daniel's Tennessee Honey. Douglas picked up the bottle before she could pour.

"This is girly whiskey," he said with a laugh.

"Now you're complaining about my offerings? Ain't that a—"

"I'm just saying, I expected a farm girl like yourself to pull out some whiskey you made in your tub."

"That's moonshine, and I'm sorry, I'm fresh out," she quipped.

"Funny," he said as he opened the bottle and Crystal grabbed two glasses from the cabinet.

They drank the first two glasses in silence. She wanted to know why his conversation had gotten so heated and what this file was that he was talking about. Their eyes met as they started on the second glass. "This is smooth," he said.

"Umm-hmm," she said. "Not girly at all."

Douglas poured himself a third glass and when he downed it, he was beginning to feel the effects of the whiskey. Crystal poured a half glass for herself, because she was feeling the alcohol lowering her inhibitions and she wanted nothing more than to kiss him. Get naked and explore his body with her tongue. She took a sip, then pushed her glass aside. Douglas boldly poured himself another glass. "Can't hang, huh?" he asked with a sloppy smile.

"I see no need to get drunk," she said, her words a bit slurred.

Douglas tweaked her nose. "You're already there, sweetheart." He closed the space between them and Crystal's heartbeat filled her ears. *Please don't let him kiss me,* she thought mere seconds before his lips captured hers. Powerless to resist him, Crystal fell into his strong arms, savoring his taste, enjoying the feather light touches on her bare arms and the bulging erection pressing against her thighs. As he coaxed her tongue deeper into his mouth, she could taste the sweet whiskey, the minty aftertaste of the tea, and the all-male desire.

Crystal pressed her body against his, rotating her hips against him as their kiss deepened.

He lifted her up and sat her on the edge of the counter, then ripped her tank top open. When her breasts spilled forward, he released a low whistle. "I knew you would be beautiful all over," he groaned. "Let me see more."

Crystal wiggled out of her shorts, revealing that she wasn't wearing any panties. And she was flawless, smooth brown skin and the roundest ass that he'd ever wanted to kiss. Douglas spread her legs apart, stroking her inner thighs. Her skin was silky smooth. Now, he wanted to taste her. He slipped his index finger between her wet folds of flesh, making Crystal moan in delight as he found her throbbing pearl. Stroking her with the pad of his finger, Douglas watched her face as waves of pleasure washed across it. He removed his finger, then planted his face between her thighs. Crystal inhaled sharply as she felt the heat of his breath against her most sensitive spot. But when his tongue lapped her bubbling juices and his lips captured her pleasure point, it was all Crystal could do to stay upright. How long had it been since her body had been pleased so thoroughly? Maybe the whiskey had clouded her mind, maybe it wasn't even . . .

"Oh, yes," she exclaimed in a voice that she didn't recognize as her own. She gripped the back of his head and pushed him deeper into her valley. Douglas sucked, licked, and gently nibbled her sweetness until he was so hard that he wasn't sure he'd be able to move into the bedroom.

"Oh. My. God!" Crystal exclaimed as she exploded and shivered. Douglas inched up her body, lifting her into his arms.

"That was only the beginning. Are you ready for more?" he asked.

Licking her lips, she nodded her head and leaned against his chest. Douglas walked as quickly as he could down the hall to Crystal's bedroom. Candles were burning on her nightstand near the bed, giving the room a golden glow and the scent of jasmine and roses. Had she been waiting for him? Did she have other plans for the evening that fell through? Why was he feeling so jealous about some damned candles and the fact that another man might have been coming over there to do what he was about to do, make love to the most beautiful woman he'd ever needed?

Needed? he thought as he laid her on the bed. He was going to blame it on the alcohol and bury himself inside her.

Douglas ran his hand down the center of Crystal's chest and her body moved to his rhythm. Crystal reached for his shirt, but he grabbed her hand and kissed it. Then he leaned against her and took her hard nipple into his mouth, licking and sucking her succulent breast until he felt her shiver. While he sucked, he stroked her wetness and she moaned, sounding like a sweet symphony. He stepped back, disrobing quickly. He climbed into the bed beside her and Crystal placed her hand on the flat of his chest as he lay on his back. She drank in the details of his flawless body. The marblelike six-pack of abs, those strong thighs, and that long, thick erection that made her mouth water.

"It's payback time, Mr. Wellington," she said with a seductive tilt to her voice. "You did things to me with your mouth that were just unfair. It's time that I return that favor." She covered his thickness with her full lips and Douglas howled out in pleasure as her tongue snaked up and down while her lips stayed in place.

How in the world did she do that? He buried his hands in her thick black hair, as she bobbed up and down taking him deeper and deeper into her mouth. She was going to make him come if he didn't make her stop.

"Crystal, Crystal," he moaned, trying to stop her. Instead, she locked eyes with him and licked the creamy drops of his essence from the tip of his penis. "I need to be inside you," he groaned as a wave of pleasure washed over him. "Now."

"Condom?" she asked, glad that she wasn't as drunk as she'd thought.

Douglas nodded, leaned over the side of the

bed, and grabbed his jeans. He removed his wallet and pulled out a condom packet.

"And I thought boys stopped carrying condoms in their wallets after high school," Crystal quipped.

"Would you rather that I didn't have one?" he asked as he slid the sheath in place.

Taking a glance at his dangling erection and feeling a throbbing between her thighs, Crystal smiled. "Thank you for still being a high school senior."

He crossed over to her, pulling her up on her knees and against his chest. "You have a wicked tongue," he said.

"Takes one to know one," she said, then licked his right nipple. *Who are you and where is Crystal Hughes?* her inner voice cried out. That voice was silenced the moment Douglas wound her legs around his waist and pressed inside her. Deep inside her. Gasping, panting, moaning, she let go of all thoughts, logic, and legal ramifications. She rode this tidal wave of passion, meeting him thrust for thrust, giving him all the lust that had been building inside her since she handcuffed herself in the lobby of Welco Industries. Lust was all it was—wasn't it? And she was love starved.

"Crystal, Crystal," he intoned. Douglas had expected good sex, something hot and quick. But this? She was insatiable. Prince's obvious inspiration. She was about to make him come again. And he wasn't sure if he'd be able to walk when he did. Because as she tightened herself around his erection, milking his essence from him and his knees went weak, Douglas knew that he wasn't going to let this woman out of his reach ever again.

Leaning back on the bed, he held Crystal against him as she shuddered from her own release. Covered in sweat, dripping with passion and need, they expelled a singular breath. Crystal leaned her head against Douglas's sweaty chest thinking one thing: *What the hell have I done?*

Chapter 10

Douglas stroked Crystal's cheek as she pretended to be sleeping. "Damn, you're beautiful," he whispered against her ear. "And I know you're not sleeping."

"Maybe if you'd shut up, I could go to sleep."

Douglas held her tighter. "Do you ever turn the feisty off? Or is this just for me?"

Crystal chuckled, belying the unsettling feeling in the pit of her stomach. "I'm sleepy," she said. The truth of the matter was that she was wondering what was next. She'd slept with the enemy. She gave him every inch of her and had a good time doing it. But when the sun rose in the morning, nothing would've changed. He'd still want Hughes Farm. Right now, before she sobered up and before reality hit her like a ton of bricks, he was just going to be the man of her dreams—for the night.

"Are you sleeping?" he whispered.

"No," she replied, turning around to face him. She smiled at his smile and sighed. "It's obvious that you don't like it when people sleep around you."

Douglas pulled her closer and kissed her forehead, then stroked her cheek. God, she liked lying with him like this. It felt so . . . natural. Right. She traced her finger across his chest, then replaced it with her tongue, causing Douglas's body to respond. He gripped her bottom, wanting to spear her, spread her wetness and make her scream until she came. He wanted to feel her bucking against him, her tight little body taking him to the heights of passion. But they needed protection and he was all out. "Shit," he muttered as he brought her head to his chest.

"What?" she asked. "I'm wide awake now."

"I don't have another condom on me," he said. "And since there isn't . . ."

Crystal tightened her thighs around his waist and leaned over to her nightstand. Opening the drawer, she asked, "Will two be enough?"

"Quite the little granola vixen, huh?" he said when he eased forward and took the condom package from her hand.

"What?" she asked as she watched him rip the package open. "Am I supposed to sit at home and wait for a millionaire to sweep me off my feet?"

"As long as I'm the one with the broom,"

Douglas said after rolling the condom in place. Crystal straddled his body, slowly twisting her hips and building the anticipation of him melting with her again.

"Let's just make it through the night," she moaned as she took him deep in her valley and slowly rode him like a cowgirl on her prized steed.

Douglas didn't often give up control in the bedroom or the boardroom, but tonight he didn't mind Crystal taking over and giving him pleasure that exploded from the tips of his toes to the crown of his head. What was this woman doing to him? Douglas exploded, filling her with all of his lust, desire, and need. He didn't want the night to end because in the morning, they would be adversaries again.

Crystal fell into the curve of his arm and nestled against him, slowly breathing in his scent. Clean, spicy, lemongrass and citrus. But she had to forget all of this. If she had half a brain, she would've kicked him out of her bed after the first round. But she was cuddling with the man who wanted to take her livelihood, her family legacy, and turn it into a business park. What was sleeping with him supposed to change? Still, she eased closer to him. Inhaled again.

"Are you okay?" he asked, noting her silence.

"I was really trying to sleep," she lied.

Douglas rolled over and eased down the bed to

face her. "You're not a good liar. That's probably what makes you a good community activist."

"I was trying to sleep," she whined. "And every time I try to go to sleep we do this dance." She glanced over his shoulder at the alarm clock on her nightstand. "It's four a.m. At some point, I'd like to sleep."

Douglas raised his right eyebrow. "So, let's have the conversation that neither of us wants to have."

"What's that?" she asked, propping up on her elbows.

"What happens in the morning? When this is all said and done, what are we going to do?"

Crystal sighed. He was right—she didn't want to have this conversation. "Let me sleep on it," she said.

"No. Because you're going to wake up in the morning and pretend you're Jamie Foxx. I know you're not that drunk. And I know that I'm not going to be satisfied with just one night with you."

"It's not always about what you want." Crystal tugged at the sheet to cover her breasts, but Douglas pulled it away, smiling at her hard nipples.

"Then let's talk about what you want," he said as he brushed his thumbs across her erect nipples. "And I know sleep ain't it."

"Douglas," she moaned. God, he loved how she said his name. He stroked her nipples again and she breathed his name as she arched her back. "What do you want, Crystal?" he whispered, then licked her earlobe. "What are you going to do?"

"Stop it," she said. "Please. Don't. Stop."

Douglas replaced his thumbs with his lips and tongue. "Dooouglasss," she gasped, and reached for his hardness. As he licked and sucked her nipples, she stroked his erection back and forth nearly bringing him to climax with her expert touch.

"Need you. Need to be inside you now," he growled.

"But what are you going to do tomorrow?" she asked. *Oh, she was cruel,* Douglas thought. His brain was mush. He didn't give a damn about tomorrow when she had her hand right there tonight.

"Crystal," he gritted. "Crystal."

She stroked him slower, feeling him get harder and harder. Douglas's knees quivered and had he been standing, he would've fallen flat on his face. "Is this all about getting my land?" she asked as she reached for a condom with her free hand.

"Hell no," he exclaimed. Crystal opened the condom and rolled it in place. She pulled him into her hot and awaiting body. Douglas slowly pumped in and out, thrusting his hips into her as he covered her mouth with his. Hungrily, he sucked her tongue as she ground against him. Her hot wetness made it hard to hold back his climax. He wanted to teach her a lesson, but once again he'd been schooled. Crystal took control of his body in ways that he'd never imagined. He'd almost expected a timid lover and she was anything but.

Douglas howled as he exploded from the inside out and she tightened herself around him as she reached her own climax. Wrapping up in each other's arms, neither of them could move, talk, or do any worrying about the question that still hung in the air. What was going to happen in the morning?

The incessant ringing of the telephone and the doorbell woke the couple up Sunday morning. Crystal hadn't slept so late in months, hadn't been so at peace in God knows how long, and if she had half the brain that her family thought she did, she wouldn't be in Douglas Wellington's arms smiling as if what happened between them last night was normal.

"Morning," he said, his already deep voice a few octaves lower. "Or is it afternoon?"

"Mmm," Crystal said as she looked over his shoulder at the alarm clock on the nightstand. That couldn't be right. It was twelve-thirty. "Damn it." That's why the phone was ringing, and knowing Dena, she was ringing the doorbell as well. "Don't move," she said.

"I have no plans to do so," he said, attempting to thwart Crystal's effort to move.

"The door," she said.

"You're naked."

Crystal wiggled out of his arms and grabbed her robe from the end of the bed. "Now I'm not." Rushing down the hall to the front door, Crystal prayed it was one of the Starlight girls at the door, but it was indeed her lawyer. Dena had her finger on the doorbell and her BlackBerry to her ear as Crystal opened the door.

"Hi, Dena," she said, attempting to keep her voice cool and even. "I was . . ."

"In bed with that man, huh? I knew this was going to happen. I knew this was a bad idea, and if we lose this land, Erin and Joel are going to kill me." Dena reached into her oversized gray handbag and handed Crystal a legal form.

"What is this?"

"An injunction. While you were getting ready to do . . . whatever, I was in court Friday. Legally, they can't touch this land for three months. Now what we have to do is prove that this farm is a value to the community and provides more than that business park will. And here's something else for you to think about," Dena said, thrusting her finger in Crystal's face. "Some of the city council are in Welco's back pocket and if Waylon Terrell is involved, they might try to use eminent domain to get this land. Did you think about that before you hopped into bed with Douglas Wellington the third?"

That was just the reality check she needed, Crystal decided. But she still needed to know what Dena and her mother weren't telling her. "Do you want some coffee? Because we still need to talk," Crystal asked.

"Is that man still here?"

"Dena."

"Crystal, you're playing with a very hot fire that's going to burn you in the end. Don't repeat history."

"What history?" she asked.

Dena folded her arms and glared at Crystal. "Ask him why his father wanted this land so badly. These Wellington men and their ilk are ruthless and your mother and I have the scars to prove it. I was really hoping you'd be smart enough to stay out of the fray."

"I don't understand. So, this is some personal vendetta?" Crystal's head throbbed as she crossed over to the coffeemaker. Dena glanced at the nearly empty bottle of Jack Daniels, the two glasses, and the shorts. She didn't say anything, but Crystal felt her eyes burning holes in her back.

"Listen," Crystal said as she pressed the button to start the coffeemaker. "I was . . . we had too much to drink."

"Maybe you did, but don't fool yourself into thinking that this man won't do whatever he has to to get what he wants," Dena said.

"Well," Douglas said from the doorway of the kitchen, "I thought my name was being dragged through the mud." Standing in the kitchen—shirtless—he couldn't help but recall the previous night's activities. And what he wouldn't do for a repeat. But the lawyer had to go.

"What are you doing in here?" Crystal asked through clenched teeth.

"Obviously eavesdropping," Dena said, not hiding her disdain for the younger Wellington.

"I was thirsty," he replied.

"I'll bet," Dena said. "Crystal, remember what I said." Then she pushed past Douglas and headed out to her car.

Crystal glared at him. "I asked you to stay in the bedroom," she said.

"I was thirsty, and how was I to know that you and your attorney were having a bash Douglas fest? So, you just used me last night, huh?"

"Are we really going there?" she shot back.

"No," he replied in all seriousness. "But I do have a question for you."

Crystal grabbed a coffee mug from the cabinet above her head and said, "What is it?"

"Do you share your attorney's view of me? Do you think last night was about the land and this business deal that I want to happen out here?"

Crystal set her mug on the counter and then turned to face Douglas. "I don't know. But I do know we have an injunction against your company." She pulled the papers from the pocket of her robe and handed them to him.

Douglas set them aside. "I'll look at that later, but I want an answer to my question." He closed the space between them and when he was less than an arm's length away from her, Crystal wanted to have an instant replay of last night. But somehow, the light of day made her realize what was really at stake.

Still, being that close to him, knowing how he could handle her body made it hard to think, breathe, and comprehend. "What was the question?" she asked.

"Do you think I'm using you?"

She shook her head. "Last night was amazing for both of us. But we know it can never happen again. I think you should take those papers and leave now."

"Is that what you want or what your lawyer said you should do?" He reached out to stroke her cheek and Crystal turned her head away from his hand as if she didn't want to be burned. Then she rounded the island in the middle of the kitchen, beginning to clean up their discarded whiskey glasses. When she grabbed the bottle and started to throw it away, Douglas crossed over to her and took it from her hands. "Since you're kicking me out, I'm going to need this."

"And a shirt. The last thing I need is one of the Starlight girls seeing you walking out of here looking like that," Crystal said, giving him a slow once-over. How was it that he looked even more delicious to her extremely sober eyes?

"The least I could do before I leave is help you clean up and cook brunch."

Crystal cocked her head to the side and slapped her hand on her hip. "You cook?"

"At times I have," he said, leaning back on the counter opposite where Crystal stood. Knowing she was naked underneath that short robe made him bubble with desire. But, he'd play her game—for now.

"What are you going to cook?" she asked as she loaded the dishwasher.

Douglas crossed over to the refrigerator and opened it. He wasn't surprised to see the fresh eggs, vegetables, and cheese in bowls. Knowing Crystal, she probably picked the veggies and gathered eggs daily.

"How about omelets, grits, and toast with some of these preserves you have back here?"

"What do you know about preserves?" Crystal asked, clearly impressed.

"I grew up here too," he said. "I bet we would've been friends if you lived in the city."

"I doubt it," she replied. "I bet you wouldn't have given me a second look in high school and you probably would've pulled my hair in elementary school."

Douglas set the ingredients for the omelets on the island and gazed at Crystal. "You're probably right. But you know why little boys do those things, right?"

"Because they're little jerks?"

"That's how we show that we like a girl. That and this," he said, quickly crossing over to her and taking Crystal in his arms. He kissed her fast, hard, and deep. The chorus of moans that escaped her throat were like a melody to Douglas's ears. He started to untie the sash on her robe when there was a knock at the back door.

"Damn," he said as they broke their kiss. "Is it always busy like this over here?"

Crystal ran the tip of her tongue across her swollen bottom lip. "I have things that I normally do on Sundays," she said as she crossed over to the door. It was MJ and Renda standing on the back porch with their gardening tools. Sunday was the day Crystal and the girls worked in the flower garden.

She opened the door and stepped outside. "Hi, girls," she said.

"Miss Crystal," MJ said. "Are you all right?"

"I'm fine, I just had a long night."

Renda folded her arms across her chest and

tilted her head to the side. "That man is in there, isn't he?"

"Renda," MJ said, slapping her sister on the shoulder. "That's none of our business." She turned to Crystal. "You like him, don't you?"

"I . . . uh . . . am just trying to work with him to save this farm and Starlight House," Crystal replied.

"Like Halle Berry in that James Bond movie," MJ said with a gleam in her eyes. "Is it working?"

"Why don't you two join us for brunch?" Crystal suggested.

"Or," Renda said, "you can bring him to the rose garden after you eat and we can bash him in the head with a rock and then get . . ."

"What did you two watch last night?" Crystal asked with a laugh.

Renda and MJ looked at each other. "There was a James Bond marathon on," MJ said.

"You two do know that things like that only work in those over the top movies, right?"

Renda shrugged. "Then what are you doing? Isn't this some Lifetime Movie Network movie plot?"

"No," Crystal said, growing tired of hearing that analogy about having Douglas at the farm. "Listen, I'm going to do whatever I have to do—aside from pretending I'm a Bond girl—to save this farm and your home."

"We believe you, but some of the others are scared," Renda said.

Crystal nodded and hugged both of the girls. "Everything is going to work out, I promise," she said, hoping that she would be able to keep her word.

"We're going to go, but if you do bring Mr. Wellington to the garden, we won't knock him out."

"That's good to know," Crystal replied with a laugh. As Renda and MJ headed for the rose garden, Crystal was left to wonder if she was doing the right thing by those girls or if she was setting them up for failure by not listening to Dena and tackling this problem in a more professional manner.

Slowly, she returned to the kitchen and was surprised to see that Douglas had finished preparing their brunch. On the island there were perfectly folded tomato and spinach omelets, cheese toast points, potatoes, peppers, and cheese, and warm biscuits smothered in peach preserves.

"This is a lot of food," Crystal said.

"I thought we were going to have guests. You and those girls are close and if they wanted to join us, I wanted to make sure there was enough food to share," he said as he picked up a piece of potato and held it out to Crystal to sample.

Watching her as she closed her mouth around the fork, he smiled, thinking about those lips around his erection and how good it felt.

"Not bad," she said. "Not bad at all."

"Thank you," he replied. "I told you that there's more to me than my millions."

Crystal took another potato slice and popped it in her mouth. "Is that so?"

"Yes," he said as he placed an omelet on a plate and some potatoes. "Do you need more convincing?"

She took a big bite of her breakfast and smiled. "Why don't you prove me wrong and tell me that you're not going to come after my farm. Otherwise, you're still everything I thought you were."

Douglas clutched his chest as if he was having a heart attack like Fred Sanford. "You know, business is business, but I'd like to think that we're getting to know each other on a different level."

"But we're still at an impasse," Crystal said, pushing her plate away. No matter how good the food was, she couldn't pretend that the gorilla in the room had moved an inch.

"Crystal, I'm not going to make promises to abandon this deal, but I can look at some things and see if there is a way we can coexist on this property," he said as he spooned grits onto his omelet.

"That's not a viable option," she said. "This land is important, not just to me and my family, but—"

"I know the story," he said. "You've been beating me over the head with it, but there has to be some sort of compromise."

"Yeah," she said. "The only compromise that I can live with is you finding another place to build this business park."

Douglas stepped closer to Crystal, feeling the heat of her breath as he stood in front of her. "Business is business, Crystal. This land is the perfect location for this business park."

"As you've said more than a million times, but what about what this land does now, gives a home to girls no one else cares about, provides food for the hungry and the throwaway people in this county that Welco—"

"Wants to provide jobs for. You and I want to do the same things."

"No, we don't," she snapped. "You want to make money and I want to make a difference. It's not the same thing."

Douglas paused, taking a fork full of food into his mouth. She wasn't totally wrong—the business park was not a charity. Yes, he wanted to make money, but what businessman didn't? Why should he continue to apologize for that? As soon as he found the file, he'd find out why this land was so important to his dad.

"You know what?" he said. "Enjoy your food. I have some work I need to take care of."

Crystal threw her food in the trash can and stormed down the hall, slamming into the bathroom and ignoring the sounds of Douglas dressing in her bedroom.

Chapter 11

By the time Douglas had dressed and left Crystal's house, he realized that the person who could give him answers had been stonewalling him and if he wanted the truth, he was going to have to contact an unlikely source—Crystal's attorney, Dena. There was something about the way she spat out Waylon's name that spoke of an untold history that was more than business.

Pulling the legal forms from his jeans pocket, he typed Dena's office address into his cell phone. Then he headed to the cottage to take a shower. He hoped that he would be able to find Dena, however since she'd already delivered an injunction on a Sunday, and he figured she wouldn't still be in her office. But he'd try there first anyway.

What is it about this farm that drives everybody crazy? he thought as he hopped into the shower.

In his case, he knew what at Hughes Farm was driving him insane and she was across the way in the big house probably plotting with her lawyer to stop Welco.

As much as he hated to admit it, the short time that he'd spent at the farm showed him that the place was special and had an impact on the community. Where would those girls go without Hughes Farm? Why hadn't his dad taken this into consideration before he decided that he had to have this farm for his business park?

Following his shower, Douglas dressed in a pair of khakis and a stripped oxford shirt. As he slipped on his leather loafers, there was a knock at the door.

"What a surprise," he said when he opened the door to Crystal standing on the front steps.

"I guess you're on your way out," she said as she gave him a cool once-over.

"I have some work to do. What's up?"

"Renda and MJ wanted to show you the rose garden," she said. "But if you're working today, you can see it later."

"I have to go into town, but I'll be back," he said. "And I'd love to see the garden."

"I'm sorry about earlier," Crystal said quietly. "I know what you were saying about business and whatnot. I don't like it, but I know you're trying to do your job. Even though you're the boss and I'm sure you could change things if you wanted to."

"If I didn't have a board, maybe. But this is bigger than me saying yes or no."

Crystal held her hand up to stop him from going further. "I don't want to argue with you and that's where this conversation is headed. So," she said, "I'll just see you when you get back."

Douglas closed the space between him and Crystal, fighting the overwhelming urge he had to kiss her. "I will do that and maybe we can share dinner without fighting."

"Maybe," she said. "I have dinner with the Starlight girls on Sundays because the girls get dressed up and practice fine-dining skills."

"Then join me for dessert."

Crystal folded her arms and started to say no, but as she stared into his eyes and felt a familiar feeling of yearning, she agreed. "Will this be another one of your homemade dishes?"

"No. But you will enjoy it anyway. A chocolate cake from Main Street Café," he said.

"Sounds good. I'll make coffee and we can talk about anything but Welco's land grab," she said.

"Agreed, but we still have to see each other in court on Monday."

"Then we will deal with it on Monday," she said as she turned toward the steps.

"Wait," he said, reaching out and touching her shoulder. Crystal turned around and speared him with a meaningful gaze. He touched her chin, lifting her mouth to his. In one swift motion, he captured her mouth in a soul-numbing kiss that she couldn't resist if she wanted to. As his tongue danced with hers, Crystal wanted to forget that he wasn't the man of her dreams, wasn't simply her lover and that Dena said she needed to avoid being personal with him. She wanted to forget that he was the CEO of the corporation that wanted what her family had worked so hard for, and that she'd shared the best night of her life with him. Wanted to forget that his kiss was addictive and left her wanting more and more. His hands, stroking her back, made her feel like pure gold. But this had to stop. She pulled back from him. "What was that for?" she asked breathlessly.

"Because you're simply irresistible," he said. "And, I figured if I didn't kiss you now, I might not get the chance later."

"You're bringing me chocolate cake, you just may get that chance again," she said with a smile on her kiss-swollen lips.

Douglas pulled her against his chest and brushed a stray strand of hair from her forehead. Her heartbeat sped up as his fingers brushed across her skin. "You know I'm going to bring you chocolate every day now."

"Really?" she quipped. "And when that chocolate sticks to my hips, will you still be coming around?"

"I'm not that shallow, and the only thing that's

going to stick to those hips is going to be me," he replied boldly.

With another quick kiss, Douglas and Crystal said good-bye. As he drove into town, all Douglas could think about was dessert with Crystal when he should've been focused on his impromptu meeting with Dena. Something told him that she wasn't going to be easily charmed.

The first thing Crystal did when she returned to her house was call her mother.

"Hello," Joel said when he answered the phone.

Crystal smiled at the sound of her father's voice. "Hi, Daddy," she said.

"Baby girl," he replied. "How are you doing?"

"I'm all right," she said. "Where's Mommy?"

"She's down on the beach. What's going on with Welco coming after the farm again?"

Crystal sighed. "Daddy, I'm going to handle this."

"Crystal, I trust that you will and I'm going to hope that you listen to Dena in dealing with this. You have this idyllic view of life and you think other people share your view, but the Wellington family is not to be trusted."

"Why?"

"Because they've been after our land for a long time and I feel Douglas Wellington's dead hand in this."

"You don't think his son could be different?" Crystal asked, hoping that she wasn't making a mistake getting emotionally involved with Douglas.

"No. I think he's just as slimy as his father and you need to steer clear of him."

Too late for that, she thought. "Dad, why do they want this land so badly?"

"Spite."

"Care to elaborate?"

Joel sighed and said, "All you need to know is that you should stay far away from Wellington and Welco. This is an old fight that I thought ended when the old man died. Your mother and I will be in court tomorrow to make sure they don't win. That little boy sounds like a carbon copy of his father; he wants what he wants and doesn't give a damn about who he has to roll over to get it."

Crystal wanted to tell her dad that Douglas wasn't anything like that—that he was sweet and caring.

"Daddy," she said. "Be straight with me."

"This is something that has nothing to do with you other than the fact that your last name is Hughes."

"Don't you think I need to know what's going on? Especially since I have to deal with Douglas Wellington in court soon?"

"Your mother and I will be in town for the first hearing," he said. "Then, we'll explain everything."

Crystal sighed and then told her father goodbye. Suddenly, having dessert with Douglas wasn't looking so appetizing.

Douglas wasn't sure if he was doing the right thing by showing up at Dena's house. He'd driven to her office and she hadn't been there. He needed to talk to her and he wasn't taking no for an answer. Hopefully, she wouldn't call the cops. He parked his truck on the street in front of her ranch style home and slowly walked to the front door, which was open. Dena was sitting on the sofa typing away on her laptop. Douglas knocked on the screen door, causing her head to snap up.

Dena set the laptop on the wooden coffee table in front of her and walked to the door with a scowl on her face. "What are you doing here, Mr. Wellington?" she all but hissed.

"Good afternoon, Ms. Hopkins. I'd like to talk to you," he said.

"We shouldn't have any contact unless your attorney is present."

"This isn't about the case," he said.

"Then we have nothing to discuss, so kindly get off my porch," she said in a sarcastically sweet tone.

Douglas smiled at her and folded his arms across his chest. "I'm not leaving until you tell me the history between you and my godfather, Waylon Terrell, and why my father wanted Hughes Farm so badly."

Dena huffed at the mention of Waylon's name and folded her arms. "If you want that information then I suggest you go and talk to Waylon. Or are you certain that he's not going to tell you the truth?"

"Why wouldn't he?"

Dena leaned forward and glared at him. "Waylon Terrell wouldn't know the truth if it bit him on the end of his nose. Tell me something—what game are you trying to run on Crystal? See, she's idealistic and believes the yarn about Hughes Farm that her family has spun over the years. But I, like your father, know the value of that land. I told my friends Joel and Erin that I wouldn't let corporate scum like your father take over that land and I mean it. You're not going to play Crystal."

"What I'm doing is a business deal. It's not personal—for me—but it seems to be for you."

"Little boy," Dena said, "I know this game you're running. What did Waylon call it? *Heart and Mine*, capture her heart and then everything else is mine. Why don't you run along and ask your godfather about that. Now, leave. I'll see you in court."

She slammed the door in his face with such force that the glass rattled. "Damn," Douglas muttered, then turned and headed back to his truck. As he climbed in and sat behind the wheel, he pulled out his cell phone and called Waylon.

"Trey, what's going on?"

"We need to talk. Can you meet me at the Main Street Café?"

"When?"

"Now."

"What's going on?"

"I'll wait for you," he said, then disconnected the call. Douglas couldn't help but wonder what the deal was between Waylon and Dena.

When he arrived at the café, which was nearly empty, the first thing Douglas did was order the cake that he and Crystal would share and a large latte with an extra shot of espresso.

"You need some extra energy today, huh, Mr. Wellington?" the barista asked as she handed him the drink.

"Something tells me that this is going to be a long evening," he said as he took the cup and handed her a five-dollar tip. Then he found a seat at a table near the door and waited for Waylon. When his godfather finally arrived, Douglas was filled with questions and doubt.

"Trey," Waylon said as he sat across from him, "why did you feel the need to drag me away from the Golf Channel?"

"What happened between you and Dena Hopkins?"

Waylon leaned back in his chair and chuckled. "She's representing Hughes Farm, isn't she?"

Douglas nodded.

"Is she still fine?"

Douglas shrugged. "It's hard to tell because every time she sees me, she's scowling, frowning, or looking like she wants to slap the hell out of me. And when I bring up your name, it's even worse."

"You have kicked a hornet's nest with this," Waylon said. "And I was hoping you'd never have to get involved in all of this."

"So, that's why you took the file?"

"This is the second time you've accused me of stealing. One more time and I'm going to treat you like I've never changed your diaper," he replied forcefully.

Douglas threw his hands up. "No disrespect, but the file isn't the only thing that's miss—"

Waylon cut him off. "Your father and Crystal's mother dated for a little while. I met Dena through them. We were young, bored, and a little reckless. Your father fell hard for Erin Hamilton. But one day, she met Joel Hughes and started working on the farm with him. They fell in love and that was the end of Erin and Doug. He never really got over losing her to that "farm boy." Then he met your mother. I thought that was the end of his obsession with Erin."

"It wasn't?"

"You know what happened with your parents."

Douglas sighed and nodded.

Waylon had witnessed Doug's parents' tumultuous marriage with both sides having affairs and doing other scandalous things for money. What they failed to do was take care of their son. Douglas spent more time with Waylon and various nannies than he did with his parents. His father had always been working, building Welco from the bottom up, and Evelyn wasn't happy about the fact that her husband didn't have time to be with her. He'd stopped being the fun man she'd married once they returned to his hometown. She'd never known why, but Waylon knew. He pondered what to tell his godson as he'd sat there staring at him.

"Trey, this was all about a woman. Listen, you and I both know Doug didn't like to lose and when he wanted something or someone, nothing could stop him."

"Then why did he marry my mother?" Douglas felt like a child, as if he was finding out that Superman wasn't real and Santa was just a big fat lie.

"Part of his plan. He wanted Erin to see the life

she could've had. To his dismayed surprise, she was already happy with the life she had."

"So, he wanted to take over the farm to punish her?"

"Her and her new husband," Waylon said. "But you've put this in motion and one thing was right about your father's plan. That farm is prime land for development."

"Are you saying I can't stop this?"

Waylon shook his head. "That's what it looks like, son. Dena thinks that I was using her because of her close relationship with Erin and Joel and hates me to this day, but I stopped your father back then."

"How?"

Waylon rose to his feet and started for the door. "Remember when I took off for a few years?"

Douglas stood as well and nodded. "Yeah, that's when I got to see that Welco was all Dad cared about firsthand."

"Well, that was my exile so that I couldn't explain to Dena what I'd done and ask her to marry me. I loved that woman and wanted a life with her. Your dad wasn't going to allow that to happen. He took great pleasure in spinning a yarn about why I left. If he couldn't be happy, no one else was going to be happy either."

"And you didn't feel the need to tell me this? Is that why you wanted me to come back and take over this damn company? So I wouldn't be happy either?"

"No. You know I don't operate like that. I wanted you here because your father was dying. Part of me hoped he'd come clean and make peace with you about everything. And I also knew that Welco wouldn't be the same without a Wellington running things. As much as you hated the corporate world, I knew you could do this."

"You also knew I didn't want to do this," Douglas shouted, then grabbed his godfather's arm. "I found something else. Dad kept a diary and it's gone too. How much trouble would Welco be in if that gets out?"

Waylon looked down at Douglas's hand and shook his head. "I'm not sure what the contents of Douglas's diary are, but knowing your father, it's nothing good. He had a lot of animosity toward many people in town. If he recorded that and it falls into the wrong hands, the results could be devastating for the company."

Douglas dropped his hand and sighed. He wondered if the diary's contents would hurt Crystal as well. Douglas was a bit surprised that he cared more about Crystal's feelings than Welco's stock prices or the reaction of the board. This was not how things were supposed to go.

* * *

Crystal paced back and forth in her living room, still reeling from the things her father said about Douglas's dad. He'd wanted the land out of spite, so was Douglas really carrying out his father's plan for vengeance? What about the time they'd spent together? Was he like his godfather, who according to Dena would use a woman's heart to get what he wanted? Had she been a big fool and now needed Mommy and Daddy to save her?

"This is nuts," she mumbled. "I don't even know how to bring this up to him. Should I?" Crystal chewed her bottom lip and continued to pace. As she was about to walk into the kitchen to get a glass of water, the doorbell rang, causing her to nearly jump out of her skin. She was happy she didn't break another glass.

Crossing over to the door, she wasn't entirely pleased to see Douglas there. "Hi," he said. "Hope you're ready for dessert."

Crystal tried to smile, but her heart wasn't in it. "We need to have a serious discussion."

"I know," he said as he stepped inside. "With or without chocolate?"

"I think we're going to need all the chocolate in that cake and some wine," she said as she took the box from his hand and headed into the kitchen. Crystal set the cake on the counter and crossed over to the cabinet to grab a bottle of Chardonnay.

"Got anything stronger?" he asked as she handed him the bottle and corkscrew.

"We don't need anything stronger," she said. "Douglas, what are we actually doing?"

"I don't know," he replied honestly, the conversation he had with Waylon replaying in his mind.

"You're the CEO, the boss, just kill the deal," Crystal pleaded, silently adding, *And prove my dad wrong about you.*

"I wish it were that simple," he moaned.

"What happens now?" she asked. "We have a court date tomorrow and one of us is going to be unhappy about the outcome."

Douglas sighed and took a sip of the wine. "That's true. Are we going to be able to separate business and pleasure or are we going to be like Batman and Catwoman?"

"Catwoman?"

He set his wineglass down and tilted his head to the side. "I'd love to see you in leather with a whip."

Crystal raised her eyebrow at him. "You're disgusting," she said, then broke out in laughter.

Douglas wished things could remain that way between them. She was going to hate him when the court case played out because he couldn't back away from the site now, not until he got to the bottom of why his father wanted Hughes Farm so badly. He needed to find that diary. If for no other reason than to show the board that this had been a bad idea because of his father's inane hatred for the Hughes family.

"Are you going to cut the cake or stand here and look at it?" she asked after catching his gaze.

"Let's take it outside. You were supposed to show me some mythical place here on the farm," he said.

"All right," she said, licking her lips and making Douglas's teeth chatter with longing. "I'll get a blanket and you cut two big slices of cake."

"Yes, ma'am," he said, offering her a mock salute.

When Crystal dashed down the hall, Douglas couldn't take his eyes off her shapely backside, couldn't stop staring at her long legs. She was exquisite.

"Ready?" she asked when she returned to the kitchen with a blanket. "And you might want to leave those loafers here."

Douglas looked down at his shoes and then caught a glimpse of Crystal's bare feet. The red polish on her toes made him think of cherries and he wanted nothing more than to lick and suck her perfect toes.

When she noticed that he wasn't taking his shoes off, Crystal shrugged her shoulders. "Suit yourself, but it's going to be really hard to get that dirt and mud off your thousand-dollar shoes."

"And how do you know they were a thousand dollars?" he asked as he kicked them off.

"Because anything less would be so unlike you."

"Is that so?" he said as he placed the shoes in the corner.

"You are the picture of a silver spoon boy," Crystal retorted as she opened the back door. She stopped short and Douglas's hot body pressed against her and she gasped when he wrapped his arms around her waist.

"I guess it's a good thing I forgot the cake on the counter or I'd have to lick chocolate from your neck and back."

She turned around quickly, poised to say something, but Douglas took advantage of having her in his arms and kissed her—slow, deep, passionate. Crystal held him tightly as she sucked his sweet tongue and moaned. This, she told herself, would be the last time she would be able to kiss him like this. The last time they could give in to passion without thinking about consequences.

Douglas broke the kiss and stared deep into her eyes. "Crystal," he intoned. "We'd better get out of here before I turn around and take you back to your bedroom and never let you go."

Turning her head away from him, she said, "Get the cake." Crystal wished she could allow him to take her into her bedroom and hide away from the court case, the personal vendettas, and her parents. Her parents! They couldn't find Douglas on the farm. Not after what her dad told her. The last thing she'd be able to explain to them was how she fell in love with the enemy.

But was he really her enemy? Maybe Douglas was simply doing the same thing she was doing—carrying on a family legacy. But why did the two things their families wanted mean they couldn't have each other?

Douglas opened the door and grabbed the cake while Crystal chewed her bottom lip and stared off into the woods. "Are you all right?" he asked, putting an arm around her shoulder.

"Douglas, we're fighting a losing battle. I can't fall in love with you at night and fight you in court during the day," she said as they walked slowly.

"So, what are you saying?"

"This is the end," she said. "This weekend was a wonderful distraction, but I can't let you stop me from saving my family's land."

"I'd be lying if I said I didn't want to stop you. But the truth of the matter is, I don't want to lose you either."

"Then stop this madness. You can't have me and my land," she said. "Stop right here."

Douglas glanced around the rose garden,

inhaling the fragrant perfume of the flowers and smiling. "I guess a man should never send you roses to impress you."

"If a man wants to impress me, all he has to do is understand my love for this land."

Douglas sighed. "Can we simply eat the cake? Nothing can change today. Trust me, I've tried."

Crystal, against her better judgment, unfurled the blanket and sat down. Douglas joined her and reached over and pulled a rose from a bush.

"Cutting roses is prohibited in the garden," she said when she took it from his hand.

"Is that why you have a vase full every morning?" he asked, grinning.

God, why did he have to have such amazing dimples? Crystal turned away from him and grabbed the cake slices. "I can do that," she said as she broke off a piece of the cake. Douglas leaned in and sucked the cake from her fingers.

"Hey!" she exclaimed as he licked the chocolate icing from her finger. "Ooh, you shouldn't do that."

"The icing is the best part," he said, then reached for a piece of cake and brushed it across her lips. "Now, let me get a taste of that." He leaned into her and slowly licked the chocolate from her lips. Then he nibbled her bottom lip, causing her to moan and forget about eating the cake. Douglas leaned her back on the plush blanket, breaking the kiss and stroking her cheek.

"If this is the end for us, then shouldn't we make it count?" he asked as he nimbly unbuttoned her blouse.

Before Crystal could protest or push away his hand, Douglas's hot mouth covered her breast. She silently chided herself for not wearing a bra and that lasted about thirty seconds before she gave in to the pleasure of his tongue. Douglas eased his hand between her thighs, touching her femininity through her wet panties. She screamed his name and arched her hips into his touch. He pushed the crotch of her panties to the side and slipped his finger between her wet folds of flesh until he found her throbbing pearl. Leaning into her, he replaced his finger with his tongue, licking, sucking, and kissing her passionately until she howled in delight.

Grasping the back of his head, Crystal expelled a satisfied sigh as she exploded from the inside. "Don't stop," she cried.

"I'm just getting started," he said as he took a brief break from tasting her sweetness. "Lift your hips." Crystal followed his command and Douglas slipped her panties off, stashing them in his pocket. Then he quickly shrugged out of his slacks and wrapped her legs around his waist. The moment he felt her wetness against the tip of his erection, Douglas wanted to bury himself deep inside her and forget the court case, forget the business park, and forget everything but the woman in his arms.

"I need you," she moaned. "Want you."

Douglas responded with a hot kiss, covering her mouth with his and drawing her tongue into his mouth. She pressed her body against his and he forgot about protection. He spread her thighs and pressed into her. Reveling in the hot wetness between her thighs, drowning deep in the flesh to flesh contact. Her moans punctuated the air as Douglas pumped in and out. She matched his strokes, adding a twist or grind to make him scream out her name. Crystal wowed him, thrilled him, and made his toes curl. And as much as he knew he needed to pull back, needed to pull out, he couldn't and wouldn't. He reached his climax inside her, unprotected. Douglas had never been so reckless, so careless, and so calm. He even thought about seeing Crystal's belly swelled with his son or daughter. He'd never had those thoughts about a woman—ever.

Crystal, on the other hand, was mortified. Had she really just had unprotected sex with Douglas? With a man who she was sure had his share of women all over the county and possibly the country? "Why didn't you protect us?" she demanded as she punched him in the center of his chest.

"Look," he exclaimed as he grabbed her wrist when she went to slug him again. "I just had an insurance physical a month ago and I have a clean bill of health."

She narrowed her eyes at him. "I don't imagine you were told that you're sterile."

Douglas shook his head and chuckled softly. "What about you? Healthy and sterile?"

"I'm healthy, but that's not the point. I don't want to have your baby," she exclaimed as she pushed him off her and rose to her feet quickly. For a moment, she'd forgotten that she was naked. "This is not good."

Douglas handed her the blouse they'd discarded earlier. "Maybe you ought to cover up and calm down."

"Calm down?" she hurled as she snatched her shirt from his hand. "My life could be really . . . Oh my God, how would I explain this to my parents?"

"Aren't you a grown woman?"

"Yes, and I certainly didn't act like one being all irresponsible with you. I . . ."

Douglas stood up and closed the space between them. "What's the problem? If you were pregnant with my child do you think it would ruin your life?"

"Yes. And I wouldn't put it past you to use my

womb as a bargaining tool in this land grab of yours!" she spat.

"That's not fair."

"This was another mistake. No wonder my parents think they have to come here and fight this battle. You have to go, Douglas."

"Wait a minute."

Crystal snatched her skirt on and stomped back to the main house.

Chapter 12

Douglas should've known when to say when. He should've just gotten dressed, headed back to the cottage, packed his clothes, and left. Crystal made it clear that the connection they had was a shallow physical one, and with what Waylon told him, he knew trying to be with her wasn't the best idea ever. But as soon as he zipped his pants, Douglas dashed toward the house, not giving a damn about the logical things he should've done. He banged on the back door as if he was trying to warn Crystal about a fire. In a way he was—the fire of longing and desire that was building like an inferno deep inside him. He wanted her more than he wanted the land, the CEO title at Welco, or his next breath. She had to understand that, even if that meant he had to lock her in that house until she realized that he genuinely loved her.

Crystal snatched the door open, her eyes red from crying, and asked, "Why are you here?"

"Because you don't understand what I'm feeling right now," he said.

"And just what are you feeling and why should I give a damn?" she snapped.

Douglas moved closer to her until they stood inch to inch. "You should give a damn because I know that I'm falling for you and I'll do whatever it takes to make you see that."

She tilted her head to the side, thinking about the words Dena said to her hours ago. Was this all a part of the grand plan? Under different circumstances, she would've fallen into his arms, told him that her heart was beating the same song. But she couldn't trust what he said nor what she felt. Lust. That's all it was. Plain and simple, it was a lustful yearning that she felt for him and that would never be enough to make her give him the main thing he wanted.

"You're a liar," she whispered. "You're falling for this land and falling for the future business park you have planned. You're falling for the idea of me being silly enough to say I love you and sign those papers. That's not going to happen and you should leave before I call the sheriff to escort you off my property."

"Oh, yeah, call Ron and see how that works

out for you," Douglas spat. "You invited me here, remember?"

"My mistake," she said. He took her face into his hands and forced her to look at him. "This was a huge mistake," she insisted.

"Why? Because you're feeling something more for me, just like I am for you?" he asked as he stroked her cheek.

"Stop," she said as she turned her face away from him. Douglas didn't stop. Instead, he sought out her full lips, kissing her tenderly and slowly. He wished his kiss told her the truth about what he was feeling, told her that he wasn't trying to use her, wasn't trying to play with her emotions. He wished he could take her away from this farm, this town, and go someplace where they could simply be Crystal and Douglas. A place where her parents and his parents never met and never had their battle. When he released her lips, he read something in her eyes that gave him hope.

"Douglas," she whispered.

"Yes?"

"I just can't . . ." Crystal stopped when she heard a commotion on the front porch.

"Just what in the hell are you doing here?" Crystal heard Dena exclaim as she and Douglas rushed to the front door.

"It's wonderful to see you as well," Waylon said as he gave Dena a slow once-over. He smiled at her, and Crystal could see that her attorney was fuming underneath his gaze.

"Up to your same old tricks?" Dena snapped as she looked from Douglas to Waylon.

"I'd like to talk to you," Waylon said, stepping closer to Dena.

She threw her hand up in his face. "Don't come a step closer to me," she snapped.

"What's going on?" Crystal asked. "And who are you?"

Waylon glanced up at Crystal and Douglas. "You must be Crystal Hughes," Waylon said. "Waylon Terrell." He never took his eyes off Dena, who was dressed in a simple pair of black slacks and a sleeveless ivory shirt. Waylon remembered days when she showed off those lovely legs in cut-off denims. This serious Dena was still beautiful, but how could he convince her that he wasn't playing the cruel games that his best friend was known for? How could he explain to her that he too was a victim of Douglas Wellington Jr.?

"You should take your godson and leave," Dena said. "Crystal may not know the truth about you two, but I do." She jabbed her finger in his face and Waylon grasped her wrist. Crystal heard Dena gasp and saw a flicker of something—desire—cross her face. Really? Crystal wondered as she looked from Dena to Waylon. As if she remembered that the others were around, Dena snatched away and stalked over to Crystal. "Have you lost all that's left of your mind?"

"What do you mean?" Crystal asked.

"I mean that these two are trying to play you and you're just being a welcome mat for them."

"I'm doing no such thing," Crystal cried incredulously.

"Why do you think Waylon is here? He's giving his godson pointers and I'm willing to bet my practice on the fact that he's using the same dirty tricks his father used all of those years ago," she said, hurling her thumb in Waylon's direction. "They don't fight fair and you're a lightweight. Do you want to lose your family's land?"

"Of course not, but—"

"Then get them off this property and let me handle this through the courts," she snapped.

Waylon walked over to Crystal and Dena. "Does this have to be ugly?" he asked, focusing on Dena.

Crystal saw a change in her attorney's body language as she whirled around and faced the tall ebony man. There was more than a legal battle going on between those two—that much was clear.

"I have nothing to say to you," Dena said.

Like Billy Dee Williams in a classic movie, Waylon stroked her cheek and smiled. "I have something to say to you. I'm sorry."

"Tell me something I don't know," she snapped.

"Why don't you take your tired-ass apology and leave?"

"I'm not going to do that because you need to hear the truth, finally," he said forcefully. Douglas and Crystal watched in rapt attention.

"Your friend told me the truth when you disappeared and left your check."

"My check?"

Dena glanced over her shoulder at Crystal. "I'm not doing this here."

"I never walked out on you—you left me first," Waylon said. "And why would I leave you a check?"

She glared at him, and as if something clicked in her head, she sighed. "You never knew, did you?" Dena asked quietly.

"Never knew what?"

As if she'd forgotten they had an audience, the unflappable Dena started to cry. "I was pregnant and *he* said you wanted nothing to do with my bastard child and that was why you left."

Waylon looked shell-shocked as well as he drew Dena into his arms. "I never knew and I would've never abandoned you."

"But you did," she said in a hushed tone, then slammed her fist against his chest. "I needed you and you weren't here for me."

"I didn't know, Dena."

"Would it have made a difference? I lost our child and suffered alone," she snapped.

"Don't you think I would've been there?" he exclaimed. "Dena, I loved you then and if you'd give me a chance, I'd prove to you that I love you now."

"Love me?" she asked. "You don't know the meaning of the word, and if you think your confession is going to change what's going to happen in court on Monday, you're wrong."

"I never gave a damn about this land or anything that Doug wanted to do out here. I tried to stop him because you're all I ever cared about. I don't know why you don't believe that."

She glared at him, dried the tears from her eyes as she spat, "You're a liar and that's all I need to believe."

Waylon, in a quick move that caught everyone off guard, lifted Dena over his shoulder and bounded toward his car—ignoring her demands to put her down.

"Wow," Douglas said as he walked over to Crystal. "That was intense."

"There seems to be a lot of history that we don't know about. Is Dena right? Was this a part of the Welco legal plan?"

"Seriously?"

Crystal raised her right eyebrow at him. "You should go," she said.

"You want to end up like them? Hating each other for years and not knowing where this could go? I can't live like that and I won't."

"Douglas, this isn't about us. This is about this land. At least that's what it looks like on the surface, but it seems as if this whole thing is bigger than either of us know."

"I don't give a damn about this land."

"But you've said many times that you can't call it off."

"And I can't turn off what I feel for you, either," he said.

"What are we supposed to do, then?" she said as he took a step toward her. "I can't let my girls down. You can't come in here and pretend that building on this land is going to benefit them or that you've had some change of heart."

"Give me a chance to make this right," he said as he reached out for her. Crystal didn't want to, but she fell into his embrace and she even believed that he would make things right between them. Still, she wondered if Dena and Waylon were a glimpse into the not-so-distant future with her and Douglas. There was no way she'd just allow him to win because she had feelings for him. Too many people depended on Hughes Farm, and just like he had family pride, she did too. "My parents are coming tomorrow and I don't think they need to find you here. So, for the last time, I'm asking you to leave."

"I don't think so," Douglas replied. "If you want me to walk away from us, I can tell you now that isn't going to happen."

"Why? Don't want to end up like your godfather? Really, Douglas, we have nothing else to . . ."

He pulled her into his arms and kissed her words away, replacing her bitter sentences with the sweetness of his tongue and the tenderness of his lips.

She moaned softly as he gently stroked her back and kissed her. Crystal pulled back from him, shaken and confused by what she was feeling. "Douglas," she said.

"Don't give up on us and don't let their past cloud our future."

"It's not that simple and you know that," she said, turning her back to him, willing her heart to stop beating so damned hard.

Douglas placed his hands on her shoulders and the heat from his touch made her shiver. "We're going to figure this out," he said, then brushed his lips against the back of her neck. She sighed, wishing that tomorrow morning wouldn't make them enemies again. But had there ever been more than sex between them? Was she being a fool like Dena said?

"I guess I'd better go," he said as he dropped his hands.

Crystal turned around and faced him. "Don't go yet," she said quietly. "Let's just pretend we're two normal people enjoying the land."

"Are you sure?"

Staring into his sparkling eyes, Crystal replied, "I'm not sure about anything anymore."

He drew her into his arms and gently kissed her forehead. Douglas knew two things for sure: he had to find his father's file and he had to convince the board to scrap the project.

As he glanced down at Crystal's radiant face, he knew the battle that he was about to confront would be well worth the risk. Maybe he could right the sins of his father and find the happiness that had eluded Douglas Wellington Jr. all of those years.

Chapter 13

Hours after Dena and Waylon left the farm, Douglas and Crystal sat on the back porch watching the sunset and sipping wine. He reached for her hand and held it as they sat in a comfortable silence.

"I see why you're so attached to this place," he said.

"No. We're not going there," she said, squeezing his hand. "Not until the morning."

"I've made a decision about tomorrow," he said. "I'm CEO of Welco and though scrapping this project is going to be a loss for our company, until I know what was behind my father's pursuit of this land, we're going to have to put a halt to the project."

Crystal's eyes widened in surprise and admiration. "Are you serious? How will you find that out?"

With his free hand, Douglas picked up his

wineglass and took a sip, then nodded. "My father, I'm learning, had some deep-seated issues with the town because of his past. Once I find out the truth, I have some changes to make."

"Why . . . ? What . . . ? I can't believe you're going to do this," she said. "How are you going to find out your father's true intentions?"

Douglas shrugged, pretending that he wasn't going to have to climb what amounted to Mount Everest to pull this off. "First, I have to find the leak in my office and get to the bottom of what was in Dad's diary."

"What do you mean a 'leak in your office'?" she asked.

Douglas set his wineglass aside and pulled Crystal onto his lap. He told her what happened the night he left the farm and went back to his office, revealing that his father's diary was missing. Then he told her about the conversation that he and his godfather had at the café. "Listen, if this was about business and business only, I wouldn't change my mind. Despite what you and others think about Welco, we have ethics. I'm not going to carry out my father's vendetta."

"I wish my parents wouldn't be so cryptic about the history between them, your father, and the farm."

"I'm thinking there are some answers in that diary and if someone makes the contents public, the fallout could be devastating for my company and my father's legacy," Douglas said as he reached out for her. "You know what—take a ride with me."

"Where to?"

"The one place where my father left a copy of everything," he said. "Our old house out in Waverly."

"Waverly?" she asked.

"I'll tell you the story on the way," he said as he held his hand out to Crystal.

"I would've never expected your family to even know Waverly existed," she said about the poorest part of the county.

"My grandparents weren't rich," he said as they walked to his truck. "When my father made his first million, he wanted to move them into a big house in Reeseville, but my grandfather was just as stubborn as my father and he refused to leave the house that he'd bought and paid for no matter where it was located. My grandfather and my father often argued about the fact that my dad seemed to forget where he came from."

"Wow," Crystal said, thinking about how much her family cherished their own history. That's why losing the farm was not an option.

Douglas shook his head and opened the door for Crystal. As he watched her climb into the vehicle, he hoped that whatever can of worms they were about to find wasn't going to ruin what they were trying to build.

"Do you think we should check on Dena and Waylon after we're done?" she asked as he slid behind the steering wheel.

"That might be a good idea. I'm a little worried about his safety. Dena's a tough woman."

"Please," Crystal said, stifling her laugh. "Waylon lifted her and pretty much kidnapped her."

"That wasn't a kidnapping," he said as he started the truck. "That was a man obviously trying to make something right."

"I wonder how many layers are in this situation. My parents are rushing back to town, my lawyer hates you because of your dad, and now your godfather has kidnapped or taken her to his love shack to make something right. This is crazy."

Douglas nodded in agreement as they headed down the street. "I hope we find something that will give me the answers I need."

"What happens if we don't find anything?" she asked as she tugged at the seat belt.

Douglas didn't have an answer. He simply hoped things would fall into place and he could get the board to agree to his plan to squash the deal.

Thirty minutes later, they arrived in the blighted town of Waverly. Crystal had been there many times with the Starlight girls delivering vegetables from the farm to the residents and the food bank. Waverly was one area of the county that Crystal knew depended heavily on Hughes Farm. It was the last place she expected the Wellington family to have roots. She figured, with all of the things that Welco had branded, that they were old money.

"After we search this place, can I show you why my farm is so important to this community?" she asked when they pulled into the driveway of a nondescript brick house.

"All right," he said after bringing the truck to a complete stop. They exited the truck and walked up the steps quietly. Douglas unlocked the door and Crystal was surprised to see that the place was decorated as if someone still lived there. When Douglas snapped on the lights, Crystal found herself drawn to the fireplace, where old family pictures were displayed. She zeroed in on a photograph of Douglas as a toddler. He had a big smile on his face as he dragged a puppy behind him. "Wow," she said with a giggle. "You've always tried to force folks to follow you."

Douglas crossed over to her and took the picture frame from her hands. "Ha," he said. "Bubbles never listened to me."

"Bubbles?"

"Like Michael Jackson's monkey. I really wanted one of those," he quipped.

"You were a cute little boy," she said.

"If you ask what happened, we're going to fall out."

Crystal tilted her head to the side. "You grew up into a devastatingly handsome and cocky man. Still trying to make the world see things your way."

He wrapped his arms around her waist and pulled her against his chest. "It works a lot better now," he whispered. "I got you, don't I?"

"See what I mean—cocky."

"And how would you describe yourself? You handcuffed yourself in my lobby until I met with you. That's pretty brash."

She placed her hand on his chest and smirked at him. "How else would I get your attention?"

"Well," he said with a seductive tint to his voice, "you could've walked in without clothes."

"And what would that have accomplished?" she asked, then smacked him on the shoulder.

"Nothing much, but I would've been paying attention immediately."

Crystal sucked her teeth and shook her head. "Not the right kind of attention."

"But attention, nonetheless. Come on, let's see if we can find this information," he said as he started down the hall. Crystal followed him closely, observing bits and pieces of Wellington family history on the walls as she walked. There were photos of who she assumed were Douglas's parents on their wedding day. She didn't miss the fact that Douglas's mother bore an eerie resemblance to her mother. A picture of Douglas on his graduation from high school and college. And was that a picture of him looking like P. Diddy?

"Mmm, Douglas?" she asked when she stopped and pointed to the photograph. "Care to explain?"

He stopped and glanced at the picture. Chuckling, he shook his head and said, "I need to take these pictures and hide them."

"That doesn't answer the question," she said, stifling a giggle.

"My first love was music," he said. "I wasn't always going to be the CEO of this company. I majored in business and my business was going to be music. I had groups lined up that I was going to sign to my label and I was about to meet with Jermaine Dupri in Atlanta before Waylon called me and said my father was dying."

"Wow," Crystal said. "So, you gave up your dreams for your father?"

Douglas nodded. "I was shamed into it. I had no intention of returning to this town or working for my father. But Waylon said my father needed me."

"That sounds like what family does," she said.

He shook his head and walked into a room that looked as if it had been converted to a storage space. "We weren't exactly your typical family. I blamed my father for my mother leaving and never looking back. Maybe it was the child inside me that thought someone else made my mother do what she did. I'm slowly learning that grown people do what they want to do and no one should stay in a loveless marriage."

"Is that what it was like with your parents?"

Douglas nodded solemnly. "From what I understand, she was simply a pawn in his game with your mother."

"What does my mother have to do with this?" she asked.

"That's a good question. If your parents are being cryptic, my godfather is doing the same thing. He did tell me that my dad was in love with your mother, but when she chose another man, he became bitter and wanted to make Reeseville pay."

Crystal hid her shock. She never wanted to think about her mother being with another man. And Douglas's father? No wonder her dad had been so angry about Douglas being on the farm. She was curious about the history of it all more than ever.

Douglas turned to her and then snapped the overhead light on. "All right," he said, pointing to a file cabinet. "Let's get busy."

Crystal and Douglas attacked the drawers, going through every file and every scrap of paper in the room.

"This looks interesting," Douglas said as he flipped through a thick file. Inside, there were pages and pages of things Douglas Jr. wanted to buy. Businesses where he'd been shunned as a child and details about how he'd make them pay.

Crystal moved closer to him and glanced over his shoulder as he flipped the pages. Douglas's eyes grew wider and wider as he read about Hughes Farm. Unlike the file he'd read before, here the pages spelled out his father's detailed plan to destroy the Hughes family and their friends—particularly Dena. Welco had other options for the business park, including a stretch of land in Waverly. As a matter of fact, Douglas realized, his grandparents' home and the surrounding acreage would be—

"That son of a bitch," Douglas muttered.

"What is it?" Crystal asked.

"Obviously, my father had two files on this business park idea," he said. "One for the board and one that's just his personal manifesto. This was a personal attack on everyone he thought had wronged him, especially your father."

"My father?"

Douglas nodded. "Everybody was a pawn to him—my mother, my godfather, hell, me! I wanted to believe that there was an ounce of decency in him and this proves just how wrong

I was. I can only imagine what he wrote in his diary."

"Are you going to show this to the board?"

Douglas sighed. "I have no choice. I just hope this changes their minds."

Crystal crossed over to him and wrapped her arms around his slumping shoulders. "I really thought I was doing the right thing. Thought I was creating a real opportunity for the county."

"I know," she cooed in his ear. His pain and hurt bothered her and made Crystal think about what she could do to take it away. Stroking the back of his neck, she nudged him to face her. Angry tears shone in his eyes as she covered his mouth with hers, gently sucking his bottom lip, kissing him with a slow passion that made his spine straighten.

Wrapping his arms around her waist, Douglas pulled back from Crystal's hot kiss. Staring into her sparkling eyes, he asked, "Was that a pity kiss? If it was, I'm feeling real pitiful right now."

"Mmm," she said, running her hand across his cheek. "What else can I do to make you feel better?"

Pulling her closer, he brushed his lips against hers and whispered, "All I need is you."

"You got me," she whispered before he captured her lips in a full-on kiss that conveyed his pain, his passion, and his need.

"Wait," he said, breaking their kiss again. "We can't do this here. Crazy as it sounds, I keep expecting my grandmother to come in and catch us."

Crystal couldn't help but laugh. Douglas Wellington III was afraid of something. It was a treat to see this side of him. Made it seem as if she'd be able to love him for real.

Stop it, she thought as they headed for the door. *Everything is too complicated to think about loving him and being with him.* Crystal glanced at him as he turned the light off and slipped the file underneath his arm.

"What was your grandmother like?" she asked as they crossed into the living room.

"Oh, she was tough. The only woman who could keep my father in check," he said. "I wish she was still here. You know, she was the one who wanted me to follow my dreams and not do what my father wanted."

She nodded. "When did she pass away?"

"Two years before my father. God, that was the most painful time in my life. My father said that I should've come back here and taken family more seriously." Douglas shook his head and sighed. "But that's neither here nor there. I just wish she knew more about what her son was planning. I can respect my father's wanting to outgrow and overcome his Waverly roots. But to use his money and power to hurt others, that's just evil."

"Maybe your grandmother is guiding you to make things right," she said, easing closer to him.

"Yeah, I don't believe in that haunting mumbo-jumbo," he said, then glanced over his shoulder. "But in case you're right: Thanks, Granny."

She leaned her head against Douglas's arm and squeezed his hand. "Come on, we have cake to finish and I have an ego to stroke."

"And you know I have a big ego," he quipped as they climbed into his truck.

Chapter 14

By the time Douglas and Crystal arrived at the farm, they could barely contain their excitement to be together. But when Crystal spotted a car parked in the driveway with Florida license plates, she could only groan. "My parents are here," she said as he brought the truck to a complete stop.

"What?" he asked.

"This isn't going to be good," she groaned. "Maybe you should . . ."

"I hope you don't plan on telling me to go away or head home. I'd really like to meet your parents—if for no other reason than to apologize."

Recalling the conversation she and her father had earlier, she wasn't sure that was a good idea. "Douglas," she began.

He brought his finger to her lips and shook his head. "I'm not running away from your parents. After all, at some point they're going to find out that I'm crazy about their daughter."

Douglas opened the door and then crossed over to the passenger side to assist Crystal down. She took his hand and smiled as he wrapped his arms around her waist. "It's going to be fine," he said, and leaned in to kiss her.

"What in the hell is going on out here?" a voice boomed from the porch. Crystal shuddered and forced a smile on her lips as she turned around and faced her father. Joel Hughes was an impressive man, even at his age. Years of farm work left him in great shape. Crystal was certain that his huge forearms, his booming voice, and no-nonsense attitude kept many suitors away when she was a teenager.

"Hi, Daddy," she said, turning around to face him.

Joel bounded down the steps and stood in front of her and Douglas. "Is this who I think it is?" he asked without saying hello.

"Daddy," she said quietly, "this is Douglas Wellington the third. He's—"

"Out to take our land and you're just hanging all over him as if nothing is going on?" Joel folded his massive arms and glared at Douglas. "I don't trust him and I see that your mother and I made the right decision returning to fight Welco. Looks like the son learned a lot from his father."

"Mr. Hughes, I'm nothing like my father," Douglas said.

"I don't think I was talking to you," Joel snapped. "Crystal, we need to talk. In private."

"Wait, Daddy," she said. "Douglas has some information that may change your mind."

Joel shook his head. "Can you just hear him out, please?" Crystal asked.

Joel looked from his daughter to Douglas. "Let's go inside," he said, then started for the front door with Crystal and Douglas on his heels.

"He's tough," Douglas whispered.

Crystal nodded and kept silent as she and Douglas entered the living room.

"Crystal," Erin said as she rose from the sofa and crossed over to her daughter. The two women hugged tightly.

"Mama, I can't believe you guys are here," she said. "So early."

Erin glanced over Crystal's shoulder at Douglas. She stepped back from her daughter and blinked as if she'd seen a ghost. "You look so much like your father," she said to Douglas. "I'm surprised Joel even spoke to you."

Joel snorted and pointed toward the sofa. "Where's the information?"

Douglas placed the folder he and Crystal found

on the coffee table. "I think I can stop Welco's plan to purchase this land."

"Being that you're CEO, you shouldn't have a problem doing that," Joel said. "I'm not as naive as my daughter. I know you could've done the right thing a long time ago." Erin squeezed her husband's arm, as if she was telling him to calm down.

Douglas flipped through the file. "Mr. Hughes," he said, "I understand that you and my father had issues. . . ."

"Issues?" Joel bellowed. "Issues? Your father was a cowardly bastard who tried to take my family's land because he couldn't have my wife. He played games with people I cared about and all of this because he had a broken heart. Boo-freaking-hoo."

"And I understand that, now," Douglas said, choosing his words carefully. "But honestly, that has nothing to do with me."

In a motion that was so quick, it caught everyone in the room off guard, Joel jacked Douglas up from the sofa, lifting him as if he were a rag doll.

"Daddy! Stop!" Crystal yelled.

"This has everything to do with you because if you're using my daughter the way Waylon Terrell used Dena, then I will snap you into two pieces."

Erin crossed over to her husband and grabbed

his arm. "Joel! This isn't thirty years ago. Let him go."

Joel dropped Douglas to the floor and glared at him. Crystal rushed to his side, whispering, "Are you all right?"

"Yeah, your dad's a strong man," he said, coughing slightly. Crystal looked up at her father and shook her head. Though she couldn't judge him too harshly because she'd wanted to do something similar when she'd first met Douglas, her father had to realize that Douglas wasn't his father and he was trying to help.

Joel dropped his head and extended his hand to Douglas. "Listen," he said, "I'm sorry about that. Obviously, I have some unresolved issues about what happened and I'm wrong for taking it out on you."

Douglas rested his back against the sofa and rubbed his throat. "I can understand where you're coming from in a way," he replied. "What my father tried to do to your family and this land was unforgivable. Welco is a publicly held company and I have a board to answer to. However, with this manifesto my father wrote, the board should see the error of our ways and fall back from trying to buy the land."

Joel folded his arms. "So, what happens with the court case on Monday?"

"Yes," Erin asked. "I want this to be over."

Douglas nodded as he rose to his feet. "So do I," he said. "I'd better go."

"I'll walk you out," Crystal said as she followed Douglas to the door. Once they were outside, she wrapped her arms around him and hugged him tightly. "I'm so sorry about that."

"Well, I can't blame your dad. My father wanted to destroy your father's family legacy. He wanted to take this farm and level it because your mother had the audacity to fall in love with someone else. Then he wanted to ruin Dena's life as well, since she introduced your mother and father."

Crystal shook her head. "What was it like growing up with him?"

"You can understand why it took a lot of convincing to get me back here. I can't believe I felt guilty about not being here and was about to . . . I will say this, I'm glad your mother and father fell in love. Otherwise, you wouldn't be here." Douglas lifted her chin and kissed Crystal with a slow, burning passion that made her light up like a candle.

Placing her hand against the flat of his chest, she pulled back from him and smiled. "That's pretty bold of you, kissing me like that, knowing that my dad could walk down those steps at any time."

"I'm not scared of your father," he said. "Just don't tell him that."

Crystal laughed and kissed him again. "We'll keep that between us," she said.

"So, do you think we should try to meet later? Maybe you can climb out of your window and meet me in the rose garden and we can just talk."

"Just talk?" she asked with a raised eyebrow. "I'm not going to fall for that one. And I'm sure when I get back inside I'm going to get an earful about being with you."

"So, your dad will be waiting by the door with a shotgun, huh?"

Crystal nodded and laughed. "I wouldn't put it past him. Tomorrow, we'll sneak away and finish what we started earlier."

Crystal watched him as he drove away, then sighed and returned to the living room where her parents were waiting.

"Daddy," she said as she crossed over to her father.

Joel shook his head and drew his daughter into his arms. "I'm sorry about how I acted, but you have to understand, there's a lot of history with Welco and our family."

"That still doesn't give you the right to act like a madman. Sorry if I sound disrespectful. Daddy, what was that really all about?"

Erin and Joel exchanged knowing looks. "That's one of the reasons why we rushed here tonight," Erin said. "Though neither of us had any idea that Douglas the third was nothing like his father. Dena didn't paint him too kindly."

Crystal nodded. "We thought we were going to be in for a big fight."

"Thought? I hope you aren't falling for his promises and lies," Joel said, showing that he wasn't convinced by Douglas's assertion that he'd back off the farm.

Erin placed her hand on her husband's shoulder. "Joel, we're not dealing with his father. You have to give him a chance."

He grumbled about Douglas Jr.'s evil soul, then nodded.

"Daddy," Crystal said, "Douglas wants to make things right. He isn't trying to pull one over on us. He's embarrassed and hurt about what his father was trying to do—not just to us, but to everyone listed in that file."

Erin beckoned for Crystal to sit down. "Joel," she said, "It's time to tell her everything."

Joel sighed and sat down beside Crystal. "It started when we were in high school," he said. "Your mother and Douglas, or Junior, as he was known back then, were dating."

"Wow," Crystal said, since she could never imagine her mother with anyone other than her father.

"Joel and I became lab partners in chemistry and he was so sweet that our relationship grew from a flirty friendship to a lifetime love. I never meant to hurt Douglas," Erin said. "I told him that I was sorry, and he said I'd be sorry when he got through with Joel."

"First he tried to fight me," Joel said. "And he ended up getting embarrassed in front of the whole school. He thought I looked down on him because he was from Waverly, but I didn't have a problem with where he was from. I simply wanted his girlfriend."

"And," Erin interjected, "we were young. I had no idea that Douglas was so serious about me or that Joel and I would fall so deeply in love."

"And we didn't know that Douglas was so damned resentful and a vindictive son of a—"

"Joel, the man is dead," Erin said quietly. "He could've done a lot more for the community if he hadn't been so bent on revenge. When Joel and I took over the farm from your grandfather and Nana, things in Duval County were getting bad and we wanted to expand the outreach of the farm and help the poor and the growing homeless population. At the same time, Junior was establishing Welco, buying a lot of property, turning Reeseville into his headquarters. Without your father's knowledge . . ."

Joel grunted and folded his arms across his chest. "And that's what started this whole mess," he said.

"What happened?" Crystal asked.

Erin sighed, rose to her feet and started pacing back and forth. "I approached him and asked for help," she said. "When I was in his office, he tried to kiss me and he told me that no one, not even his wife, had his heart the way I did. He even told me that he'd leave his wife if I would give him a chance to love me the way he'd always dreamed of doing. His wife was pregnant at the time and I thought he was so cruel to even suggest that. It was as if he'd just come back to town for me—despite the fact that he left town to start a family and I was dedicated to my husband."

Erin stopped talking and glanced at Joel, who had a far-off look in his eyes, as if he'd returned to the moment she'd been describing. "Right then and there I should've taken him out," Joel mumbled. Erin stopped in front of her husband and stroked his forearms gently. Her touch seemed to calm the storm of the past and he wrapped his arms around her waist, pulling her closer to him.

Crystal had always admired the love her parents shared; simple touches and a smile said so much between them. She just had no idea that their love had been tested so seriously. Now, the closeness and the tenderness between them made so much more sense. You had to go through hell to have that kind of connection.

"Junior tried to pretend that he was better than everybody else," Erin said. "But he was still a scared boy from Waverly, no matter how many suits he put on or how much money he made. He always thought that I chose Joel over him because of this farm."

"And," Joel said with a little laugh, "your mother has always hated this farm."

Erin playfully smacked her husband's shoulder. "I did not hate this farm. I just didn't know, until we got married and started living here, the sheer amount of work that went into it."

Joel pushed a stray lock of Erin's salt and pepper hair behind her ear, then kissed her forehead. "Thanks to you, we made this farm mean something to the community and not just the Hughes family."

"I thought Junior would've bought into what we were doing here," Erin said. "That's why I was so taken aback when he came at me about our long-dead relationship. I turned him down and he said he'd make me and my whole family pay."

"Is that how Dena got involved?" Crystal asked.

Erin nodded. "Dena and I have always been close and when she started dating Waylon, I thought they were going to make it. It really seemed as if he loved her."

"I think he still does," Crystal said. "He was here earlier as well."

"What?" Joel exclaimed. "He certainly has a nerve. I wonder if he has a backbone now?"

"Joel, you need to let your anger go, too," Erin said. "You and Waylon were friends once. He even worked on the farm with you. Hasn't enough time and bitterness passed?"

He sighed. "We need to find Dena and see what her plan is for court tomorrow. And, Crystal, you need to stay away from that Wellington boy."

"Daddy," she said, "he's not his father and I . . ." Her voice trailed off. "He said he was going to talk to the board and see what he can do to stop this. Can't we just give him a chance?"

"I don't know what lines he's been feeding you or what you think you two have together, but I don't trust him any more than I trusted his father," Joel said.

"We'll have to take Douglas at his word and see what happens," Erin said cautiously. She locked eyes with her daughter and winked.

Crystal knew her mother would have a long talk with her father later. She nodded and slowly rose to her feet. Joel padded into the kitchen, leaving mother and daughter alone.

Erin crossed over to her daughter and wrapped her arms around her shoulders.

Placing her hand on Crystal's cheek, she said, "You really care about him, don't you?"

"I don't know," she said.

"You could never lie to me," Erin said with a chuckle as she and Crystal took a seat on the sofa.

"When I first met him, I wanted to just bash his head in. I even handcuffed myself to a desk in the lobby of Welco," Crystal said.

Erin laughed, then pointed her finger at her daughter. "You're too much. Sometimes you can just write a letter or have a real meeting with people. You should've been around in the sixties with that spirit of yours."

Crystal rubbed her forehead and leaned on her mother's shoulder. "But when he came here, something changed," she said quietly.

"Before or after you slept with him?" her mother sagely asked.

"Ma!" Crystal exclaimed. "How did you know?"

Erin smiled. "Do you think sex started with your generation? I see how you looked at him. I look at your father the same way. Crystal, I wish you hadn't gotten so involved with him before this issue was taken care of; now you're in a horrible position."

She dropped her head in her hands. "Do you think Daddy will ever accept him?"

Erin shrugged. "I knew your father still held some bitterness about what Junior tried to do, but I had no idea that he was this angry about it still. Maybe he looked at Douglas and it brought back all of the hurt and hard feelings about the situation."

Crystal nodded. "I hope Daddy will change his mind because . . ."

Erin smiled. "You love him and want a future with him?"

Crystal leaned against her mother's shoulder and sighed. "I never said that I loved him," she said, her words not ringing true to her ears or Erin's.

Chapter 15

Douglas paced his office waiting for Crystal's call. After about twenty minutes, he figured that she wasn't able to get away from her parents, so he called Waylon to see what happened between him and Dena. When he didn't get an answer, he could only smile and assume that his godfather had worked something out with the fiery attorney. Part of him wondered why his father felt the need to play with people's lives the way that he had. From all accounts, his father grew up loved by both of his parents. But Douglas knew what a hard man he'd been when he was a child. Ignoring his mother, flaunting his numerous affairs and disdain for their marriage while he crafted an image of a man who cared about Duval County and had brought Welco in to provide jobs for people who grew up poor as he had.

The truth about his father was a bitter pill to

swallow. He couldn't understand how a man who claimed to want to do so much good for others didn't give a damn about his family. That's why Douglas had wanted to get far away from Welco and what it stood for when he went to college. That's why he'd majored in music, despite the fact that his father and Waylon told him that it would be a waste of time and energy.

Douglas Jr. had tried to make peace with his son before he died, at least that's what Douglas thought his father was doing. Now, he wondered if his father had been adding another layer to his revenge plot. Did he want this to extend from the grave?

I have to stop this, Douglas thought as he sat behind his desk and began typing a memo to the board on his computer about halting the purchase of Hughes Farm and moving the business park to Waverly. As he hit "Print" on the keyboard, he heard footsteps outside his office. Slowly rising to his feet, Douglas quietly crossed over to the door and locked eyes with Amy, his secretary.

"What are you doing here?" he asked.

"Mr. Oldsman asked me to come in and—"

"You don't work for Clive, you work for me. If you want to keep your job, you'd better start talking about what you and Clive have been doing behind my back."

Amy shivered and began to cry. Douglas wasn't

sure if it was an act or if he'd scared the girl and he really didn't care.

"After the hearing tomorrow, the board is planning a secret vote to remove you as CEO. Mr. Oldsman had me come in to print the information that he needed for the meeting."

"So, you've gone behind my back to work with the board against me?" he snapped.

"What choice did I have? If I didn't do what he wanted, then I wouldn't have a job. I don't have anything but this job."

Douglas clenched his fists and grunted. "Haven't I always looked out for you? You don't have to worry about Clive firing you—you're done right now."

"But—"

"Save your sputtering for Clive and get the hell out of my office!" Douglas bellowed.

Amy ran from the office, dropping the tote bag she'd been carrying. Douglas saw the diary he'd been looking for a few nights ago and Clive's letter to the board spill across the floor. The letter had been an indictment on Douglas's handling of the business park and why the board needed to relieve him of his duties as CEO. That wasn't a surprise to him. Clive wanted his job and he'd known that for a while. What he didn't know was what the old man's plans had been for his father's diary.

"That son of a bitch," he groaned as he scanned

the letter, which said the board could no longer have confidence in Douglas's leadership, nor his ability to keep Welco profitable in the new economy. The letter went on to question Douglas's ideas for the future of the company and his loyalty to the standards set by his father. Clive suggested that the board appoint him as CEO until a better candidate was hired.

Part of Douglas wanted to fight, but he knew there was a different route he needed to take. Someone else could run this company, but it damned sure wasn't going to be Clive Oldsman. The board was scheduled to meet at nine, the same time he was supposed to be in court.

Douglas dialed his attorney, despite the hour, and ordered him to show up in court with a motion to make the case against Hughes Farm go away. His last act as CEO would be to right the wrongs that his father had created all of those years ago. More than anything else, he was going to finally follow his heart.

Crystal lay in her bed, frustrated, confused, and missing the heat of Douglas's arms around her. She missed his lips, his hands touching her intimately, and even his soft snoring. She couldn't help but wonder if her father would accept him and their relationship. . . . Wait, were they in a relationship?

Her mother was right; she had fallen for Douglas. But would she lose her father because she found love with him?

Crystal flipped over on her stomach and buried her face in her pillow to stifle a scream. Things had gone from complicated to damned near impossible. Sitting up, she sighed and reached for her robe. Since she couldn't sleep, she decided that she would have some honey tea and sit on the porch until she either fell asleep or saw the sun rise. Slipping into her fluffy slippers, she made her way to the kitchen and fixed her late night snack of tea and oatmeal cookies. She remembered her last late night in the kitchen and how a little too much whiskey turned into one of the most passionate nights of her life. She couldn't help herself as she thought about sharing that drink with Douglas, so she poured a shot of whiskey into her teacup. Heading for the porch, Crystal took a seat on the wide steps and slowly sipped her drink. Though she was an adult, drinking under her parent's nose still seemed wrong. She broke off a piece of her cookie and nibbled at it as she heard a vehicle creeping up the driveway. Looking up, she smiled when she saw Douglas's truck without the headlights on come to a stop. Setting her cookie and teacup aside, she met him on the sidewalk.

"What are you doing here?" she asked quietly as he drew her into his arms.

"When I didn't hear from you, I got impatient and decided to come over and risk the wrath of your dad for this," he said, then captured her lips in a hot kiss that made the tea she'd been drinking seem absolutely frigid. Crystal melted in his arms, allowing herself to be completely enveloped in the strong embrace she'd been missing. Douglas smiled as they broke the kiss. "Whiskey?"

"Not as much as the last time," she replied.

"Good, because when I carry you into that dollhouse and make love to you, I don't want to hear you blaming it on the alcohol this time," he said, then scooped her into his arms.

"Wait," she said, pressing her hand against his chest. "I have to know something."

"What's that?"

Crystal sighed, closed her eyes, and then asked, "This is just about us, right?"

Douglas tilted his head and peered deeply into her eyes. "Babe, I know what that file showed you about my father and I understand your family may not trust me, but after tomorrow you and everybody else will know this is just about us."

She stroked his cheek and smiled. Crystal felt

that she could believe him and that she could even open herself up to him even more, allowing herself to easily love him. She could stop telling herself that it was lust, because the way her heart swelled when he touched her, she knew it was love.

"Crystal," he intoned, "I hope you know that I would never do anything to hurt you."

"I know," she replied quietly, then kissed his cheek.

Douglas headed for the cottage where he had yet to sleep. Once he and Crystal entered, Douglas placed her against the wall and untied the sash on her robe. Even though she stood there in a pair of Happy Bunny boxer shorts and a white tank top, she was still the sexiest woman he'd ever laid eyes on. And the way her erect nipples pressed against the cotton tank did nothing but make his mouth water like a fountain. In a quick motion, he lifted the shirt up and covered her rock-hard nub with his hot mouth, making her scream out in pleasure. With his free hand, Douglas slipped inside her boxers, happy to find that the only barrier between them was that sarcastic bunny's face. Slowly, he pressed his finger inside her, circling her sensitive clitoris with the tip of his finger.

Crystal's knees shivered, shook, and nearly turned to liquid as Douglas used his finger to bring her to the brink, while he still sucked and licked her nipple. Before her head could catch up with what was happening, she was naked with her legs on his shoulders as he kneeled in front of her, his mouth covering the most sensitive part of her body. Crystal couldn't hold back the orgasmic wave washing over her as Douglas's tongue flicked across her throbbing bud.

"Ooh, that's it," she cried as he began to suck her essence as if it were fresh honey. Looking down at him, their eyes locked in an expression that needed no words. Her pleasure turned him on. Quenching her desire seemed to be his only need, the only thing he wanted. Pulling back from her, Douglas quickly stripped out of his clothes, revealing his dangling erection and how much he needed Crystal.

"Come here," he commanded. "I want you right now." Douglas lifted Crystal in his arms and she wrapped her legs around his waist, her chest pressed against his as they kissed deeply and fell back on the sofa. He gripped her hips, positioning her on his erection. And she took him inside her, slowly riding him as if he was a prized steed in a main street parade.

"Damn," Douglas moaned. "Damn, you feel so good."

She groaned, drawing him deeper and deeper into her hot valley. Crystal had never felt so hot and passion filled. Douglas matched her pace, her heat, and her desire, thrusting in and out—forgetting that they hadn't been protected as he felt a hot stream of release explode from him. Crystal reached her own climax, collapsing against his chest with a satisfied sigh.

Douglas held her tightly and kissed her cheek. "What do you think would happen if your father walked in right now?" he whispered in her ear.

"You'd better be able to run really fast," she quipped.

"Or, maybe I should tell him how much I love his daughter."

"Is that so?" she asked, propping up on his chest with her elbow.

Douglas drummed his fingers lightly on the back of her arm. "That's so," he replied. "Who would've thought after you locked yourself up in my office that we'd be here right now?" He ran his finger down the valley of her breasts.

Douglas smiled and inched up in a seated position, holding Crystal around her waist, and said, "I have something that I need to tell you about tomorrow."

This was it, the other shoe was about to drop. Crystal steeled herself and waited to hear what he was about to say. Douglas felt her body tense in his arms and stroked her shoulders in an attempt to calm her.

"It's not that bad," he said. "But things are going to change with me and the company."

"Change how?" she asked, hoping her voice didn't convey how tangled in knots her nerves were.

"I found out what happened to the file that I'd used to start this project and my father's diary. The chairman of the board, Clive Oldsman, took it."

"Why would he do that?"

Douglas shrugged. "I have my suspicions. If my father's diary is as dark as what was in the file at my grandparents' house, I'm sure Clive planned to use it to damage Welco's image. If the stock prices dropped, he'd be able to convince the board to fire me."

Crystal tilted her head to the side, confused as to why Clive would do something like that. Just as she was about to ask Douglas that very question, he continued. "Oldsman never wanted me to be the CEO of Welco. He's been trying to undermine me my whole career. He thought since I'd moved away and he had become my father's right-hand man that when he died, the job was his. I guess Waylon knew my father wanted to have a Wellington in that job and he made sure I came back to learn how to continue his legacy."

"So, Clive would risk the company just to get his way?" she questioned.

Douglas nodded. "Not only that, but he was willing to risk people's retirement plans, jobs, and future projects to get what he wanted. That sorry bastard."

Crystal rolled her eyes. "Seems as if he's the one I should've gone after."

"And deprive me of the pleasure of your company? I think not. The funny thing about this is, until you marched into my office with your granola and handcuffs, I didn't really care. Truth of the matter was, after this deal was done, I was going to get out of town. Be a CEO who lived someplace else, spend my money and chase women who weren't from Reeseville."

Hearing his plans sent a ripple of jealously down her spine. Had those plans changed now? Where in the hell was he going with this story and why did he want to talk about other women while she was lying there naked in his arms? She cleared her throat and Douglas smiled again. "It's a good thing plans don't always get followed," he said. "But I did obviously fall into a trap."

"A trap?"

"Clive's trap with this business park," he said. "This was built for failure. And he wants to present that to the board tomorrow at an emergency meeting."

"What?"

Douglas explained what happened when he found Amy in his office earlier and the letter that he'd read about his shortcomings as CEO. "How can he do that?" Crystal asked.

"It's a cut-throat world in business and when you make it to the top you can only go down," he said.

Crystal shuddered. "I'm glad that I'm not in the business world."

Douglas wondered if he could have a quiet, sleepy life on the farm with Crystal. He didn't mind giving up the top spot at Welco—provided that Clive didn't get it—but would he be able to trade in business suits for overalls and boots? *Of course,* he thought as he looked into Crystal's eyes, *this woman may not want me around at all if Welco still comes after this farm. I have to make sure that doesn't happen.*

"What?" she asked, catching the look in his eyes.

"I'm going to need a job tomorrow evening," he said. "Know anyone who's hiring?"

Crystal laughed heartily and rolled out of his embrace, standing and stretching her arms above her head. "Are you seriously asking me for a job? You want to muck stalls and shuck corn?"

"A brother has to eat," he replied as he stood behind her and cupped her naked bottom in his hands. "And being here and seeing everything that you all do here, I seriously want to lend a hand, starting with doing some renovations on the Starlight House."

She turned around and searched his face as if she expected him to be joking. Crystal wrapped her arms around his neck and hugged him tightly. "I'm floored, I can't . . ."

"It's the least I can do for those girls and you," he said.

"Me?"

"At least you have a family legacy worth believing in, and I see how important this place is to you. So, when I ask you for a job, I'm asking you if I can make you happy for the rest of your life," he breathed into her ear.

Crystal felt weak, felt as if she were melting in his arms. "Yes," she said. "You can."

Douglas leaned in and kissed her slowly and passionately. "I never thought I could love a woman this much," he said after breaking the kiss.

"Douglas," she intoned.

He held her face in his hands, peering deeply into her eyes. "First things first," he said. "We have to make sure this place is protected from companies in the future."

"What, other than your father's file, made Hughes Farm so attractive?"

Douglas sighed. "Honestly, this is prime real estate. It's far enough from downtown to build factories without hearing the environmentalists complain about the fumes and smoke. As we were looking into purchasing this land, things have changed. Ordinances and rules for zoning have changed, and you can expect more land grab attempts in the future. I'm not proud to say that my company and I had a lot to do with that."

Crystal sighed and closed her eyes tightly. "Then, how in the world are we going to keep the farm out of the hands of developers? I refuse to be the Hughes who loses this farm after everything that it means to our family and this community."

Douglas brushed a tear from Crystal's cheek. "I know, babe. But I have a plan."

She shook her head and began to gather her clothes. "This is really your fault," she snapped.

"What?"

"Douglas, you're here now because of some underhanded tactics at your company, but it doesn't seem as if you're above that yourself! It's because of you that this farm is going to be in jeopardy in the future."

"Do you think I thought this was going to happen?"

Pulling her clothes on, Crystal headed for the door of the cottage. "I don't know what the hell I was thinking. I tell you what—keep your plans and everything else to your damned self. I was taking care of this place long before I met you and I will continue to do it without you!"

She stormed out and Douglas quickly dressed and then followed her outside. When he caught up with Crystal, he grabbed her arm and forced her to face him. "You know what?" he said. "I'm not going to apologize for decisions I made as a businessman. I'm not going to say that I didn't cross the line to try to get what I wanted, but you can't allow what I did in the past to cloud our present and future."

Crystal folded her arms across her chest and blinked. "Future? According to you, my future is going to be fighting off Welco and other companies because *you* got laws and ordinances changed to suit your needs!"

"Not if this place is turned into a historic landmark," he said. "I've been looking into doing just that."

Crystal's pulsing heart rate calmed slightly. "Why would you . . . ?"

"I told you, you have a family legacy that you should be proud of and I want to help you keep it. But damn, woman, you have to give me a chance to do it."

"I'm sorry," she said. "It's just . . . I'm afraid."

"You don't have to be. Let me just say, if I couldn't have this farm, then I'd be damned if someone else tries to pressure you into selling."

Crystal chewed on her bottom lip and focused her intense stare on him. "But what if you don't lose your job tomorrow and your board still wants you to move on with the construction of the business park out here?"

"I know that Waverly is a better location for the park and if we get Clive out of the top seat, then the rest of the board will see what's best for the company and will go along with the new plan," he said.

"You can't know that for sure," she said.

"That's why I always have a plan B, C, and D," Douglas said with a smile. "No matter what happens in the morning, Hughes Farm is going to be fine. And I know that for sure."

"How can you be so sure?" she questioned.

"Trust me," Douglas replied, "no one will get a piece of this property."

"What should I tell my parents?" she asked.

Douglas folded his arms across his chest and smiled confidently. "Let me take care of that," he said with a smile.

Chapter 16

It was a little after dawn when Douglas left the farm. As Crystal crept inside the main house, she was greeted by her father holding a steaming cup of coffee.

"Do I want to know where you're coming from?" he asked, then handed her the cup.

"Daddy, are we going to argue every time I see Douglas?"

"Baby girl, I don't trust him. The apple doesn't fall too far from the rotten tree," he said as he started for the kitchen.

Crystal followed him, hoping that her father would keep an open mind about Douglas. Sure it was hard, but would she have to suffer because of things that happened years before she and Douglas were even born?

"What if he's different?" Crystal asked when they arrived in the kitchen.

"What if global warming isn't caused by cows?" Joel asked. "What if we could fix the eroding beaches with egg shells? There's no way of knowing what kind of asshole he is until he hurts you, and I don't want to have to harm that boy."

"Douglas said he's willing to give up Welco and help us protect the farm," she revealed.

Joel snorted. "Don't believe that. One thing I know for sure about this entire situation is that any man who holds a grudge and takes it to the grave with him passed that same thing on to his son."

"That's not what happened, Dad."

Joel held his hand up and shook his head. "Please don't defend him until we know for sure that our land is safe. I'm wondering what Dena is going to do in court today. Your mother wasn't able to reach her at all."

Crystal stifled a giggle, sure that Dena was with Waylon making up for lost time. Or perhaps they'd killed each other. "Dad," Crystal began, "what happened between you guys? This much hate and bitterness makes it seem as if there was something deep here. Deeper than that man being in love with Mom."

"There was a lot of betrayal in this circle," Joel said. "Waylon worked for the farm in the summer and because your mother and Dena have always been friends, they met and allegedly fell in love."

"Allegedly?"

Joel pouted as he opened the refrigerator and

began to remove ingredients for breakfast. "Have you stopped keeping chickens?" he asked when he pulled out a paper carton of eggs.

"No," she said. "We've changed the packaging on the eggs. But those are Hughes Farm Fresh Eggs."

Joel laughed, then grew serious. "That's the one thing that Waylon did for us. He gave us that slogan before he put the knife in our back."

"What happened?" she asked. Before Joel could answer, the phone rang and Crystal grabbed the extension. "Hello?"

"Crystal, it's Dena," she said.

"Your ears must have been burning; we were just talking about you."

"Let me guess who the other half of the 'we' is," Dena said with a snarky tone to her voice.

"Actually," Crystal replied, "I was talking to my dad."

"Joel and Erin are there? I'm coming over to let you guys know what's going on."

"All right," Crystal said, then hung up. She turned to her father. "Dena said she's coming over with news."

Joel grunted. "I hope it's good news," he said as he cracked three eggs into a mixing bowl. "French toast still your favorite?"

Crystal kissed her father on the cheek. "Only when you make it."

"Crystal, I don't want you to think that your

mother and I aren't proud of what you've done with this place, and we want you to keep running the farm and expanding on what we do in Reeseville."

"I know that and I hate that you had to come here because of this mess," Crystal said.

"This is not your fault. It's an old fight that I'm sorry you were ever involved in. Your mother and I never wanted you or this farm to be touched by the past. If I could, I'd dig Junior up and smash his face in for everything that he did and tried to do to my family."

The anger in her father's voice made Crystal cringe. Her dad had always been easygoing and laid back. She had to know more about what Douglas Wellington Jr. had done to leave such bitterness in her father.

"But," Joel said, noting the worried look on his daughter's face, "that's the past and we're looking toward the future and saving this farm."

"Daddy, that's what Douglas is trying to do," she said quietly. "You know, Douglas showed me his father's plan, but you've never told me what happened and why you're still so angry."

Joel stopped whisking the eggs and looked up at his daughter. "Junior was an evil son of a bitch who thought his money would give him carte blanche in this town, and what he couldn't buy, he tried to take," he said.

"And he tried to take this farm?"

Joel nodded as he sprinkled cinnamon in the eggs and began to whisk them again. "Your grandfather was in the early stages of dementia when you were two months old. Douglas came around here talking about wanting to help us and tried to get Dad to sign away the property. He knew my father was sick and so did Waylon. I think he's the one who told him about my father's condition. For Waylon to do that and then leave Dena after he'd proposed to her was the ultimate betrayal. I have no respect for that bastard either. He was just as bad as his friend, using people to get what he wanted and not giving a damn about their feelings or needs."

"How do you know Waylon told him about Grandpa?"

"He had to," Joel said. "Besides your mother and myself, no one knew about Dad's condition. What makes matters worse is that Waylon was down and out when we gave him a job on this farm. He was smart, but came from a poor background. He went to college on a scholarship, but couldn't find a job after he graduated. He moved back to Waverly and was working in one of the textile mills making pennies. When your mother and I took over the operations of the farm, Dena suggested hiring him. He had great ideas and we were trying to modernize the place. Then he betrayed us."

"And that started the chain reaction?"

Joel nodded and dipped the bread in the egg mixture, then dropped the bread in the frying pan. "I can't and don't trust Welco or Douglas Wellington's son. I hope that you haven't misplaced your trust in him like Dena did with Waylon."

Crystal sighed and realized that her father would probably not accept her relationship with Douglas or him working to make the farm a historic landmark. "That's not going to happen again," she said as she heard her mother open the front door.

"Dena's here!" Erin called out.

"We're in the kitchen," Joel replied.

"Well," Erin said as she stood in the doorway of the kitchen. "She's not alone and you don't need to be around knives."

Joel raised his right eyebrow. "What do you mean?" he asked as he turned the heat down on the stove.

"Just stay calm," she said. "Stay calm."

"I get the feeling that I'm not going to like this," Joel said as he followed Erin and Crystal into the living room. Erin held her husband's massive arm as he locked eyes with Waylon. Crystal watched as her father narrowed his eyes into slits like a snake about to strike.

"What in the hell is he doing here?" Joel boomed, his voice seeming to make the walls vibrate. "Has everyone lost their damned minds around here?"

"Joel," Dena began, "let me explain . . ."

"No," Waylon said. "I need to explain what's going on and what has been going on."

Joel broke away from his wife's grip and stood nose to nose with Waylon. "You have the unmitigated gall to set foot on this farm when you were part of this scheme to wrest control of this farm from my family. Maybe Dena's dumb enough to forgive you, but I'm—"

"Wait a minute, Joel!" Dena exclaimed.

"Never going to forget . . ." Joel grabbed Waylon by the throat.

"Joel!" Erin and Dena called out as they attempted to separate the men. Crystal stood there in shock and awe as her father tossed Waylon to the floor like a rag doll. This was the second time in her life that she'd seen her father act out in rage.

Waylon coughed and sputtered as he slowly rose to his feet. "Well," he said once the pain in his throat subsided, "I can't say that I'm surprised that happened."

"I ought to—"

"Joel. Calm. Down," Erin said as she grabbed her husband's shoulder when he flexed as if he was going to grab Waylon again.

"Joel," Waylon began as he eased a few inches back from his former friend, "I know you have every reason to hate me and what I tried to do when Doug and I were working together. But you have to know that I wasn't trying to hurt you and your family."

"No, you were just trying to take advantage of my father, knowing that he was suffering and not of sound mind."

"That's not true. Honestly, I thought I was helping."

Joel clenched his fist. "Helping? Are you out of your damned mind?"

"This farm was bleeding money and Doug had money to help. He'd said that Erin had reached out to him, but he turned her down because she wouldn't betray you," Waylon said.

"I know this, but that has nothing to do with the underhanded bullshit you pulled, bringing him here with those papers that would've made this farm a subsidiary of Welco because he wanted to own me and have me work for him. You know this was about Erin and you went along with it."

"It was never about you, Joel. Doug and I grew up wondering every night if we'd get enough to eat, if we'd have lights or heat in the winter. And when he made it, it went to his head. All I wanted to do was provide a future for me and Dena."

"To hell with everybody else, you just wanted to cement your future while robbing my family of our history," Joel exclaimed.

"Looks like you're the winner," Waylon snapped. "You were able to have a life with the woman you love and I spent years apart from the only woman who mattered to me."

"And you couldn't tell Doug's son about the history of this place when he decided to grab the land?" Erin asked.

"That's why I'm here," Dena said. "I got a call from Welco's lead attorney and the company isn't going to fight the injunction. He even hinted that Welco might be backing off the development of the business park here."

"What?" Erin and Joel exclaimed.

Crystal beamed, though inside, she wondered how Douglas had faired at the board meeting. He said he didn't mind losing his job, making her wonder if he felt as connected to his father's company as she did to her family's farm.

"Now," Erin said, "can we come to a peaceful resolution? Can we let the past go? Dena and Crystal need us to do that."

Joel sighed and looked around the room. Maybe Waylon had a point. The farm still belonged to the Hughes family. He'd spent his life with Erin and he was still above ground to enjoy many more years with his wife. Still, he didn't trust that Douglas Wellington III was any better than his father or Waylon, and Joel wasn't going to allow his daughter to be hurt or used.

"Listen," Dena said. "I don't expect everything to be hugs and smiles today, but Joel . . ."

"I can leave the past in the past," he said. "If you want to be with this clown, then that's on you." Joel turned to Crystal. "I still don't trust that Wellington boy."

"Daddy—" she said.

"That's not fair, Joel," Waylon said.

"You shouldn't say another word to me."

"Right now, Trey is giving up everything for your daughter and this farm," Waylon said. "You should give him a chance."

When Douglas walked into the conference room, the silence of the board members spoke volumes. He locked eyes with Clive. A beat passed before either man spoke. "Why aren't you in court?" Clive demanded.

"Ladies and gentlemen, I have two announcements today," Douglas said, focusing his cold stare on the board. "First, Welco is backing off the business park construction on the site of Hughes Farm."

A rumble rippled through the room and Douglas held up his hand like a conductor leading his orchestra. "I made a huge mistake, and Clive here"—he pointed his thumb at his nemesis as if he were nothing more than an afterthought—"was more than happy to sacrifice the company's bottom line to force me out. Trying to purchase Hughes Farm was a bad idea that came from an incomplete file that contained outdated information."

"That's a lie, and it was your job to vet this project before you garnered all of this bad press and accrued legal fees."

"Save it, Clive," Douglas snapped. "This is precisely what you wanted to happen. I don't blame Amy for helping you; she needed her job. But I fired her when I saw her trying to replace the file about Hughes Farm that you asked her to steal from my office. And let's talk about the diary that you took as well. Did you plan to use my father's private thoughts to run this company into the ground, so that you could force the board to fire me? After all, you've been going behind my back trying that for years, you just didn't have cause."

Douglas crossed the room and stood in front of the older man. "Being that you worked with my father for more than twenty years, you knew this wasn't business, but rather a personal vendetta that would cause the protests, send Welco into court, and cost this company millions. Did I make mistakes on this deal? Yes. I allowed my past success to lull me into a position of complacency. After all, since I've been CEO, haven't we enjoyed record profits? I foolishly thought this would be another cake walk." Douglas glanced around the room and shook his head. Then he perched on the edge of the oak table. Clive glared at Douglas as he picked a piece of lint from his trousers. "But," Douglas continued, pointing his finger at Clive. "This guy put his ego before the company, before profits and everything else. All he wanted was my job. To be honest with you, I don't give a shit about this job."

There was a collective gasp in the room as Douglas rose to his feet. "But, there is no way in hell that I'm going to allow Clive to replace me as CEO. I returned to Reeseville and came to Welco out of some misguided loyalty to my father. My father was a lot like Clive, selfish, ruthless, and heartless. Maybe that's the kind of man who needs to lead Welco. I'm willing to step aside, but I'll be damned if that bastard will take my job. Now, we can handle this quietly or I can air all of our dirty laundry, then watch the Welco stock free-fall like a rock dropped from the top of the Empire State Building."

"This is blackmail!" Clive exclaimed.

"Let's not pretend that you weren't above playing the blackmail card," he shot back. "What did you find in the pages of my father's diary? I'm willing to bet it was pretty dark. I'm sure you promised a certain reporter exclusive rights to the story."

"You don't know a damned thing, little boy. You've been living off your father's name for too long. But you don't have the balls to make the tough calls. You're nothing like your father. He would be ashamed of you. As a matter of fact, he was. You should've stayed in Atlanta trying to be a record executive because you're a shitty businessman."

Douglas folded his arms across his chest. "And you're so much better? You were willing to risk the company, our employees' retirement plans, and the profits of the board because you wanted to teach me a lesson?"

Fred shook his head. "Any truth to this, Clive?"

Clive snorted. "He's trying to save his ass and shove this new project down our throats. Don't fall for this."

Douglas rose to his feet and rounded the table. "How did Deloris Tucker know I was staying at Hughes Farm?" He eyed Clive intensely.

"You're the one who has a relationship with the media, always in the paper and on TV cleaning up your mistakes," Clive sputtered.

"At least I'm man enough to own up to what I've done wrong," Douglas snapped. "Tell the truth, Clive. You were attempting a coup. It failed. Own up to it."

The older man glared at Douglas and his body tensed as if he wanted to hit the younger man.

"What should we do about this?" Fred asked.

Douglas laughed and looked at the other board members. "You all have a choice and I suggest you make the right one. Clive can't be trusted. After all, I wasn't supposed to know about this meeting."

"If you were thinking with your head and not your libido, we wouldn't need this meeting. Everybody knows about you and Crystal Hughes," Clive spat. "You just want to keep her happy and in your bed—at the expense of the company."

"Because you made sure they found out, so it would look as if I was choosing her over the company," Douglas said as he approached Clive. "You know what? Maybe I am. See, I don't want to be like my father or you. Bitter. Old and lonely."

"I just . . ." Clive uttered.

"If anyone is going to run this company for the near future, it will be Waylon Terrell," Douglas ordered. "Then the board, without Clive as the chairman, can hire a headhunter to find the right man or woman to do the job."

"Wait a damned minute!" Clive exclaimed. "You can't waltz in here and think you're going to fire me. That's not what this meeting was about. My performance isn't the issue."

Douglas folded his arms across his broad chest. "It is now. Let me ask you all this," he said as he turned to the other board members. "Do you want someone on this board who isn't thinking about making Welco better? Do you want a leader who will sell out just to make himself look good? Everything Clive says I am is exactly what he is. So, if you came here to vote me out, you might want to think what you're getting if you vote him in."

Clive pounded his fist on the closed door. "Are you all going to listen to this little punk?"

Douglas smirked as he watched Clive try to save face. He'd shown his hand and proved everything Douglas had pointed out.

Fred spoke up again. "You know," he said, "I haven't been this entertained at one of these meetings in a long time. But Clive and Douglas make very good points."

"I don't like this," Willis said. "I wasn't going to vote to replace you, Douglas. Because despite this project, you have done a great job with the company. Your father would've been proud. Why do you want to give it up?"

Douglas toyed with telling them the truth—that he didn't want to be anything like his father and that Crystal's love meant more to him than running this company. He wanted to admit that he never planned to spend more than five years there, never wanted to be Mr. Welco. Instead, he shrugged and said, "I've done as much as I can with this company."

"And it hasn't been nearly enough," Clive chimed in.

"But what in the hell have you done?" Willis questioned. "Why should we turn the control of this company over to you when you were willing to sabotage us to get what you want?"

"I'd like to make a motion," Dorian said. "All of those in favor of removing Clive Oldsman as chairman of the board, say 'aye.'"

Everyone but Clive said "aye." He glared at his colleagues and hissed, "You spineless bastards. I would've never called this meeting had I known—"

"I'd like to make a second motion," Douglas said.

Clive glared at him. "You're out of order! You're not a member of the board."

"I'll make the motion then," Willis said. "I move that we remove Clive Oldsman as a member of Welco's board of directors." The motion was quickly seconded and passed.

Douglas gladly picked up the phone and called for security to come and escort Clive from the building.

"You all are going to regret this and I can't wait to watch how much money this company will lose," Clive spat out. "You're all going to be penniless and I'm going to laugh at your stupidity and smugness."

Douglas shook his head. The burly security guard appeared at the door and Douglas pointed him in Clive's direction. "And never allow him in this building again," he ordered.

After Clive left the room, the other board members looked up at Douglas. "So, what happens now?" Willis asked.

Part of him wanted to say "not my problem,"

but Douglas knew he owed it to the board to try and make sure Waylon would agree to take over.

"And," Fred asked, "what happens to this business park?"

"We can move it to Waverly," he said. "By the end of the day, I'll have the specs and a price comparison on building in Waverly versus Hughes Farm."

"So, this isn't just about a girl," Willis said. "You have a sound business plan behind this."

"I won't take credit for it as my father wrote this plan before he decided to use this company to settle a personal score. For whatever reason, my father held on to a lot of shame about his Waverly roots. That town needs this business park and those jobs even more than Reeseville."

"We look forward to seeing the proposal and getting started on this project, for real this time," Fred said.

Douglas nodded as the board rose to their feet and headed for the exit. Once he was alone, he pulled out his cell phone and called Crystal.

Chapter 17

Crystal sat on the sofa ignoring the whispers of her parents, Waylon and Dena. Her mind was on Douglas and what happened at the board meeting. Had he given up everything for her? As she was about to head outside, the phone rang. She rushed to the extension on the end table. "Hello?"

"Hey, babe," Douglas said. "Miss me?"

"Yes. What happened at the meeting?"

"I tell you what—meet me at the Main Street Café and we can talk about it."

Crystal glanced around the corner and saw that her parents were still involved in a deep conversation with Waylon and Dena. "All right," she said. "I'll see you in about fifteen minutes."

She padded down the hall and dashed into her bedroom so that she could change out of her pajamas. After selecting a pair of leggings and a sleeveless tunic, Crystal took a quick shower and dressed.

When she headed for the front door, she noticed her father pacing back and forth on the front porch. Crystal stepped outside and touched his elbow. "What's wrong, Daddy?" she asked.

"I don't trust that this is over," he said. "I know I should forgive and forget, but that's a little hard for me to do."

"Why?" she asked. "Daddy, Douglas's father is dead and he can't come after you and Mom anymore."

"Baby girl, I'm not worried about me and your mother. I'm worried about you and this thing you have going with Junior's son. I'm guessing you're about to go and see him."

Crystal nodded. "He's going to tell me what happened at the board meeting."

"And you trust him? Because I swear . . ."

"Not only do I trust him, I think I love him, Daddy."

Joel shook his head. "It's amazing that a Wellington can even know how to love. Crystal, I don't want you to be hurt and I don't want to find out down the line that son is more like father than you realize."

Crystal hugged her father tightly. "Give him a chance," she whispered in his ear.

"I'm only doing this because I see that smile on your face. Your mother still does that to me."

"Ooh, Daddy, TMI," Crystal quipped as they broke their embrace. "So, if Douglas comes back to the farm with me, do you promise to be nice?"

"All I can do is try," he said. "It's bad enough Waylon is still in there."

"Daddy, you really should give him a chance as well. He made a mistake, but he did it for love. I guess sometimes when your heart is in the right place, you make mistakes."

Joel smiled at his daughter. "I'm glad you have more of your mother in you than me. You see the best in people and I never want that to change." He leaned in and kissed Crystal's forehead. "But be careful. Wolves come in sheep's clothing all the time."

"Got it. See you later," she said as she bounded down the stairs and headed for her car. Crystal drove slowly, her mind filled with questions about what happened at Douglas's board meeting and if her father really would let go of the past and get to know the man she loved.

Wait . . . *Loved?* Was that even smart? She hadn't even known him that long and though he said he loved her, was she ready to admit the same? And what was going to happen now that he wasn't the CEO of Welco? Suppose he wanted to move to a more exciting place or follow his dream of being a music executive? There was no way Crystal could leave Hughes Farm and honestly, she didn't want to. She enjoyed the quiet beauty of the farm, harvesting vegetables and working with the Starlight girls. Could Douglas be satisfied with a simple life like that?

You are so getting ahead of yourself, Crystal chided silently as she pulled into the parking lot of the café.

As she exited the car, Crystal tried not to let her doubts cloud her excitement to see Douglas. When she walked in and saw him sitting at the table with an older man she didn't recognize, she couldn't help but be curious. Was this one of the board members trying to talk him out of leaving his job?

"There she is," Douglas said when he looked up and locked eyes with Crystal. He rose from the table and crossed over to her. "Hey, babe." Douglas leaned in and kissed her on the cheek.

"You seem as if you are in a good mood," she said.

"Oh, I am, and you will be too when you meet Dr. Emory Taylor." He nodded toward the man sitting at his table.

"Who is he? Are you sick?" she asked, her voice filled with concern.

Douglas laughed and linked his arm with hers.

"I'm not sick. Come on and allow me to make the introductions."

When they approached the table, Crystal smiled at the older man, who reminded her of Frederick Douglass with his snow white afro and chocolate skin.

"Well, hello," he said, slowly rising to his feet to shake her hand. "You are a vision."

"Thank you."

"Dr. Taylor, this is Crystal Hughes," Douglas said. "Crystal, this is Dr. Emory Taylor, head of the Duval County Historical Society."

"It's great to meet you," she said, excitedly shaking his hand.

"I wish we would've met a lot sooner," he replied. "I've been following the developments at Hughes Farm for years and I've always wondered why you all weren't on our registry already."

Crystal shrugged. "I guess I didn't know how it worked."

Douglas nodded. "I figured, so that's why I wanted you two to meet. We need to make sure Hughes Farm is protected from now on," he said.

"How do we make that happen?" Crystal asked.

"First," Dr. Taylor began, "we have to write to the National Registry of Historic Places. Second, I'm going to need you to get me the history of the farm so that I can write the letter to the registry. And finally, we wait."

"And," Douglas said, "since Welco has backed off building the business park on your farm, we should have enough time to wait for the decision without worrying about court cases and bulldozers."

Crystal smiled. "And this is the perfect time to do this because my father's here and he knows all about the history of the farm."

"Joel Hughes is back in town? Why, I haven't seen him since he was knee-high to a grasshopper."

"Why don't you come to the farm?" Crystal asked. "We can have dinner and you and my dad can catch up."

Douglas leaned in to Crystal and whispered, "Hopefully they will spend a long time catching up so that we can play a little game of our own."

She fought back a smile and squeezed his thigh underneath the table. "Shall we go, gentlemen?" Crystal asked as she slowly rose to her feet.

"Yes," Dr. Taylor said. "Now, Crystal, tell me something. Do you all still grow that sweet corn?"

"Oh, yes. I think Mom was talking about roasting some for dinner."

Dr. Taylor rubbed his round belly and smiled.

The trio left the café and Crystal felt a warmness inside her as she and Douglas locked eyes. She couldn't believe that he'd gone so far out of his way to help save her family's farm. It made her believe that he cared for her just as much as she'd grown to care for him. Now, if she could get her father to see the kind of man that Douglas was, she'd be free to love him without worrying that she would lose her father.

Once they arrived at the farm, Crystal was surprised to see Waylon's car was still there. She hoped she wasn't about to walk into more arguing. Crystal took a deep breath and waited for Dr. Taylor and Douglas to join her.

She locked arms with Douglas. "Here goes everything," she whispered in his ear.

"It's going to be fine," he replied.

Crystal opened the front door and was greeted by the sound of laughter and calm voices. "What in the world?" she whispered as she led everyone into the kitchen. Inside, she found her parents and Dena and Waylon chatting like old friends.

"Well, well," Dr. Taylor said. "If it isn't all of my old students."

Joel rose from the table and crossed over to the older man and gave him a tight hug. "It's great to see you," he said. "What brings you to our farm?"

"I'm now the head of the Duval County Historical Society. Retirement didn't suit me," he said.

"Crystal, when Dr. Taylor taught history at Reeseville High School, he was the toughest teacher around," Joel said as Waylon nodded in agreement.

"He took points off for everything," Waylon said.

"Because I knew you all could do better. I expected nothing less. To allow you folks to slack off would've done a disservice to you all. Besides, none of you seem to be any worse for the wear."

"You're right about that," Joel said. "Care to join us for dinner?"

"I thought you'd never ask. Tell me, will there be roasted corn?"

"Of course, Dr. Taylor," Erin said. "Please have a seat."

Once the doctor sat down, Joel turned to Douglas and Crystal. "So, what's going on here?"

"Well," Douglas said. "Don't you think it's time that Hughes Farm becomes a historic landmark?"

Joel smiled. "Well, I'll be damned. I just keep getting proved wrong today."

"What will having this farm declared a historic landmark do?" Erin asked as she crossed over to the stove.

"It means that no one will be able to tear it down or purchase it," Douglas said. "And everyone will know how important Hughes Farm has always been to this town, county, and state."

Crystal stroked the back of Douglas's hand as he explained his plan.

"And," Crystal interjected, "once the farm is

safe from future corporate takeovers, we're going to work on expanding Starlight House and using more land to grow more fruits and vegetables."

"That's a great idea," Erin said.

"I want to do what I can to help those girls," Douglas said.

"Wait a minute," Waylon said. "You're funding this?"

Douglas shook his head. "No, I stepped down as CEO of Welco today."

Waylon leapt to his feet. "You did what? You let Clive force you out? Why would you do that?"

"I didn't let Clive force me out. As a matter of fact, he's no longer a member of the board, provided that you take over as temporary CEO."

Waylon blanched. "I'm retired."

"Aww, Waylon," Dena said. "If you expect to marry me, you're going to need a job. After all, you have years of gifts and make-up diamonds to buy."

Waylon turned to Dena and smiled. "I guess I do, but I said I wouldn't work for . . ."

"You set the rules, this time," Douglas said. "You have a board in place that's going to be hands off and you know you want to do it."

Waylon looked over at Joel, who shrugged. "No offense, son, but it's not like you're being Junior's lackey—you're going to be in charge this time," he said.

Douglas held up his hand. "No offense taken. So, will you do it?"

Waylon nodded. "But only because you asked me, Trey. And if I do this for you, you're going to have to do something for me."

"What's that?"

Waylon nodded toward Crystal. "You better treat her real good and don't let anyone or anything come between you two."

Douglas wrapped his arms around Crystal's shoulders. "Those are the easiest terms I've ever agreed to."

Joel cleared his throat. "Keep in mind that I'm going to be the one enforcing the penalty if you don't live up to those terms." He flexed his muscles to drive home the point.

"Oh, Daddy," Crystal said with a laugh.

Dr. Taylor shook his head. "The more things change, the more they stay the same. These two always played good cop/bad cop in school."

"Oh, we weren't playing," Joel said with a laugh.

Crystal crossed over to the refrigerator and poured Dr. Taylor a large glass of fruit juice and set it on the table in front of him. He smiled at her, then patted the back of her hand.

"You know, most of the young people in this town want to leave as soon as they graduate from high school, but what you have done on this farm has been amazing," Dr. Taylor said.

"Thank you," Crystal said with a slight blush. "This farm is a big part of me."

Douglas glanced over at her and swelled with pride as he listened to his woman talk about how important the farm was to her, and he couldn't wait to start working the land with her. Make love with her on the lush land in the middle of the night when everyone was sleeping. He could envision having picnics with Crystal and the Starlight girls on summer afternoons and soon adding a little Wellington baby to the mix.

Wait. Here he was with the baby thoughts again. He gave Crystal a slow once-over, imagining her belly swelled with his seed. *A daughter that I can spoil and give all the love I never received from either of my parents,* he thought with a smile.

Crystal caught his stare and the smile on his face as she crossed over to him. "What's going through that mind of yours?" she asked as she wrapped her arms around his waist.

"Hmm, that's a conversation best saved for later. Maybe in the dollhouse."

"You're going to stop clowning my cottage," she quipped.

"Oh, I'm not clowning it," he said. "We made quite a memory there."

Crystal stroked his cheek. "Then we should make another one tonight. I have to properly thank you for all you've done for Hughes Farm."

Douglas twirled her around and pulled her

close to his chest. "I did it all for you. I see how important this was to you."

"Ahem," Erin said as she approached the couple. "We have to get started preparing dinner, and all this lovey-dovey stuff is going to spoil my food."

"Yes, ma'am," Crystal said as she and Douglas broke their embrace. He turned to leave the kitchen.

"Young man?" Erin called out. "You can get started shucking the corn."

"Yes, ma'am," he replied with a smile. Then he turned to Crystal. "I see where you get it from."

She jabbed him in the side with her elbow. "Funny."

While Crystal, Douglas, and Erin prepared dinner, Joel and Dr. Taylor talked about the history of the farm for the historical society. Though Dena offered to help in the kitchen, Erin shooed her away, telling her that she and Waylon should continue their talk.

After preparing a dinner of sweet corn on the cob, homemade biscuits, roasted chicken and rice, the group headed outside to dine on the porch.

"I think Hughes Farm meets all of the requirements to be considered for the national registry," Dr. Taylor said between bites of corn. "Now, have you all kept a written history of the farm?"

"Yes," Joel said.

"But it hasn't been updated lately," Crystal admitted.

Joel glanced at his daughter. "I guess fighting off a corporation trying to bulldoze your property doesn't leave time to update the history books." He shot a pointed look at Douglas and then broke out into laughter. The rest of the table joined in.

"Listen," Douglas said, "I messed up. I admit it."

"It wasn't all your fault," Joel said. "You were pulled into a fight that began way before you were born."

"And I didn't give you the counsel you needed about this property," Waylon said. "Had I known that you thought this project was your father's final wish, I would've told you what it was all about."

Dena cut into her chicken and turned to Dr. Taylor. "Now, we can leave this part out of the history book," she said, eliciting laughter from the group.

"Of course, Dena," Dr. Taylor said.

Erin smiled as she looked around the table and squeezed her husband's hand. "This is nice, isn't it?"

"Yes, it is, but I still need to have a conversation with young Mr. Wellington. Alone."

"Daddy, please," Crystal pleaded, hoping that her father wasn't about to cause a scene. He'd promised to give him a chance, didn't he?

Joel rose to his feet and motioned for Douglas to follow him. Crystal started to follow, but her mother stopped her. "It'll be fine. You know your father isn't good with public apologies," she whispered.

Crystal could do nothing but watch the two men walk toward the rose garden.

Chapter 18

Douglas didn't get nervous often, but walking into the rose garden with Joel Hughes gave him pause and made his heart beat a little faster. Was all truly forgiven?

Joel glanced over at Douglas and smiled. "Calm down, son. I just want to talk to you and thank you."

"Thank me?" Douglas asked.

Joel cleared his throat. "Yes. Thank you for what you've done to protect this farm, even though it came at great expense to your career."

"Mr. Hughes, I never knew what my father's plan was."

"I believe that now, even if it took me some time to come to that conclusion. I'm sorry that I prejudged you without getting to know you. Obviously, my daughter is pretty smitten with you."

Douglas couldn't help but smile. "As I am with her."

"That's good to know, but I wouldn't be a good father if I didn't tell you that if you hurt my daughter, I'm going to hurt you."

Douglas nodded. "I understand and I wouldn't do anything to hurt Crystal. Who knew I'd fall for the woman who handcuffed herself in the lobby of my building?"

Joel guffawed. "That's my baby girl. When she gets a head of steam about something, nothing can stop her. You'd better get used to it," he said.

"I'm just glad we're on the same side now," Douglas said.

Joel nodded. "Do you plan on helping her run the farm now that you've stepped down from Welco?"

"I do. Being here and seeing what the farm means to the community gives me a lot of ideas—how we can produce more and even turn a profit."

Joel held up his hand and shook his head. "This isn't your typical business, and I hope your changes aren't going to interfere."

"No, not all. I'm thinking once the farm becomes a historic landmark that we should offer tours, and the profits would go to support the Starlight House and other charities as well as the day-to-day operation of the farm."

"That sounds amazing."

Douglas looked down at his watch. "I have one

bit of business I have to take care of before I'm officially done with Welco."

"I'd like to discuss this proposition of yours further before Erin and I head back to Florida. It sounds like a really great idea."

Douglas smiled proudly, happy that he had impressed Joel. One thing he knew for sure about Joel was that he was a hard man to impress. "I'll have a proposal ready that we can discuss over breakfast tomorrow morning."

"I guess having a former CEO on our side isn't going to be that bad either," Joel said, extending his hand to Douglas. "Thank you."

Douglas shook Joel's hand firmly. "Thank you for giving me a chance."

"That you should thank Crystal for." Joel pointed his thumb toward a pink rosebush. "She planted this bush when she was twelve. I think she'd appreciate a dozen or so of them when you come back to visit this evening."

Douglas and Joel returned to the house to a bunch of silent questions. "Well," Douglas said, breaking the silence, "I have to go back into town. Dr. Taylor, are you ready?"

The older man rubbed his belly. "I think I've eaten enough corn," he said as he slowly rose to his feet. "Mr. and Mrs. Hughes, thank you for your hospitality and this wonderful meal. I can't wait to get started on the history of Hughes Farm."

Douglas crossed over to Crystal and pulled her

into his arms. "I will see you tonight," he whispered. "In the dollhouse."

"I'll be waiting," she replied quietly.

As Douglas and Dr. Taylor headed for the car, he glanced over his shoulder at Crystal standing on the porch. Yeah, he needed to hurry so that he could get back to her as soon as possible. He couldn't wait for the time when he woke up to that face every morning.

Erin, Dena, and Crystal cleared the dinner dishes and cleaned the kitchen while Joel and Waylon sat on the back porch smoking cigars and preparing the smoker to roast some meat that Erin and Joel planned to take back to Florida. "Did you ever think you'd see the day?" Dena asked Erin.

"Not in a million years. You know, when we were in Florida, if I brought up Waylon's name Joel would just walk out of the room. I'm glad it's all been cleared up. Joel finally knows that Junior was scheming to take this farm by himself and Waylon didn't tell him about Pop's dementia."

"If that bastard Junior wasn't dead, I'd kill him," Dena spat. "When I needed Waylon, he made sure that he was nowhere around."

Crystal was so taken in by her mother and

Dena's story that she could only stand there with her mouth open.

"Thank God his son seems to be the total opposite of his father," Erin said, stroking her daughter's arm. "I had no idea that Junior was that obsessed with me."

Dena rolled her eyes as she dried a serving tray. "You obviously never saw his wife."

"What do you mean?" Erin asked.

"She was a clone of you, E. I don't know if he had her built or if it's true that we all have a twin out there."

"Wow," Crystal said. "I thought the same thing when I saw the wedding picture. It's scary to know someone could be so obsessed with another person and would do all of this."

Dena pointed her dish rag at Crystal. "Be glad you don't have to deal with him."

"Where is Douglas's mother now?" Crystal asked Dena.

She shrugged. "When Trey was eleven, she just left. Waylon says that Junior paid her to leave and she did. Were it not for Waylon, Trey would've probably been just as cold and evil as his dad. I think that's why he wanted to get away and do his music thing. But Waylon asked him to come back when Junior got sick."

"That's so sad," Crystal said.

"Junior caused a lot of sadness wherever he

went, as if a dark cloud of doom followed him," Dena said bitterly.

"He's dead, Dena. Let him rest in peace," Erin said. "We all had our issues with him. But we're still above ground. I imagine he died a lonely man."

"You're right," she said.

Crystal wondered what was in the diary that Douglas found. Was he going to read it? How would knowing his father's deepest and darkest thoughts affect him? Crystal couldn't imagine how she would handle things if she were in his shoes.

Erin looked at Crystal. "Girl, those dishes aren't going to wash themselves and I'm not letting you out of here to see your boyfriend until this kitchen is clean."

Crystal laughed, feeling like a young girl again. "Yes, Mom."

Dena glanced out the window as if she was checking to see if Waylon and Joel were still getting along. "I hope it doesn't take long for Welco to find a CEO. I don't want Waylon to get drawn back into the corporate rat race."

"Sounds like you two are going to pick up where things left off," Erin said. "I'm glad to hear it. Remember when we were supposed to have a double wedding?"

Dena laughed. "Yeah, that was the plan. Wow, the seventies."

After the kitchen was cleaned, Crystal headed

to her room to get ready for her evening with Douglas at the cottage. She couldn't wait to feel his arms around her and his lips pressed against hers. Hopping into the shower, her mind was filled with all of the erotic things they'd do the moment they were alone together. If her parents weren't here, she'd simply cross over to the cottage in nothing more than her towel and wait for her man.

Following her shower, Crystal dressed in a strapless maxidress and a pair of wedge sandals. She decided to skip the underwear so that there wouldn't be much between her and Douglas's touch. Now, she had to practice patience until he returned to the farm.

Douglas pressed "Print" for the Waverly Welco Business Park project report. "Amy," he called out of habit, then remembered that he'd fired her. It didn't matter; he could get the copies of the report himself and place them in the conference room for the board. He was sure that Waylon would hire a great staff and get a personal assistant whom he could trust.

"Wait," he mumbled. "Why am I even concerned about what happens here now? I left the company in good hands and my future is with Crystal." Douglas returned to his office and began packing his personal belongings. When he picked up a picture of him and his father, he stared at it and wondered why his father had been such a bitter man.

"If you would've known real love, you wouldn't have had time to scheme and try to ruin people's lives," he said, then tossed the picture in the box with his other belongings. Glancing at his father's diary, Douglas toyed with the idea of tossing it in the trash. Did he want to know what had been going on in his father's mind? There'd been a reason why he'd put off reading the diary. Now that he wasn't the CEO of Welco, did it matter what his father had planned? Did he want to know how his father felt about him? Was Clive telling the truth when he said that his father was disappointed in him?

Sighing, Douglas tossed the book in the box with his other belongings. One day, he would crack it open and read it. It wasn't going to be today.

Once he was certain that he had all of his personal belongings packed away, he left a note on the computer with the password to log on and for the protected files that he'd saved on the hard drive. He gave his corner office one last look, turned off the lights, and headed out the door. He couldn't wait to wrap his arms around his lady. Then he remembered what her father said about the roses, so he returned to his office and grabbed a pair of scissors from his desk and then left.

After dropping his things off at his place, taking a quick shower and changing into a pair of dark blue jeans and a white T-shirt, Douglas headed to the farm. Before going to the cottage, he headed for the rose garden and cut a dozen pink roses. Douglas wished that he'd brought a vase to place the flowers in. Then he remembered the newspaper he had in the car. He dashed to his truck and grabbed a section of the paper and wrapped the flowers. Finally he headed to the cottage.

Crystal had been sure she heard Douglas's truck pull into the driveway, but what was keeping him? She stood and crossed over to the door just as Douglas arrived.

"There you are," she said with a smile when she opened the door and noticed the crudely wrapped but beautiful roses in his hands. "How did you know?"

"I had a little help from your dad. You planted the bush when you were a little girl. And guess what? You and that rosebush both grew up to be beautiful."

"Sweet, but cornier than our dinner," she quipped as she took the roses from his hand. "Let me put these in water."

Douglas pressed her against the wall. "Not yet.

I've been wanting to do this all day." He captured her mouth in a hot and randy kiss that turned her knees to jelly. Dropping the flowers to the floor, Crystal wrapped her arms around his neck and lost herself in the sweetness of his kiss. Douglas slipped his hands underneath her dress and immediately felt her hot wetness on his fingertips.

Pulling back from her kiss, Douglas smirked. "I see you have been waiting for me," he said as he stroked her damp folds of flesh until he found her throbbing bud. Crystal moaned as his fingers skillfully played her body as if it was a saxophone. Each touch elicited a different note, a different moan, a louder cry that was a sensual melody to his ears. Slipping his finger out, Douglas lifted her dress higher, then dropped to his knees, kissing every spot he'd touched with his finger. When his tongue lashed her clitoris, Crystal howled in delight and turned to hot liquid melting into Douglas's kiss. He lifted her hips closer to his mouth until he was filled with the essence of her desire. Douglas throbbed and yearned to be inside her hot and wet valley.

"Let's try out that little bed back there," he moaned as he pulled back from her. "I need you."

The couple dashed into the bedroom, Douglas holding on to Crystal as if he never wanted to let her go. She ran her hand across his chest. "I like you in a T-shirt," she said. "But I'm going to love to see it on the floor." She clawed at the shirt, pulling it over his head and tossing it aside. He laid her on the bed and peeled off her dress. Her naked body against the lace was innocent and erotic at the same time, and Douglas was brick hard as he kicked out of shoes, jeans, and boxers.

Crystal inched to the edge of the bed and took his dangling erection in her hands, slowly stroking him. Leaning forward, she took the length of him into her mouth, sucking and licking him until Douglas felt an explosion brewing in the pit of his stomach.

"You win, you win," he exclaimed as he pulled back from her hot mouth. Smiling, with a devilish gleam in her eyes, Crystal stroked his thigh, then wrapped her arms around his waist.

"Just what did I win?" she asked.

Douglas looked down at his crotch. "You got me all night," he replied as she eased back on the bed, giving him room to join her. Crystal couldn't help but wonder if this would last. What would happen when reality set in? Would he be a part of the Starlight girls' lives? Could he find satisfaction tilling the land to plant seeds and watering rosebushes? Would he miss the life that he gave up just for her?

"You got quiet and still on me," he said as he drew her into his arms. "What's wrong?"

She wrapped her arms around his neck and her legs around his waist. "Nothing's wrong," Crystal covered.

Douglas traced her full lips with his finger as she slowly ground against him. He wanted to bury himself inside her and stay there forever. He wanted to fill her with his seed and watch her grow with his child. But he couldn't do that until she was finally his wife.

"Protection," he groaned.

Reaching backward with the flexibility of a ballet dancer, Crystal grabbed a condom from the nightstand and handed it to him. "I like that move," he said as he ripped the package open and sheathed himself. Crystal drew him inside her and ground slowly while his hands roamed her back.

"Umm, but I like this move. Right. Here," she moaned as he thrust deeper and harder. Their bodies moved in sync, their hearts shared the same beat, and Crystal felt as if they were the only souls in the world. With Douglas, she could be naked and bare.

"Tell me how you feel," he commanded softly.

"I feel . . . umm . . . so good."

He stroked her breasts, thumbing her rock-hard nipples as they rocked slowly, keeping time with their beating hearts. "I love you, Crystal," he moaned as he felt the bubbling of his orgasm rising.

She tightened her grip on him, leaning in close and whispering, "I love you, too."

Hearing her declaration made Douglas explode and seconds later, Crystal reached her own climax. Collapsing into each other's embrace, Crystal laughed when she saw Douglas's long legs hanging off the foot of the bed.

"Okay," she said once her laughing subsided, "I was wrong to stick you in here."

Douglas raised his left eyebrow and propped up on his elbow. "You think? But I have a confession to make."

Tilting her head to the side, she asked, "What's that?"

He pointed to the window. "That is a direct view into your bedroom. I was so looking forward to a show."

Crystal popped him on his shoulder. "Are you serious? Wow. I need to invest in darker curtains."

"Yes, especially since I don't want anyone watching what we're going to be doing when your house is empty again," he said, then kissed her collarbone. "You know, I was talking to your father about some plans for the farm."

"Do I really want to hear about this?" she asked.

"Yes," he said. "You're going to like these plans."

"Am I?" she questioned.

Douglas ran his hand down her thigh. "Yes. When this property becomes a historic landmark, I think we should consider doing tours. I was ignorant about the history of this place, and we should make sure other people don't have those same issues."

Crystal loved the way he said "we." It made her hopeful about their future together. But she wasn't too sure if she was down with the idea of having strangers traipse through the farm. What about the Starlight girls and their privacy? Historic landmark or not, she didn't want hundreds of people gawking at the property.

"I don't know," she said. "It sounds disruptive. This is a working farm and we have to consider the Starlight girls and their home here."

Douglas paused. "It's just an idea. We could work out trails and historic areas that are only for the tours."

Crystal shook her head. "And my father agreed to this?" she asked.

"In theory, he thinks it's a good idea," Douglas said. "It would be a great revenue stream."

"This farm is not some division of Welco that you can market to the masses."

"Whoa," Douglas said. "You need to calm down."

Crystal rose from the bed and paced the room. Douglas found it so hard to focus on what she was saying as he was distracted by the sway of her hips, the swell of her breasts, and the fact that when she was angry, she had the rosiest glow on her cheeks.

"You can't think that you're going to come here and turn this place into your vision of Hughes Farm. Your new job isn't CEO of . . ."

Douglas leapt from the bed and closed the space between him and Crystal. Placing his finger to her lips, he said, "Did I say I wanted to take over? You really are resistant to change, aren't you?"

"And just what is that supposed to mean?" she asked, narrowing her eyes to tiny slits.

"Just what I said. You act as if you're afraid to give a damned inch. Haven't I shown you by now that I wouldn't do anything to hurt you or what you love?"

Crystal expelled a breath and allowed Douglas to draw her into his arms. "Look at me," he said, lifting her chin upward. "I'm on your side no matter what happens. But you can't look at my help so suspiciously all the time."

"Honestly," Crystal began, "I can't be sure that this will be enough for you."

"This?" he said as he stroked her round bottom. "Or this?" Douglas leaned in and kissed her on the neck. "I will never need more than this."

"Douglas, I'm not just talking about the bedroom. And, for the record, I know I have that on lock." She placed her hand on his chest. "I'm talking about this lifestyle, a quiet, sometimes mundane farm life. Before I put my eggs in the Douglas basket, I need to know if the bottom is going to fall out."

This was an important conversation and Douglas would've been an active participant if Crystal's erect nipples weren't calling out to his mouth.

"This isn't going to work," he said.

"What?"

"I can't have this conversation with you until you put some clothes on."

"Will you be serious?" Crystal snapped.

"Oh, I'm very serious," he said.

Crystal begrudgingly crossed over to the bed and grabbed her dress. "Happy?" she asked.

Douglas, who had pulled on his boxers, nodded. "Now, let me tell you this, and I hope I don't have to repeat it again. I want nothing but your happiness. I want to grow with you and I want to see what you love flourish. Forgive me if I still have a bit of CEO inside me."

Crystal sighed and leaned in to him. "I'm sorry," she said. "But I don't want to think that you gave up everything just to make me happy."

"I learned a lesson when I came to town to run Welco. That was when I gave up everything for someone else's happiness or to satisfy the needs of someone that didn't mesh with mine. And I promised myself that I would never do that again. So, anything that I'm doing is because I want to do it and it's where my heart is and where it will stay. Don't you ever doubt that."

"Douglas," she cooed.

"I love it when you say my name like that," he said as he tugged at the top of her strapless dress. "Now," he said. "Let's make a pact."

"A pact?" she asked as her dress fell to the floor with a flourish.

Douglas nodded as he drank in the lush curves of her naked body. "No more serious conversations in our dollhouse. This is the pleasure zone."

"Now, that's some change I can believe in," she said as she reached for his boxers.

Chapter 19

Dawn found Douglas and Crystal naked on the floor, spent from their all night lovemaking. Instinctively, Douglas thought about reaching for his phone and checking his e-mail. Then he remembered his job was right there with Crystal. Welco wasn't his business or his problem anymore. Yawning and stretching his arms above his head, he tried not to wake Crystal, but his efforts were in vain as she opened her eyes and smiled at him.

"Morning," she said.

"Didn't mean to wake you," he replied.

"Well, sleeping late on a farm is really not an option. I hope you brought a change of clothes. I wouldn't want my parents to know what we have been doing over here, though I'm sure they have an idea."

Douglas smirked. "I do have fresh clothes in

the truck. So, what's on the agenda for the day?" he asked.

"Good question. Normally, I go over the orders for the farmer's market and some of the girls will help me getting the orders ready. Then, there's the weeding of the flower gardens, making sure the irrigation systems are properly flushed and running. Breakfast and then a delivery to the soup kitchen in Waverly."

"All of this before breakfast, huh?"

Crystal nodded, but snuggled closer to Douglas. "But today, I think I need to eat first. I'm a little drained."

"Is that so?"

"Mmm, you know you kept me up all night," she said, kissing him on the side of his neck.

"And I did it all by myself, huh?"

Crystal laughed. "You know, we should really give more thought to your tour idea."

"No, ma'am. You're breaking the pact already. This is the pleasure zone and I never ever discuss business before I've had my first cup of coffee."

"And there's no coffeemaker in here, so we'd better shower and head to the house if we're going to get any work done today."

Douglas pulled Crystal on top of him. "Before we get started with work and business," he said, "I got some pleasure I want to share with you."

Crystal smiled as she spread her thighs apart and ground against his morning wood. "Maybe this is the best part of waking up," she said with a grin.

It was after eight a.m. when Crystal and Douglas emerged from the cottage. Douglas, clad in blue jeans and Timberlands, was ready for his first day of work on the farm. When he and Crystal walked into the main house, Joel and Erin were finishing up breakfast.

"Late start today?" Erin asked with a knowing smile for her daughter.

"A tad bit," Crystal replied. "Had to talk to our new employee about his duties."

Joel snorted. "So, Douglas, have you told Crystal about your ideas to make the farm more profitable?"

Crystal and Douglas exchanged deep looks. "Let's talk about that over coffee," he said. Crystal agreed and crossed over to the coffeemaker and grabbed two mugs.

"Well," Erin said. "While you all talk business, I'm going to see Brooke and the Starlight girls. Do I need to hide the knives or can you all play nice?"

"We're all on the same team now," Joel said. "I think we can be good."

Erin moved closer to her husband and kissed him on the cheek. "I like the sound of that." As she walked toward the door, she patted Douglas on the shoulder as if she was wishing him good luck.

"Mr. Hughes," Douglas said after taking a sip of coffee, "Crystal doesn't like the idea."

"I never said that," she exclaimed.

Joel sipped his coffee. "I'm not surprised at all. My daughter likes to do things her way because for whatever reason, she thinks every idea for the farm has to be her own. Yep, I know how that goes."

"So, you two are going to talk about me as if I'm not even sitting here?" Crystal said.

"Yes," Joel said. "I've noticed something about the farm and about what you've been doing over the years, baby girl. You're going to work yourself into a frenzy because you haven't allowed yourself to put your spin on the farm. You're running everything just as your mother and I left it, aside from the Starlight House."

"But . . ."

Joel held up his hand to quiet his daughter. "Listen, your mom and I are retired. As long as you don't let some company come in here and try to take our property, everything else that you do we're all for it. I'm even open to allowing little Mr. Wellington to offer his two cents. You could do worse."

Douglas sipped his coffee, keeping his comments about Joel's less than glowing recommendation to himself.

"Daddy," Crystal said, "I don't believe you. I thought you wanted the farm to—"

"You've been running this farm for five years," he said. "I trust whatever you do will be the right thing. Your mother and I have never lost confidence in what you can accomplish and have never been more proud of you. But we have to look at the reality of the economy."

Crystal nodded. She had been so focused on fighting Welco and saving the farm that she hadn't given much thought to moving forward. Still, did she want to . . . ? Wait, she had to make a business decision and be an adult.

"All right," she said. "I'm open to new ideas."

Douglas and Joel exchanged a smile. "I have a proposal in my truck for you two to look over," Douglas said.

Joel drained his coffee cup. "I'm retired. You two can handle this. I'm going to take a walk." He rose from his seat, kissed Crystal on her forehead, and headed out the door.

Once they were alone, Douglas grabbed Crystal's hand. "This is going to be a good thing, trust me."

"I'm putting my trust in you," she said. "Don't make me regret it."

"You won't regret it. I'll be right back." Douglas stood up and headed out to his truck.

Sitting in the kitchen alone, Crystal sighed. Why was she so afraid to allow Douglas to help her? She trusted him. She was just as stubborn as her father, but he had a point. For the last five years, she did want everything that happened on the farm to be her idea. Maybe it was time to look at other ideas. Taking the empty coffee mugs to the sink, Crystal closed her eyes and imagined growing old on the farm with Douglas at her side. She hoped they'd last that long and their relationship would continue to grow. Despite their conversation last night, Crystal couldn't stop wondering if he'd decide to leave one day. Now that he was free to follow his dreams. Suppose they didn't include her or Hughes Farm?

"Crystal, are you all right over there?" Douglas asked as he encircled her waist with his strong arms. "What's the matter?"

"Nothing," she said. "I was just about to do the dishes."

"And you're so into clean dishes that you didn't hear me call your name?" he asked. Crystal twirled around and faced him. The smile on her face didn't reach her eyes and Douglas noticed immediately. "Crystal, don't tell me there isn't something going on in that pretty little head of yours."

"Douglas, let's go over that proposal so we can start looking toward the future," she said, pushing her insecurities down. Looking into his sparkling eyes, she decided that she'd take Douglas at his word. He said he wanted to be there with her and she couldn't let fear and doubt cloud what she was feeling.

He stroked her cheek. "You know what?" he began. "You worry too much. We need to work on that."

"Really?"

He led her over to the table and dropped the file in the middle of it, then looked into her eyes. "Listen, babe, what I said last night I still mean today. If you're afraid for whatever reason, stop it."

"Maybe it's all the talk of this farm's history, seeing how each generation of Hugheses made it better. I'm a little worried about what the history books will say about me and what I've done."

Douglas stroked the back of Crystal's hand. "Well, if I had to write that chapter, I'd say Crystal Hughes shook up Welco Industries, forced the extremely handsome CEO to take stock in what's important in life, made him realize that love is more important than profits, and saved her farm."

She smiled at him and leaned across the table, kissing him on the tip of his nose. "Is that so?"

"Yes. Now, let's get down to business so that we can go back to the pleasure zone and please each other," he said.

"Not until we go over this and get some other work done," she said. "You're forgetting, I'm the boss now."

Douglas tweaked her nose. "Yes, ma'am," he replied as he watched her read the report.

"You're very thorough and I like how you took the privacy of the Starlight House into consideration," she said.

Douglas nodded. "So, are you willing to give the tours a chance?"

She closed the file and sighed. "You knew last night when I was ranting that you had everything under control, didn't you?"

"Sometimes you just have to let people have their say," Douglas said. "I figured that protecting those girls would be important to you."

Crystal rose from the table and went over to Douglas, sitting in his lap and kissing him slowly and sweetly. "Thank you," she said after finally pulling away. "For everything."

"You're welcome and I'm not done," he said.

She raised her right eyebrow and smirked. "Is that so?"

Douglas nodded. "So, we'd better get our chores done asap so that we can play." He winked at her and moved her off his lap.

Crystal and Douglas began cleaning the kitchen, then headed to the vegetable garden to assist with gathering the orders for the homeless shelter and the farmer's market. To say Douglas was surprised by the amount of work that was done on the farm was an understatement. He was impressed by how hard the Starlight girls worked and the pride they took in what they were doing.

MJ caught Douglas watching her sister as she piled corn cobs in a basket. "Excuse me," she said.

"Yes?" Douglas asked.

"Don't you think you owe all of us an apology now?" MJ asked.

Douglas laughed. "Yes, I do."

"So, since you're here and working, does that mean our home is safe?" she questioned as she filled her basket with peas.

"Your home is safe, the farm is safe, and I want to offer you the first apology," he said.

"You'd better be nice to Miss Crystal," MJ warned. "She deserves to be treated well because she's the only person in this stinking town who wanted to give us a chance."

Douglas smiled at MJ. "You don't have to worry about me not being nice to Crystal," he said, glancing at her as she and Renda loaded the corn on the truck.

"We better not," MJ said.

"You know what?" he said, leaning into her. "I want to do something really nice for Crystal, but it has to be a surprise. Will you help me?"

MJ eyed him suspiciously, then she nodded. "I'll help. But we're going to have to tell Renda too. She can't keep a secret if she isn't involved in it."

"All right," he said, and began whispering the details of his plan and what he needed from the two girls.

Crystal and Renda stopped to grab a bottle of water after loading another bushel of corn for the farmer's market.

"Miss Crystal, is everything good now?" Renda asked.

"Yes," she replied, stealing a glance at MJ and Douglas. What were they discussing so intently? she wondered.

"Why is he here?" Renda asked, following Crystal's gaze.

"Well," Crystal said, "Douglas is going to be working with us."

"But I thought he wanted to tear the place down. Why did he change his mind and how can you trust that he won't change his mind again?"

Crystal placed her hand on Renda's shoulder. "He had a change of heart and, trust me, he's not that bad."

"Hrump," Renda said. "But he thinks we're delinquents."

"He didn't mean . . . You know what? Maybe you need to get to know Douglas. I know he's sorry he said those things."

Renda smiled at Crystal. "You like him, don't you?"

Crystal looked at Douglas again as he shook

hands with MJ. "I do. He's really a nice guy once you get to know him."

"If you say so," she replied. "Well, I'm going to get showered so I can go to class tonight."

"Thanks for your help today, as always," Crystal said, then gave Renda a tight hug.

"I'm going to keep my eye on that guy, just in case he tries to come after our land again," Renda said, and Crystal knew the young woman was very serious.

"You don't have to worry about that," she said. "I got a feeling he won't try that ever again."

"He'd better not," Renda said as she watched MJ and Douglas walking in their direction.

"Renda," MJ said, "we need to talk about something important."

Crystal watched as the sisters walked away talking in hushed tones. "What's going on with them?" she asked.

Douglas simply shrugged. "You know how girls are. I like MJ," he said, "but she reminded me of something."

"What's that?"

"That I need to tell the Starlight girls how wrong I was to say those things about them in the newspaper," he said.

Crystal nodded. "You should do that, because some of the ladies are still holding a grudge."

"How about I throw a party for them? Nice dinner, a DJ, and a break from work?"

Crystal smiled and nodded. "That would be really nice, and I imagine that the girls would enjoy it. I just need to check with Brooke."

"Leave that to me. All I want you to do is get a new blanket for that bed in the cottage."

"A new blanket?" she asked.

Douglas nodded. "All of that lace is too much. After all, Barbie and G.I. Joe are playing in there now."

"G.I. Joe, huh?" she teased. "I see you more as Businessman Ken."

Chapter 20

A month later, Douglas was starting to get used to the early mornings on the farm. More than anything else, he was enjoying waking up every day with Crystal in his arms. Today, though, he had to sneak out of bed to make sure his plans were going to come together.

He, Renda, and MJ had been planning a party that would celebrate three things: the success of the Starlight girls who were about to graduate and head off to college, the addition of Hughes Farm to the Duval County Historical Landmark registry, and his engagement to Crystal—provided that she said yes.

Glancing at her sleeping body, he smiled. She was so beautiful when she slept, Douglas wanted to kiss her before he left, but he couldn't wake her up just yet. Slipping into a pair of jeans and a

V-neck T-shirt, he crept out of the room and met the girls on the back porch.

"Do you have the ring?" Renda asked, not bothering with a good morning greeting.

"Renda," MJ said, nudging her sister in the ribs, "you can be a little rude sometimes."

"I'm just making sure he isn't going to change his mind," she replied.

Douglas glanced over his shoulder, checking that the coast was still clear. He pulled a small black velvet box from his pocket. "Listen," he said, "I'm not changing my mind and we have to be quick about this because Crystal's going to be up soon."

Renda took the box from his hand. "Tell us the plan again," MJ said as Renda opened the box.

"This ring is so pretty!" Renda exclaimed.

MJ nudged her again. "Don't wake up Miss . . . Ooh, she's going to love this."

Douglas grinned at the pink-diamond-encrusted ring, which was shaped like a rose. He'd had the ring especially made for Crystal. He hadn't wanted to get her a regular engagement ring because she definitely wasn't a regular woman. "All right," he said as Renda snapped the box close. "When the champagne comes out, this ring has to be in the bottom of Crystal's glass."

"Right," MJ said.

"We're going to toast to the farm being included

on the historical registry and then I'm going to ask her to marry me."

"What if she doesn't say yes?" Renda asked. "Will you try to tear the place down again?"

"No one will ever be able to tear this place down," Douglas said. "And I have a pretty good idea that she will say yes."

"I hope she does," MJ said. "She smiles a lot more now."

Renda nodded in reluctant agreement. "I guess you are good for her and the farm."

Douglas really liked Renda's suspicious mind because he knew underneath, she was a sweet little girl who wanted to be happy. That's why he'd established a college fund for the Starlight girls. It was the least that he could do, since his words had caused them a lot of pain. They'd finally gotten over that hump when Douglas treated all of the Starlight girls to dinner and offered them a public apology. He'd even gotten his godfather to get Welco to provide the products and volunteers to do some renovations on their home.

Waylon had been happier these days himself, even if he was in a job that he claimed he didn't want. Douglas knew that the man's happiness came from his reunion with Dena. At some point, Douglas wanted to know the story about how his father broke the couple up. Why had his father been so hell-bent on keeping everyone around him unhappy? Maybe that's why his mother left and never came back. He was sure those details were in his father's diary, but he wasn't ready to allow that negativity to infringe on his happiness. Today was about his future. His future with Crystal.

"All right, girls," he said. "Now, make sure no one else knows about this."

"You got it, Mr. D.," MJ said.

"But," Renda said, "you're going to have to load those eggs for us so that Ms. Fey and Miss Crystal think that we got up early to work."

Douglas shot them the thumbs-up signal as they headed to the Starlight House and he grabbed his boots.

Crystal rolled over on her side expecting to collide with Douglas's body. Instead, she found the bed empty and cold. Sitting up and yawning, she wondered where he'd gone so early. These last few weeks with Douglas practically living on the farm with her had been blissful. She'd begun thinking about a future with him and worrying less about him deciding to leave her and Reeseville. Still, that whisper of a thought rippled through her this morning. Swinging her legs over the side of the bed, Crystal decided to start breakfast. Walking into the kitchen, she wondered when they would hear from the historical society about the farm's status as a landmark.

"Morning, beautiful," Douglas said as he walked into the kitchen.

"Well, you're up early this morning," she said as she kissed his sweaty cheek.

"Wanted to get a jump-start on some things since we have a big party coming up."

"The girls are really excited about this," Crystal said. "So, Mr. Wellington, since you've been so busy, why don't you sit down and I'll make you breakfast."

Douglas yawned and took a seat at the kitchen table. "Thank you," he said.

"Still having fun?" she asked as she prepared the coffee machine.

"You could say that," Douglas replied as he looked down at his hands. "I'm forming my first callus."

"Umm, that's not exactly a good thing," she said.

He laughed. "I know."

Crystal crossed over to the refrigerator and grabbed eggs, cheese, bacon, and a bag of grits. "My grandmother had a secret remedy for callused hands."

"Is that so?" he asked.

Setting the ingredients on the counter, she turned to him and smiled. "Yes, because when you touch me, I want to feel nothing but your smooth hands."

Douglas rose from his seat and crossed over to her. He ran his hands down her hips and then pulled her against his chest. "You know," he whispered. "I did a lot of work this morning, so there's no rush for you to get out there."

"And what do you suggest we do instead?"

He didn't reply; he simply kissed her slow and deep. Crystal moaned softly as he lifted her up on the counter. The cotton gown she wore was quickly discarded and Douglas planted his face between her thighs, sucking and licking her throbbing pearl as she clamped her thighs around his neck.

"Yes," she cried as he licked the sweetness of her pleasure. "Oh . . . That. Feels. Good."

Pulling back after she'd reached a second climax, Douglas lifted her from the counter. "Let's go back to bed."

"Umm," she said breathlessly. "I like that idea."

Douglas rushed down the hall with Crystal in his arms. He needed to melt with his woman. His future wife.

Entering the bedroom, Douglas laid Crystal in the middle of the bed, then stripped his clothes off. As he joined her, she ran her hand down the center of his chest. His skin was so smooth and so silky. Douglas moaned as her fingers circled his nipples, and his erection grew harder. The anticipation to feel her wetness wrapped around him made him shiver.

Crystal locked eyes with Douglas as he spread her thighs and thrust into her. "Douglas," she moaned, meeting his long, slow strokes. Her body hot, wet, and tingling as he touched her in the most sensitive spots.

"I love you," he called out. "Love you." He dove deeper into her, imagining the look on her face when she accepted his engagement ring. He wanted this to be the rest of his life. Wanted to make love to her every morning before they started their day. Wanted to carve out time to sneak away in the middle of the day to taste the sweetness and saltiness of her skin at lunch.

Never did he think they'd fall in love when he met her all of those months ago. He never thought she'd change his life in the manner that she had. Douglas closed his lips around her neck, gently licking and sucking as she tightened herself around him, milking his essence from him. He didn't pull back or out as he reached his explosive climax. Douglas wanted to give her everything, even if that meant giving her his child. Crystal clutched his back and the waves of her own orgasm flowed through her body.

Spent from their lovemaking, the couple held on to each other, neither feeling the need to speak—or rather, having the energy to do so. Crystal stroked his arm and nestled closer to him.

This felt good. This felt right. She didn't want this feeling to ever end. Crystal loved this man, loved him so much that she couldn't think about her life without him. How unreal was it that this multimillionaire, former CEO was working on her farm? The same man who she'd expected to have horns and breathe fire had shown her how tender and caring he could be. Crystal was touched by how he got along with the Starlight girls, especially Renda and MJ.

She sucked her bottom lip in and sighed. Her life had worked out better than any Lifetime movie she'd ever seen. And there was no stalker.

"What's wrong?" Douglas asked.

"Nothing," she replied. "Everything is just fine."

"I know you better than that, and when you suck that luscious lip in and sigh like that, it's not because everything is all right," he said as he propped up on his elbow.

"I hate to be a pessimist," she said, knowing she was going to mar their afterglow. "But, are you sure this is enough?"

Douglas stroked his chin. "Nope."

"What?"

"That's what you wanted to hear, right?" he asked with a low chuckle. "Crystal, when are you going to understand that I'm right where I want to be? If I had my way, you'd let me hire some people to do all the work we do here and we'd spend all of our mornings in bed just like this."

She smiled and stroked his cheek. "I'm being ridiculous," Crystal replied. "But I keep looking for the other shoe to drop and hit me on the head."

"It's not going to happen," he said. Douglas glanced at the clock on the nightstand and smiled. He needed to go into town so that he could talk to Waylon about the party, and despite himself, he was a bit curious about what was going on at Welco. Moreover, he wanted to make sure Waylon and Dena were as happy as he and Crystal were. "I have to go into town to get some things for the party tonight, and to see Waylon at Welco."

Crystal smiled, thinking that she should give Dena a call since she hadn't seen her in a while. "Do you miss it, at all?" she asked as Douglas climbed out of bed.

"I don't miss the work, but I can't say that it's easy to simply turn my back on Welco. No matter what he did, my father built that company. I'm hoping that Waylon can erase the bitterness and one day our children can be proud of all sides of their family legacies."

Crystal didn't say anything, simply smiled at the thought of having Douglas's children. Just how in the world would they explain the strange history of the Wellington and Hughes families, though?

"And just how many children are we talking about?" she asked as she rose from the bed.

Douglas laughed. "We could be like the Duggar family, nineteen kids and counting."

She playfully smacked him on his shoulder. "You're out of your mind," she quipped.

"Come on, you don't think you can handle that many kids?"

"You can't handle that many kids," she said. "Because you will be hands on, especially in the diaper-changing department."

"I'm guessing you're against nannies," he said as he headed for the bathroom.

"Nannies?" she called out after him. "Are you serious?"

"Not at all," he replied. "Who needs a nanny when our kids are going to have the sweetest and most beautiful mother ever?"

Crystal followed him into the bathroom and wrapped her arms around him. "And our kids are going to have a father who will love them unconditionally and teach them to follow their dreams and desires."

Douglas's insides clenched and he wondered if he could be the father that Crystal described. She had been lucky to grow up with parents who cared and loved her, and he'd never had that. Not a loving mother to offset the coldness of his father nor a father who gave a damn about anything but himself.

"Don't worry," she said. "We'll be great parents."

"You can read my mind now, huh?" he asked before kissing her forehead. "Join me in the shower?"

"Sure," she said as he turned the water on.

After another round of lovemaking, Douglas and Crystal finally pulled themselves apart and he headed to Welco. On the drive over, his smile was plastered on his face. Talking about a future with Crystal made him even more excited about his proposal.

Crossing the lobby of Welco, Douglas did feel a slight tug. If he was honest with himself, he'd admit that his time as CEO wasn't all bad, despite the fact that his work was now tainted by his father's need for revenge.

"Mr. Wellington," a security guard said. "Do you have an appointment?"

Douglas tilted his head to the side and walked over to the elevator without saying a word. He might not be CEO anymore, but he wasn't a guest in the building that he built either.

When he made it to Waylon's office, Douglas laughed at the irony of the situation. Waylon had been so happy to be retired; now he was working and Douglas was living the life of a nearly retired man. Knocking on the open door, Douglas walked into his old office.

"What's up, godfather?"

Waylon popped his head up from the file he

was reading and sneered at his godson. "I could punch you in the chest, boy," he said.

"What?"

"I'm supposed to be retired, living a stress-free life, and here you come looking like you're having a great time doing nothing," Waylon quipped.

When Douglas saw the smile plastered on his face, he realized that Waylon wasn't as stressed as he'd led him to believe. "So, how's Dena doing?"

"Wonderful. As a matter of fact, I'm trying to convince her to come on Welco's legal staff, since I see how much pleasure one can get working with the woman he loves. She's having a hard time dealing with the history of this company, though."

Douglas nodded. "I can understand why, I guess."

Waylon leaned back in his chair. "Dena and I should've been married and celebrating our anniversary. But, outside forces—"

"My father."

"Yes, your father stepped in and altered our destiny. We're working our way back to where we should be," Waylon said, his smile telling Douglas that things were going very well on that front. "But, I'm sure you don't want to hear about that. You're going to ask Crystal to marry you tonight, right?"

Douglas nodded. "I wish her parents could be

here, but Joel said he and Erin are on their way to Jamaica."

"He told me that he expected this sooner or later. He really likes you and that shocked the hell out of me."

"What? Everybody loves me."

Waylon snorted. "Your dad and Joel had a bitter battle. I'm surprised that he was able to get past your lineage."

Douglas leaned against the wall, still trying to wrap his mind around the evilness of his father's deeds. "Why did he do it all?"

Waylon shrugged. "Your dad was very smart and in a small town none of that mattered because he was from Waverly. He was poor and thought that defined him."

"But when he created this company and . . ."

"As much as he tried to pretend that he wasn't, your father remained that same little boy from Waverly who thought he didn't measure up. When we were growing up, the Hughes family was the talk of the town. You know, people took pride in what that farm meant. To your dad, when Erin chose Joel as the man she loved, she was just like everyone else—thought he wasn't good enough."

Douglas wished he could say he understood why his father took everything so personally, but it was too hard for him to wrap his mind around what Waylon said. Hearing about his father's coldness further solidified his decision not to read the diary. Douglas wished his father would've been proud of the life he'd built for himself, treated his mother with more love and opened his heart. Maybe things would've been different and he would've had a happier life.

"Trey," Waylon said, taking note of the pensive look on his godson's face, "what's done is done. Your father could've done so many things differently, but he made the choice to be consumed with anger and resentment. I wanted to shield you from that."

"How? By leaving the company?"

"And not letting your father's bitterness shape you. I was glad when you wanted to abandon business and do your music thing. Your father wasn't happy about it at all. He made me promise I wouldn't let him die alone; that's why I begged you to come back."

Douglas shrugged. "A lot of good it did."

"You did more good than you think," Waylon said. Before Douglas could reply, the phone rang. "I have to take this. The headhunter is having a hard time finding a qualified replacement."

"Welco without a Wellington running it seems odd."

Waylon raised his eyebrow before picking up the phone. "Second thoughts?" he asked.

"No," Douglas said quickly. "Take your call and I'll wait for you outside so that we can talk about the party." As he left the room, he wondered if he could really cut his ties with Welco forever. Even if his father had tried to use the company for revenge, it was still a part of his family's legacy. He could make it something that he and his future children could be proud of, couldn't he? Shouldn't he?

"Trey," Waylon called out from his office. "So, this party is going to be when you ask Crystal to marry you, huh?"

Douglas smiled brightly. "Yes, but I'm wondering if she's going to accept my proposal when I tell her what I'm thinking about doing."

Waylon folded his arms across his chest and looked up at his godson. "You want your job back, huh?"

Douglas nodded. "While I've been working to get Hughes Farm on the historical registry, I can't help but think about the Wellington family. My grandparents worked hard, tried to help out in Waverly as much as they could, and then there was my father and Welco. I want to be as proud of my Wellington roots as Crystal is of her Hughes roots. If I come back to Welco with a board that supports my ideas, Welco can do some serious good in this county."

Still, Douglas was worried about Crystal's reaction to him returning to the job in the company that she hated.

"This company is a part of you and no matter

how you feel about what your father did, you have every right to want to be a part of this place. I don't know if the board will be willing to vote you back in though."

"That could be a good thing."

"Maybe you should just become a board member. It will keep your home happy and you'll still have a say in Welco."

Douglas smiled. "When I grow up, I need to be smart like you," he said as he shook his godfather's hand.

"Keep living and maybe you'll be as smooth and as smart as I am one day," Waylon said as he gathered the files from his desk. "I have a meeting and lunch with Dena before heading to Hughes Farm for your big announcement."

"All right, I'll see you tonight. I have to go and pick up a cake for Crystal."

Crystal couldn't put her finger on it, but Renda and MJ had been acting strange all day. Whenever she approached them, they'd stop talking and exchange the oddest looks. Finally she had to ask, "What's going on with you two today?"

"Umm, we're just excited about the party tonight," Renda said as she tied a ribbon on a balloon.

"Okay," Crystal said.

"It's going to be a good time," MJ said.

"MJ," Renda chided, "shouldn't you go talk to the caterers?"

She smiled brightly. "I'm on it."

Crystal watched her retreating frame as she tied another set of balloons. "Why do I get the feeling that you two are up to something?"

"Us? Come on, Miss Crystal. We're just excited about the party and MJ going off to college," Renda said.

"I'm so proud of everything that you and your sister have accomplished here. Next year it will be your turn to go to college."

Renda shrugged. "I want to stay here," she said. "Work at Starlight House and on the farm so other girls can see that even when people write you off, you can still make a difference."

"But what about furthering your education?" Crystal asked. Though she admired what Renda wanted to do, she didn't want her to sacrifice too much.

"I can go to college online. I just want to be like you and help other people," Renda said.

Crystal enveloped the girl in a tight hug. "I'm glad you feel that way."

"Well," Renda said, holding back happy tears, "I'd better take these balloons into the cafeteria."

As Crystal stepped out on the porch of the Starlight House, she saw Dena walking up the driveway carrying gift bags and wearing a huge grin. "Are you going to stand there or help me?" Dena asked.

"This was so sweet of you," Crystal said as she took half of the bags.

"Well, I know how you feel about these girls and how you've fought for them. I just wanted them to know that there are others who care," Dena said as they entered the house and dropped the bags on one of the tables.

"I haven't seen you in a while," Crystal said. "Not since you and Waylon reunited."

Dena's grin broadened. "That man," she said.

"Seems as if that man is making you happy."

"Well," Dena said with a sigh, "he was until he suggested that I start working at Welco."

"Doing what?"

"Head of their legal staff. Waylon doesn't trust a lot of the people working there because of loyalties to the old board, and when he brings the new CEO in he wants him or her to have a staff that can be trusted. I've tried to move forward, but that company represents a lot of pain and suffering."

Crystal sighed. "But things are different now, right?"

Dena nodded. "Still, Douglas Wellington did everything in his power to keep me and Waylon apart because he was unhappy. He used Welco to do it, sending Waylon away on 'business' and making it seem as if he'd left me on his own accord. Left me and our baby."

"Baby?"

"I was so angry because I had a miscarriage, alone. I spent years hating Welco, Waylon, and everything Wellington," she said. "That's why I filed all of those lawsuits every time Welco started a development."

"If you work for the company, you'll be able to make changes from within."

Dena shrugged. "Some things aren't worth saving," she said. "Douglas walked away and that place is his family legacy. What does that tell you?"

Crystal sighed and thought about the conversation she and Douglas had had earlier that day. Part of her wondered if she'd been the reason he left Welco.

"Let's get ready for the party," Dena said as she walked over to the helium machine with Crystal.

Chapter 21

Douglas waited in line at the café for two slices of the rich chocolate cake he and Crystal loved. As he stood there, he couldn't stop thinking about Welco. Why was this so important to him now?

"Mr. Wellington," the clerk said. "Long time no see."

"I know," he said, remembering that he used to stop in every morning for coffee and a pastry before heading to the office.

"It's a little late for breakfast, isn't it?"

Douglas nodded. "I'm here for dessert. Two big slices of chocolate cake."

"All right, I'll get that for you."

Douglas took the cake and walked out of the café slowly, wondering if he could explain to Crystal why he wanted to go back to work at Welco—simply as a board member. Would she understand? Should he tell her before or after he asked her to marry him? Maybe he should just scrap the idea. Something inside wouldn't let him do that, though.

When he arrived at the farm, Renda and MJ rushed over to his truck. "Mr. D," Renda said excitedly, "everything is all set. Dr. Taylor called and said he's going to bring the proclamation and the sign for the farm."

"And after he does that, then are you going to ask Miss Crystal to marry you?" MJ asked excitedly.

"Yes," he said.

"I can't wait," MJ said.

"Wait for what?" Crystal asked as she walked up behind them.

"Umm, the party," MJ said.

Crystal looked from Renda to MJ to Douglas. "Is that what I think that is?" she asked when she saw the Main Street Café box in Douglas's hand.

"Maybe," he said, grinning.

Renda and MJ told the couple they'd see them at the party and took off toward Starlight House. "Those two are a trip," Crystal said. "I think there's something going on that you don't want to tell me about."

Douglas shrugged and pretended to be offended. "Do you think I would hide something from you?"

She took the box from his hand and opened it. "Maybe."

Douglas closed the top of the cardboard box. "That's for later, much, much later." He leaned in and kissed her cheek. "Let's go inside. I need to talk to you about something."

"All right," she said as they turned toward the front door. Douglas opened the door with one hand and held it for Crystal. She looked up at him and saw the serious expression on his face. "It seems as if I'm not going to like this," she said as she took the cake box from his hand and started for the kitchen.

"It's possible that you won't," he said. "Coffee?"

Crystal placed the cake on the bar and tilted her head to the side. "What's going on, Douglas?" she asked.

He sighed and moved closer to her, placing his hands on her shoulders. "I'm thinking about going back to Welco."

"I knew this was coming," she said quietly.

"I don't want this to be a problem," he said. "I won't be the CEO, but I'm thinking of joining the board."

She nodded. Douglas stroked her cheek. "You have to understand," he said. "Despite what my father did, Welco is a part of me and my family history. Maybe I can undo some of the wrongs that my father did."

"So, what will this mean for us?" she asked.

"I don't see much changing. Are you okay with this?"

Crystal stroked the back of his hand. "How can I tell you to turn your back on your family's legacy? I wouldn't—didn't—and I can't expect you to do anything differently."

He drew her into his arms and hugged her tightly. "I love you."

"I love you, too," she said. "But Hughes Farm is still off limits."

"No doubt," he replied. "Besides, this place isn't going to be touched by anyone."

Crystal raised her right eyebrow. "Is that so?"

He nodded. "Well, that was a lot easier than I thought it would be. I know Waylon wishes things could be like this with Dena. He wants her to work for Welco and she's not even considering it."

Crystal shook her head. "I can understand why," she replied. "What's Waylon hoping to accomplish by asking her to work there, knowing the history she has with the company?"

Douglas sighed and released her. "I guess it's his way of trying to make up for the past. It's confusing, you know. . . ."

Crystal crossed over to the coffee machine and loaded it with water. "Are you going to read your father's diary? He probably wrote about why he did those things."

Douglas stroked her arm and shook his head. "I don't know if I want to see the darkness that shrouded his heart, not when—" Douglas stopped short because he was about to reveal his plan to ask her to marry him. "One day, I'll read it, but right now, I'm looking forward to the future."

She turned to him and grinned. "Everybody's looking forward to the future today, especially Renda and MJ. I'm so proud of those girls."

Douglas nodded. "They are special."

Placing her hand on her hip, she asked, "So, what are you three scheming?"

Douglas feigned ignorance. "What are you talking about?" he asked.

"I've seen you guys having these hushed conversations, and don't tell me it's just about the party," she said.

"It's a surprise and I'm not saying anything else about it, Miss Hughes," he replied.

Crystal groaned. "I hate that tone. You sound like the pompous jerk who tried to have me arrested," she quipped.

Douglas winked at her. "I have a question for you, Miss Hughes," he said.

"Well, Mr. Wellington, I may have an answer."

Douglas closed the space between them and wrapped his arms around her waist. "Whatever happened to those handcuffs you used in Welco that day?"

She tilted her head and eyed him with a seductive gleam in her eyes. "And you want to know that piece of information because . . . ?"

"Because the moment I saw you handcuffed in the lobby, I wanted to see you handcuffed in bed," he replied in a low growl.

Crystal glanced at the clock on the wall. She and Douglas had just enough time to play a little game before the party started. "Follow me and I'll show you just where they are," she said as she took his hand and led him to the bedroom.

Douglas and Crystal entered the bedroom, surrounded by a crackling sexual energy that was almost overpowering. She pushed him back on the bed.

"You know," she intoned as she lifted his shirt above his head, "you've had me handcuffed once already. I think it's time that I return the favor."

"Is that so?" he asked as she unzipped his jeans. His erection nearly burst out of his boxers as Crystal eased his pants down his hips. Once he was naked on the bed, she went to the closet and retrieved the handcuffs.

"It's payback time," she quipped. Crystal sauntered over to the bed and straddled Douglas's body.

He lifted his hands above his head and she locked the cuffs on his wrists. "Mmm," he moaned as she kissed his neck. Next, she eased down his body, sucking his nipples and stroking his hardness. Her expert touch sent his body into overdrive and Douglas regretted the decision to allow Crystal to restrain him. He wanted and needed to touch her.

The moment she took the length of him into her mouth, Douglas cried out with desire. "Yes, yes," he moaned. They locked eyes as she gave him oral pleasure and Douglas fought the urge to climax.

Pulling back from him, she stripped out of her cotton dress and mounted his erection. Leaning forward, she unhooked the cuffs. "Hold me," she moaned as he thrust his hips forward, filling her wetness with his throbbing hardness. Douglas wrapped his arms around her waist and sat up, pulling her against his chest as they ground against each other. She felt so good, so hot, so wet. When Crystal threw her head back and screamed his name, Douglas lowered his head and suckled her nipples. She dug her nails into his back as she reached her climax.

"Come for me, baby," he ordered as he continued thrusting into her. "I want to feel it."

"I—I," she moaned as she climaxed again. When Douglas felt her tighten around him, he was unable to hold back his own orgasm.

Covered in sweat and spent from their session,

Douglas and Crystal held on tightly to each other and drifted off to sleep.

Two hours later, the ringing of the doorbell awakened the couple. "What time is it?" Crystal asked through a yawn. Douglas glanced at the clock on the nightstand.

"Damn, we've got to get ready," he said as he leapt out of the bed and threw on his discarded clothes. He knew who was at the door—either MJ or Renda. They had to go over the setup for Crystal's proposal one last time and he had to give the girls something special. Since MJ was heading off to college, he wanted to pay for her books and provide her with a monthly stipend so that she could focus on her classwork and not worry about financial issues.

"I'll get the door," he said as he pulled his shirt over his head and rushed to the front door.

Crystal slowly pulled herself from the bed and went to the bathroom to take a shower. She wondered, though, what Douglas was up to.

"We'd better make this quick," Douglas said when he stepped on the front porch with Renda and MJ.

"Okay," Renda said. "Now, when Dr. Taylor makes his announcement, we're going to have the caterers bring out the drinks."

"And Mrs. Fey said we have to include sparkling

cider because most of us are underaged and can't drink Moët," MJ said.

Douglas nodded. "That's a good idea. And the ring?"

Renda smiled. "I told one of the waiters—the guy who's going to have the champagne for you and Miss Crystal—that we're going to put the ring in her glass."

"Maybe we shouldn't put it in the glass," he said, stroking his chin. "But I love what you girls have done. This is going to be a special night for Crystal." He drew MJ and Renda into his arms and hugged them tightly.

"Now, you make sure you don't mess it up," Renda said. "Because I'm going to be here and if you hurt Miss Crystal . . ."

"I told you before, you don't have to worry about that. As a matter of fact," Douglas said, reaching into his back pocket, "I have something for the both of you." He handed the girls two prepaid debit cards. "This is for all of your help and hard work."

"Credit cards?" Renda asked.

"Preloaded debit cards, a few hundred bucks for you to do whatever you want with," he said. The girls giggled excitedly.

"Thank you," MJ said.

"You know," Renda said as she stuffed her card in her jeans pocket, "I guess you're an all right guy. But I have to know, if Miss Crystal hadn't changed your mind and your company bought this farm, what would've happened to us?"

Douglas rubbed his throat. "I'm not sure. But after tonight, that's not going to be a concern ever again. I'm glad I got a chance to see what this place means to people and especially to the girls who live here."

"So are we," MJ said. "We'd better go get dressed." Renda and MJ dashed off.

Douglas stood on the porch looking out over the farm and smiling. No one could have paid him to believe that spending time there would change his mind about what he wanted to do with the farm. Now, he couldn't imagine tearing down anything on Hughes Farm. This place was as magical as Crystal described that first night he was there.

Just as he was about to return inside the house, Dena flagged him down as she made her way to the front porch. "Douglas," she said. "I guess congratulations are in order."

"For?" he asked.

She looked over his shoulder to make sure Crystal wasn't in earshot. "I know about the landmark proclamation and the proposal," she whispered. "Waylon is very excited for you, as am I." She gave him a quick hug. "I'm glad I was wrong about you."

He smiled. "You're wrong about something else," Douglas said.

"And what would that be?"

"Working for Welco."

Dena sucked her teeth and placed her hand on her hip. "You know, I don't want to have this conversation."

Douglas sighed and shook his head. "But, Dena, you have to understand what Waylon is trying to do," he said.

"I hate to speak ill of your father, but that man was a monster, an evil son of a bitch, and I don't want anything to do with his company."

"It's not his company anymore. We have a chance to make it better. Something we all can be proud of. Don't you want to be a part of that?"

She narrowed her eyes at him. "You walked away."

"But I'm going back," he said.

Dena rocked back on her heels. "And Crystal is okay with that?"

Douglas nodded. "Despite what my father did and how he used Welco, it's still a part of my legacy. I'd like to see good people like you and Waylon making Welco a much better place for the community."

"I'll think about it, but I'm not making any promises, young Mr. Wellington."

"You can call me Trey," he said with a laugh.

Dena looked into his eyes as tears sprang into hers. "I wonder if Waylon and I would've had a son or a daughter," she whispered. "We lost a lot of time together and a lot of our dreams died. We'll never be able to have a family and we'll never be able to get back what your father stole from us. When I think about Welco Industries, I can't separate it from your father. He used that company to try to lord over this town because he thought people did him wrong. He ended up doing so many wrongs while paying off the right people so that folks overlooked his evil. I couldn't. I can't."

"Dena, he's gone now."

"And as cruel as this may sound, thank the Lord," she retorted. "I'll be glad when Waylon finds a new CEO and I simply hope he will walk away. Then we can have the life we should've had."

Douglas wanted to apologize, tell her that he was so sorry his father had caused her so much pain and suffering. He couldn't imagine how he would feel if someone kept him and Crystal apart for decades.

Dena noticed the pensive look on Douglas's face and tapped the back of his hand. "Enough about that," she said. "It's not your fault and you can't change the past."

"That's true. And if you want my godfather to walk away from Welco sooner rather than later, then I will see what I can do," Douglas said.

"I can't ask you to do that," she said. "You and Crystal are just getting ready to start your life together. Don't let my past intrude on your future.

Waylon and I will be fine." She gave him a tight hug. "But you're sweet for offering."

"I want my godfather to be just as happy as I am. And you make him happy."

Dena smiled brightly. "Not as happy as he makes me," she said. "Tell Crystal I'll see her tonight at the party."

"All right," he said, then headed inside. He was surprised to see Crystal standing in the living room. "How much of that did you hear?"

She frowned and then crossed over to him, wrapping her arms around him. "Enough to know that I love you even more than I thought I could," she said. "That was really sweet of you."

"A lot of good it did," he said.

"Douglas, if you want to return to the CEO position at Welco, then I'm behind you. What you said to Dena makes sense. That company is just as much your family legacy as this farm is to me. Turning your back on it is wrong and I wouldn't do the same."

"Crystal, that job requires long hours, late nights, and early mornings," he said.

"And as much as you tried to pretend you'd be a good farmhand and could stay away from Welco, you belong there. We'll still have our time together."

You got that right. We're going to have the rest of our lives to be together, he thought as he brought his mouth down on top of hers and kissed her with a heated passion that made her shiver.

Crystal pulled back from him. "We'd better stop," she said breathlessly. "Kiss me like that again and we won't make the party."

"We can't have that," he said.

"And you're not going to give me a hint as to what you, Renda, and MJ are up to?" she asked.

Douglas shook his head from side to side. "Well, I'll give you one little clue," he said. "You're going to love it."

Slapping her hands on her hips, she poked her lips out at him. "That's not a clue."

"You need to work on your patience," he replied before jogging into the bedroom to get ready for the party.

Crystal had just finished glossing her lips when the phone rang. She rushed into the bedroom and grabbed the extension. "Hello?"

"Hey, baby girl," her father said.

"Daddy," she replied excitedly. "Have you and Mom made it to Jamaica?"

"Oh yes," he said. "I just wanted to call and check in with you. Tonight is the big night, huh?"

"Yes. The girls are really excited about this party and the fact that their home is safe and three of them are going off to college," Crystal reported.

"That's great," Joel said. "I know I told you before, but I have to say it again. I'm so proud of what you've done at the farm. Your mother and I should've been a lot more forthcoming about our history with Welco; it might have saved you some stress."

"It would've been helpful, but that's behind us now," she said as she watched Douglas emerge from the bathroom dressed in a pair of dark denim jeans, brown leather loafers and a tan oxford shirt. He smiled at Crystal and headed across the room to get his watch from the dresser.

"It is, and I'm glad, because I like that young man a lot. He's nothing like his father and I know he loves you."

Crystal watched Douglas as he snapped his watch on his wrist. "I feel the same way," she replied.

"Have a good time tonight and remember, your mother and I are so proud of you."

"I love you, Daddy."

"Love you too, baby girl. Tell Douglas I said hello."

"Will do," she said, then hung up the phone.

"Your dad?" he asked.

Crystal walked over to him and hugged him tightly. "Yes, and he said hello." She kissed him on the tip of his nose. "Have I told you how happy I am?"

"Not in the last couple of hours, but I don't mind hearing it again and again," Douglas said as he patted her bottom. "You better get dressed."

"I know," she said. "We don't want to be late and have people assuming what we're doing."

"Yeah," he said. "We're going to be doing that a little later."

"And we get to eat the cake."

"Among other things," he said with a wicked gleam in his eye.

Returning his sultry look, she said, "I like the way you think, Mr. Wellington."

Douglas couldn't wait until the day she was Mrs. Wellington. He nervously wondered about the proposal. What if she said no? *Nah,* he thought as he glanced at her. *This is right. We're going to spend the rest of our lives together right here in Reeseville. Who would've believed that I'd actually find love and happiness in the last place I wanted to be?*

"Douglas, did you hear me?" Crystal asked as she dropped her robe and reached for her dress. He drank in her sensual image; the black lace bra and matching panties looked so good on her.

"No," he said as he closed the space between them. "You keep trying to have conversations with me when you're looking like this." Douglas slid his hands down her hips and was tempted to forget the party.

"All I asked was for you to hand me my earrings," she said in a low voice as he toyed with the waistband of her panties. "But if you don't stop, we're not going to make it out of here."

"Would that be so bad?" he joked, then dropped his hands. Reaching for her silver bangle earrings, Douglas handed them to Crystal and planted a kiss on her cheek. He headed outside and saw Waylon walking toward the house.

"Trey," he called out. "Are you ready?"

"Just waiting on Crystal," he said as he stepped off the porch to meet his godfather.

"Women. I told Dena I'd meet her here. Interestingly enough, she said she might consider joining the legal staff at Welco. I guess I should thank you for talking to her earlier this afternoon."

"You don't have to thank me," Douglas said. "But you can help me convince the board to give me my job back."

"Oh, I'm already there. Fred and I were discussing you after you left the office and he said if you wanted to come back, he'd support your decision. Of course, Clive is lobbying for a return as well."

"Over my damned dead body," Douglas boomed. "He's what was wrong with Welco. Still playing by my dad's old rules."

"Yes, but he has his supporters as well. I know

one thing is for sure. I'm too old for this shit," Waylon said with a chuckle.

"But you're going to have to become a board member," Douglas said. "I'll need someone I know I can trust on my side."

"You got it, Trey. Now, about this proposal of yours . . ."

"Keep it down," he said, looking over his shoulder. "Everything is set up. Hughes Farm is going to be presented with the historic landmark proclamation and then I'm going to pop the question."

Waylon nodded. "This is good. I'm glad to see you happy and that you're not acting like so many other young moguls. Crystal is just what you need."

"Truer words have never been spoken," Douglas said as he turned around in time to see Crystal step onto the porch.

"Hello, Waylon," she said. "I'm glad you could make it."

"Oh, I never miss a good party. And I have an announcement to make tonight," he said.

"What's that?" Crystal asked as Douglas linked his arm with hers.

"I've established a scholarship foundation for the girls who live in the Starlight House," he said, then looked pointedly at Douglas. "Things with Welco and these girls got off to a rocky start, but we've all seen the error of our ways."

Crystal gave Waylon a tight hug. "Thank you so much. This is going to make such a big difference in these girls' lives."

Waylon smiled. "I'm just following Trey. He told me a lot about these girls and they deserve this."

Dena waved to the group from the steps of the Starlight House as they approached. The look she and Waylon exchanged made Crystal's heart melt. It was easy to see how much they loved each other and she wished them the best.

Douglas stroked her arm as if he was having the same thought.

Chapter 22

As Crystal looked around Starlight House, she was amazed at the number of people who'd come to celebrate with the girls. The mayor was there, as well as two of the city council members who'd voted against having the house in the city limits. Though she wanted to say "I told you so," Crystal graciously greeted them.

Brooke approached Crystal with a huge smile on her face. "Crystal, I just spoke to Mr. Terrell. He told me about the scholarship fund. It's such a great thing to know people in the community actually care about these girls and want to see them succeed."

Crystal nodded. "Yes. I'm glad the tide is turning in our favor. These girls are working hard to be productive members of society."

Brooke nodded. "And I'm sorry that I questioned your concern about them. Your faith in them and teaching them how to fight the right way has made a big difference."

"You don't have to apologize. You were simply doing your job and putting these girls first," Crystal said, then offered Brooke a hug. "We make a great team, though. I know you'll keep me in line."

Brooke nodded and smiled. "Well, looks as if I have help with that now." She nodded in Douglas's direction. "He's taken a liking to Renda and MJ."

"What's going on over here?" she asked Douglas as he wrapped his arms around her waist and kissed her cheek.

"You'll see soon enough," he replied. "Dr. Taylor just arrived."

"Oh my goodness. This is about the historic landmark registry, isn't it?" she said excitedly. "You've known all along?"

Douglas played dumb. "I don't know anything."

"Funny," she said, popping him on the shoulder. "Did the farm make the registry or what?"

"You're going to have to wait. I told you, you need to work on your patience," Douglas quipped. "I'm going to talk to Dr. Taylor. You stay right here."

Crystal pouted and watched Douglas cross the room to catch up with Dr. Taylor.

The party was in full swing when Douglas and Dr. Taylor took the stage. The DJ cut the music and Douglas handed the microphone to the older man.

"It gives me great pleasure to make this announcement about Hughes Farm tonight with all of you," he said. "If I could have Miss Crystal Hughes on stage with us."

Crystal smiled and made her way through the crowd. Douglas held his hand out to her and assisted her up the steps. She looked so beautiful in her peasant-style yellow dress and her hair curled loosely and pulled back in a trendy bun. The rose on the side of her head made Douglas smile and think about the ring that she'd be wearing shortly. He kissed her on the cheek.

Dr. Taylor smiled at the couple. "Tonight," he said, "It is my humble honor to present you and Hughes Farm with the recognition of being included on the Duval County Historical Landmark registry."

Applause erupted from the crowd. Dr. Taylor held up his hand and quieted the group. "This farm is such a place of inspiration. The Hughes family kept this land at a time when African Americans were thought of as less than human. And as their riches increased, this family gave back to the community. Miss Hughes continued her family's legacy when she allowed Starlight House on her land, a haven for these girls in need. She did it because it was the right thing to do. A lot of us in Duval County could learn a lesson from her example. It is with great pleasure that I present this proclamation to Miss Crystal Hughes, declaring Hughes Farm a historical landmark."

Once again the room erupted into cheers and applause. Two waiters began circulating the room with sparkling cider and champagne. Another waiter climbed on stage and offered champagne to the trio on stage. Dr. Taylor passed the microphone to Douglas, then exited the stage.

"Crystal," Douglas said into the microphone, "I want everyone in the room and this town to know how much you mean to me and what loving you has taught me. You showed me how to give without expecting anything in return, but getting more than I deserve."

He turned to the waiter, who was holding the tray with the champagne and the engagement ring, and took the ring. Douglas dropped to one knee and tears sprang into Crystal's eyes. A chorus of oohs and ahhs rippled through the crowd.

"Crystal Hughes, will you marry me?" he asked as he took her left hand in his and slipped the ring on her finger.

"Say yes!" MJ called out. Crystal smiled, figuring out what MJ, Renda, and Douglas had been plotting.

"Of course," she said. "I'll marry you."

Douglas rose to his feet, dropped the microphone, and took Crystal into his arms. He kissed her slowly, tenderly, and passionately as the crowd cheered.

Dena and Waylon looked on and he got a romantic notion of his own. "Look at them," he said. "Reminds me of a life I missed out on."

Dena nudged him in the side. "You were never that over the top," she said.

Waylon draped his arm around Dena's shoulders and pulled her closer. "I love you," he said. "And my life without you was empty and miserable. Then, when you looked at me with hate in your eyes, I was broken."

She looked up at him. "Waylon, we can't—"

"We can't change the past, but we can fly into the future together. It's not what we planned, but I want to spend the rest of my life with you."

Hot tears sprang into her eyes. "Waylon, I . . ."

He brought his finger to her lips. "Just think about it. We have a lot of lost time to make up for."

"Let's go congratulate Douglas and Crystal," she said, and started to walk toward the stage.

Waylon stopped her. "Tell me something," he said quietly. "Do you believe that we deserve a chance to get it right? Don't you think we belong together?"

"Waylon . . ."

"Dena, we can congratulate them and then I'm taking you away from here to plead my case, because I'm never going to let you walk out of my life again."

Dena didn't—or rather—couldn't say another word because she agreed with everything Waylon said. But for the first time in her life, Dena was afraid.

The party began to wind down and most of the well-wishers had left. Douglas and Crystal found a quiet corner near the stage to share a quick kiss. She couldn't take her eyes off the rose-shaped engagement ring on her finger. Douglas held her close at the corner of the stage. "Do you like it?" he asked.

"I love it," she said. "And I love you."

"I meant what I said on stage," he said. "Every word."

She stroked his cheek and leaned forward to kiss him. "I'm going to hold you to what you said. But right now, I want to get you alone."

"I thought you'd never ask," he exclaimed, and stopped short of picking her up and carrying her outside.

Holding hands, they told the girls and a few partiers still left at the Starlight House good night. Renda and MJ crossed over to them. "Were you surprised, Miss Crystal?" Renda asked.

"I was. You guys got me big time," she replied, then hugged the sisters. "Thank you."

"Now remember," Renda whispered. "Our offer still stands if he messes up."

She laughed and looked over Renda's shoulder at Douglas. "I don't think that's going to be necessary."

"All right," she said, then pointed at Douglas as if she was telling him *I'm watching you.* Douglas gave her a mock salute as she and MJ headed back inside.

"You'd better be on your best behavior, Mr. Wellington," Crystal said as they walked toward her house.

"Renda and MJ gave me the same warning several times," he said, then scooped her up in his arms. "But I'm at my best when I'm a little bad."

"Well, why don't you show me exactly what you're talking about?" she said, grinning.

Douglas nodded and then kissed his fiancée slow and deep. He couldn't wait to spend tonight and forever basking in the glow of Crystal's love.

Don't miss
Recipe for Desire
On sale now wherever books are sold.

Chapter 1

The only thing Marie Charles enjoyed more than being the center of attention at someone's party was hosting one of her own. Either way, she was instantly the center of attention. Charlotte's resident party girl was always on the cutting edge of fashion, dressing in clothes that were always tailored especially for her svelte body. And she knew how to keep everyone's attention—by either walking into a venue exchanging air kisses with the most high-profile man or woman who caught her eye so that she could get her picture snapped, or by dating the hottest ball player, singer, or actor she wanted. She was a professional public-relations maven, so it was her business to be in the know. But if you asked the right people, Marie Charles—daughter of civil rights attorney Richard Charles III—was just a girl seeking the wrong kind of attention.

Tonight, she was playing hostess at Mez, where her public-relations and event-planning company, M&A Exclusive Events, was sponsoring a party for the Charlotte Bobcats' second playoff win in franchise history. She'd checked the VIP list and kissed a couple of the players on the cheek, telling them congratulations. And, of course, she basked in the compliments the men lavished on her and how she filled out her gold Alexander McQueen dress. As Bobcats center Drayton Neal reached out and grabbed Marie so that they could take a picture, she turned to her intern, Hailey, and said, "This is how you host a party."

Hailey, a shy Central Piedmont Community College student, offered her boss and the six foot nine basketball star a slight smile as the *Carolina Nightlife* photographer snapped photos.

"Have some bubbly," Drayton said to Marie as he held out a glass of Ace of Spades Champagne Blanc de Blancs. She happily accepted the flute of six-hundred-dollar champagne and sipped with Drayton. He palmed her bottom as if it were a basketball and brought his lips to her ear. "You know you're sexy as hell. What do I have to do to make you my good-luck charm?"

"Get your hands off me," she replied through her smile. While most women would've welcomed the advances of an NBA baller, it was just another night on the town for Marie. "I'm not a trophy."

"Umm," he said, taking a step back and watching her sip her champagne. "You look like one to me. You are wearing that gold, baby."

Marie drained her glass and turned to Hailey. "We all look amazing when they're drunk."

"Okay."

Marie took Drayton's bottle and refilled her glass. "Thanks for the bubbly and good luck in New York," she said with a flirty wink. As she and Hailey walked away, she told the intern, "When you're hosting an event, don't spend too much time with one group of people. You have to make everyone feel special so they'll come to your next event. I need you to check the table and make sure everyone has drinks. Have you seen Adriana?" Marie glanced at her watch and fingered her curls. It was almost time for DJ Chill to start his set.

"She was talking to the DJ," Hailey said. Marie nodded.

"I'm going to check on the bartenders and make sure they're making the Bobcat rum punch," she said, then strutted downstairs to the wraparound bar. Marie had carefully selected the drink menu and had worked with the bartenders to make sure everything was perfect. Landing the Bobcats as a client had been a huge get for M&A. *Tonight has to be perfect,* she thought as she crossed over to the crowded bar. Smiling, a half an hour into the party, Marie was sure that everything was going to be . . .

Wait! Was that William Franklin, her fiancé, walking in the door with *that woman*!

William was holding hands with his ex-wife, Greta Jones, looking at her as if they were still together. "Oh, hell no," she mumbled. She started to stalk over to them, but a hand on her shoulder stopped her.

"Marie," Adriana Kimbrell, the *A* in M&A Exclusive Events, said. "Please don't trip."

"Do you see this? He came to *my* party and brought *her*!" Marie hissed.

"DJ Chill is about to start and we don't need to have a scene," she said. "Let's just sit down, and you need to calm down."

"I simply don't believe this bull," Marie snapped as they sat down at the bar.

Adriana waved for the bartender. "Patrón and two glasses. Leave the bottle." Turning to Marie, she said, "Ignore them. She's only sniffing after him again because you two are together," Adriana said as she poured Marie a glassful of tequila. "She can't beat you in any other way, so she wants her loser ex back. Let her have it."

Marie downed a shot and then snatched the bottle off the bar and took a big swig. "If either of them thinks that I'm going to let this go, then they don't know who the hell I am."

"Marie, this isn't just about you and Willie. Our name is on this event. Do you know what I had to do to get Mez to agree to let us have this party here after what you and Tia did during the last event we hosted here?"

Marie took another swig. "We had a good time and got all kinds of press for this place, so they need not trip. I made Mez a hot spot."

"Neither should you," Adriana said as she tried to take the Patrón away. Marie quickly moved the bottle out of her friend's grasp.

"I'm cool," she said. "Look at this outfit." Marie stood up and twirled. "Not trying to mess this up by slapping that slut silly." She glanced out on to the dance floor and watched as William and Greta danced closer than close, but when they kissed, she felt a tug of embarrassment. Everyone knew that was her fiancé, and there he was pretending that she didn't exist. Sure, she wasn't in love with him; her relationship was simply a means to an end. Respectability in her father's eyes. But the longer she watched him, the more the alcohol began to kick in. Marie took a shaky step, with the liquor bottle in her hand, toward the dance floor, shaking off Adriana's hand and ignoring her as she said, "Don't do it, Marie!"

Marie thought she'd saunter over to William and Greta, but the Patrón made her stumble, bump into patrons, and cause quite the scene before she grabbed Greta's shoulder.

"Oh, shit, Marie," William said. "Look . . ."

"This is pretty cozy," Marie slurred. "Funny that you're kissing her when I'm wearing your engagement ring." She threw her left hand up in the air.

Greta shook her head and giggled, which infuriated Marie to the point that she took a swing at her. But, in her drunken state, she stumbled and landed on the floor flat on her bottom.

William bent down and helped her up. "You're embarrassing yourself and you're drunk."

"And you're kissing this bitch as if you're still married," Marie shouted, bringing the music and movement around them to a halt.

Greta shook her head. "And this is what you left me for? Have you gotten it out of your system?"

William turned to Greta and shot her a look that cried for silence. "Marie, I wanted to tell you that Greta and I had been seeing each other, but . . ."

"You know what! Go to hell. Both of you go straight to hell!" Marie yelled. She fumbled with the ring on her finger, trying to pull it off and toss it in William's face. But the ring slipped off and flew across the dance floor. "It was a cheap-ass stone anyway. It wasn't even flawless. So, kiss my flawless ass good-bye, loser!"